PRINCES AT EWIN

FIRST CENTURION KOSNETT, BOOK 4

BLAZE WARD

KNOTTED ROAD PRESS

Princes at Ewin
First Centurion Kosnett, Book 4
Blaze Ward
Copyright © 2022 Blaze Ward
All rights reserved
Published by Knotted Road Press
www.KnottedRoadPress.com

ISBN: 978-1-64470-267-3

Cover art:
ID 1-0270 © Luca Oleastri

Cover and interior design copyright © 2022 Knotted Road Press

Reviews
It's true. Reviews help. Even a short one, such as, "Loved it!" So please consider reviewing this book (and all of the ones you've read) on your favorite retailer site.

Never miss a release!
If you'd like to be notified of new releases, sign up for my newsletter.

http://www.blazeward.com/newsletter/

Buy More!
Did you know that you can buy directly from my website?

https://www.blazeward.com/shop/

ALSO BY BLAZE WARD

First Centurion Kosnett

Encounter at Vilahana

Consensus at Aditi

Hegemony at Dalou

Princes at Ewin

Empire at Gloran

Domain at Yaumgan

The Jessica Keller Chronicles

Auberon

Queen of the Pirates

Last of the Immortals

Goddess of War

Flight of the Blackbird

The Red Admiral

St. Legier

Winterhome

Petron

CS-405

Queen Anne's Revenge

Packmule

Persephone

Additional Alexandria Station Stories

The Story Road

Siren

Two Bottles of Wine With A War God

The Science Officer Series Season One

The Science Officer

The Mind Field

The Gilded Cage

The Pleasure Dome

The Doomsday Vault

The Last Flagship

The Hammerfield Gambit

The Hammerfield Payoff

The Bryce Connection

The Science Officer Series Season Two

Alien Seas

Buried Among the Stars

The Lazarus Alliance

Escape

Return

Rebellion

Revolution

Liberation

Retribution

Alliance

Shadow of the Dominion

Longshot Hypothesis

Hard Bargain

Outermost

Dominion-427

Phoenix

Princess Rualoh

The Handsome Rob Gigs

Can't Shoot Straight Gang

Can't Shoot Straight Gang Returns

Hunting Handsome Rob

Handsome Rob, Assassin

Earth Force Sky Patrol

Birth of the Star Dragon

Flight of the Star Dragon

Call of the Star Dragon

Shadow of the Star Dragon

Trial of the Star Dragon

Hunter Bureau

Mirrors

Latency

Pleasure Model

Inhuman

PROLOGUES

PROLOGUE: KOSNETT

Phil studied the plot of ships at anchor from a screen in his office, rather than out on the flag bridge. He'd spent an extra day at this point getting everything prepared, because he had swapped out two excellent ships that had sailed great distances with his squadron and replaced them.

As if you could replace the Heavy Escort *Morninghawk*. The Command Cruiser *Storm Petrel* was much heavier, as you measured mass. More weapons. More than twice the tonnage.

But they lacked the sorts of heart that *Morninghawk* and its captain, Makara Omarov, had brought. That willingness to go for the throat against any threat, any size, anywhere. As Iveta Beridze had said at the beginning, other captains had nightmares about *Morninghawk* coming for them.

Storm Petrel was more of a showboat than a warrior. A vessel where important men were trained for important jobs. Sons of semi-feudal lords such as Omarov or Sugawara. Men, but he could see revolution breaking out there as well, like had happened in the *Fribourg Empire*.

Storm Petrel's Command Centurion was Captain Malachi Yukimura, of a clan that was favored by the Shogun. The man who was the true Hegemon of *Dalou*.

Today, it carried the Imperial Crown Prince himself, nineteen-year-old Shingo Yosan, as a trainee officer. Phil doubted that the man would be allowed to truly serve or be put at any sort of risk, but the mere fact that he was in a black naval uniform had apparently been something of another revolution, according to what Phil had learned. No emperor had served in the navy in centuries before this.

Storm Petrel also carried the fourteen-year-old middle daughter of the Shogun, Lady Kohahu Kugosu. Fourteen going on forty, as his wife Xue Yi liked to say about their oldest, Yi Wen Kosnett, who was planning to join the navy like her famous father from the most recent letters he had gotten from home.

Phil would have liked to carry the young woman representative of her dangerous father aboard *Urumchi*. He had the ambassadorial space forward from removing the bubble gun. She had insisted, however, on traveling aboard *Storm Petrel* instead.

Phil had a number of theories, but hadn't pressed for answers. Nor had he insisted on her joining him here. There had been any number of undercurrents that night when Lord Morninghawk was awarded the Republic Cross and elevated to become his own lordship. Lady Kugosu had spent an interesting amount of time speaking directly with the crown prince.

None of it properly chaperoned, according to *Dalou* custom.

But *Dalou* was in the first chapters of a social and political revolution at least as troubling as the civil war centuries ago that had elevated the Shogun and reduced the Emperor to a figurehead.

Phil checked the time. Close enough. He rose and moved to the door, pausing to put on his game face as it were, before emerging.

Markus Dunklin was seated just outside his door, two travel mugs of coffee waiting, but he could read a clock as well as anybody.

"Ten?" he asked his assistant.

Markus held up both hands, palms out and grinned.

"Ten."

The man liked to play with power tools and occasionally things that went boom. As long as he had all ten fingers, he kept this job. Otherwise, he had to return to Engineering.

A fate, he had assured Phil on more than one occasion, worse than death.

Phil had a good crew. His arrival in the larger space got a few looks, nods, and then folks went right back to what they'd been doing. Nobody needed to pause, stand up, and salute him. That was stupid. Even *Fribourg* was starting to break themselves of the habit, though it might take them a generation.

Harinder Abbatelli was seated in her usual spot, directly across the main table from where he sat, with her own screens to watch and the big hologram projector between them. Everyone else in here answered to her as Command Flag Centurion, but she had assembled one of the best teams of such folks Phil had ever known.

They were comparable to the folks that had been aboard *RAN Vanguard* with Jessica Keller during *The Expedition*. Their legend would hopefully shine as bright.

Phil sat. Markus dropped the other travel mug into a holder and clicked it shut.

The command table on the flag bridge could be set up to display holographic images of all the Command Centurions in an *Aquitaine* fleet. However, Phil had eleven vessels in this squadron, and only five of them hd *RAN* hull numbers. The holograms were just presentations of flat screens now. Easier, though it lacked some of the warmth.

But this was a war fleet on a war footing.

Even *RAN Varmint* had been sent back to *Meerut*, but they were a former pirate Picket and had no business in the middle of the thing Phil was about to do.

He paused, confirming that all the images were frozen and

overriding the switch himself, then addressed himself to Harinder. She was as close to him as anybody in the fleet, having spent years preparing for this, after having been trained by the legendary Enej Zivkovic himself, Keller's old Flag Centurion.

She knew Phil's moods and foibles. She was watching him now with interest and empathy.

"I won't ask if anybody thinks this is a dumb idea," he told her quietly. "Most of them are chomping at the bit, if I had to guess. Do me one favor, Harinder?"

"Done," she said. "What is it?"

Just like that. She would agree, then find a way to move heaven and hell to do it. But that described most of the force around him.

"If I look like I'm going too far, poke me," he said.

"Too far?"

"*Dalou* behaved and *Ewin* launched a surprise attack when they knew I wasn't going to be around," he reminded her. "Just about the opposite of what I expected. Today, we are going to make an example of someone. I don't think I will let it get out of hand, but I might. Your job is to ask me at the critical moment."

She nodded. She would do that.

Phil took a breath and opened the line to the squadron.

PROLOGUE: KUGOSU
COMMAND CRUISER STORM PETREL

Kohahu had worked assiduously to keep Captain Yukimura from growing nervous, but the man was not prepared to deal with her aboard his ship. She doubted that any captain would be.

Female. Young. Well-connected. Highly intelligent. Deadly. For most of the gentlemen of *Dalou*, about as intimidating as it could possibly get. A few looked on her with covetous eyes, but that was the connection to her father, where she was just an image.

It was the ones who saw her as a woman who were interesting. Most of those were foreigners. Unsurprising, as Kosnett's force was nearly equally split by gender, with many of his closest officers women.

Dalou captains didn't know how to deal with Harinder Abbatelli or Heather Lau. They were all pitifully out of their depth with the Tactical Officer Iveta Beridze.

Kohahu had much to learn. Fortunately, she had excellent examples. Perhaps her dear father would figure out that aspect of things eventually as well. Or not.

He had three daughters, in a culture that did not allow women to wield power as anything but dangerous dowagers.

Kohahu knew that there were Houses out there maneuvering to marry favored sons to the three Kugosu daughters, so that they might be in position to claim the Shogunate at some point.

She planned to keep it. If it took years, she had years, as her father wouldn't retire or announce an heir any time soon.

Looking around the chamber, she noted the players today.

Captain Yukimura in command. Short, stout. Of the ancient African ethnotype that was somewhat rare in *Dalou* and other places. Gray hair kept severely short but not shaved, a rough stubble intended to convey something fierce. Dressed in black. Polite but not obsequious. He ran a warship entrusted with training well-bred sons of the nobility.

Crown Prince Shingo sat next to the captain. Young, though who was she to say. Nineteen, so five years her senior, though his years had been spent in the gilded cage of the Sunflower Palace, rather than the Shogun's realm. In that, she had an advantage.

The other officers were an interesting mix. *Storm Petrel* was an important vessel in the Shogun's fleet, and she herself had caused it to be here with Kosnett, rather than back someplace safe.

Kohahu didn't think that they were at risk, given the immense firepower Kosnett's people had demonstrated previously, but they were still going to do something rare and dangerous.

The screen at the front of the conference room came live now, showing the First Centurion in the center and ten other captains around him so that everyone could see each other.

"All vessels, this is Kosnett, aboard *Urumchi*. I have the flag," he said in a dark, sober voice.

She watched the man's face for clues. Here was a terrible warlord who had chosen instead to be an explorer. Most folks would see the latter and forget the former.

At least for one more day.

She shivered at the thought of what was coming.

"When we went to *Ellariel* to honor our friend Lord

Morninghawk, my fear had been that *Dalou* might launch a sneak attack behind us," Kosnett continued, laying things out more starkly than the Shogun's Court would do. Especially with serving officers. But this was Kosnett. "Instead, we found many new friends among the folks of the *Dalou Hegemony*. People committed to doing the right thing, just as Morninghawk."

He paused there. She watched his eyes shift around, as though taking in all the small images of his own captains, either *Aquitaine* or forwarded on to assist him in dealing with pirates. She thought that they were perhaps stretching their writ some, but she also understood just how immensely angry the man was.

That much she had seen in one of their final, private meetings before departure, when she had asked him the important question.

Why are you doing this?

"Instead, *Ewin* chose to try my patience," Kosnett continued, syllables like a hammer driving nails into hard wood. "I have suggestions that Baron Russand is a renegade to his own Duke and King. That his attack at the moorage at *Meerut* was similar to what Utkin did previously. Except that he failed. Badly failed. *Viking* and our reformed pirate friends saw them off with terrible casualties. Russand lost half his fleet in an afternoon. I am still not satisfied."

Kohahu watched the men around her stir uncomfortably now. Previously, demonstration raids were all anybody truly engaged in. Wars among the Five Nations were rare, as piracy had been the biggest issue until recently. Each held their borders as hard as they could, but few worlds actually changed hands.

Kosnett was introducing a new kind of warfare. The men in this room were only now internalizing what that meant.

Kohahu already knew.

Tsunami. The terrible wave, where the waters pulled back sharply, followed by utter devastation.

It was a thing for planets, not starships, but Kohahu

understood that Kosnett's anger would not be assuaged any other way.

She just blessed whatever deities would listen that they had chosen someone else to be made an example of.

"Understand this," Kosnett said after that short break. "They respect us, the folks of the Balhee Cluster. That is good. However, they have not been taught to fear my wrath, so they may choose to continue pushing their luck when they think I might not strike them down. Baron Russand is about to learn the hard way what a poor choice he has made."

Even Kohahu quailed inwardly at the lurid images his words painted. Many would call the foreigners barbarians, but that was a mistake. Merely alien. And folks who had just spent more than a century engaged in a series of wars for their very survival.

It bred strong, deliberate warriors. *Ewin* would be learning what that meant shortly.

"As Striker Solo of *Shadowbolt* has reminded me, we are also about to make a political statement," Kosnett said. "Because Russand is renegade, and not acting under the orders of King Doysan IV. We are making a larger statement as well."

He stopped and his eyes seemed to grow enormous as Kohahu watched.

"You will not try my patience," he growled.

It was like a beast at the edge of the firelight growling.

"*Shadowbolt*, you will have the van," Kosnett said now. "Come to three-five-five, down five, and begin accelerating standard. *Forktail*, you will switch places with *Shadowbolt* for this run. All ships conform to *Shadowbolt* in three lines astern. Ladies and gentlemen, today we are going to teach someone better manners. *Shadowbolt*, as you bear."

He cut the line and Kohahu felt like the temperature in the room had just fallen chill enough that she needed a jacket over her half-kimono.

Captain Yukimura turned to her now, sober and focused.

"He intends to attack them without any warning?" the man asked, mostly confirming.

She had seen the original orders Kosnett had transmitted.

"They had their warning to behave, Captain," Kohahu replied. "That the Baron chose to ignore it is simply bad decision-making on his part."

"Kosnett intends us to sail down prepared for battle," Yukimura countered.

"No," Kohahu corrected him. "Kosnett intends you to destroy the moorage at *Jacoby* and anyone who disputes his ownership of it today. Whether the *Ewin* king chooses to accept that or cause a larger issue is secondary, as I doubt that the entire *Ewin* fleet is a threat to Kosnett. And if they are, he might return to *Meerut* and summon all his little pirates, plus the three vessels he left there."

"That would be sufficient?" the Crown Prince spoke up now.

Technically, he was the lowest ranked officer in the room. He was also the son of the Emperor.

"With *Viking* and the rest, I expect he could annihilate them," she said. "If truly pressed, he might send home for a fleet capable of sweeping the entire Cluster clear of threats."

The men around her were all older. Generations in some cases, with Captain Yukimura being in his early fifties. Every one of them still trembled a little at her words.

Kohahu was just happy someone else had chosen to try Kosnett's patience.

JACOBY

ONE

Heather had worked with Iveta and the rest on this, taking everything Striker Solo of *Shadowbolt* had been able to tell them about how *Ewin* forces usually worked. Barnaby Silver, Command Centurion off *Viking*, had also sent his full scan logs.

Baron Russand had attacked *Meerut* with a Hunter as his flagship. A cruiser-sized hull that carried a squadron of snubfighters like the famous Jessica Keller had done when she transferred to *Auberon*. Russand's people weren't nearly as good.

He'd also brought a Heavy Bombard, which was the other thing that *Ewin* did with cruisers, and a Light Bombard like *Shadowbolt*.

Throw in four missile frigates and he must have thought he was the king shit. Certainly, most fleets around here weren't equipped to deal with that many missiles tracking down on you at once.

Fool had severely underestimated the *RAN*. And Bedrov-designed Expeditionary vessels. All those Pulse-Twos and Type-3-Pulse were tailor made for annihilating missile swarms.

And now, Phil was pissed.

You just had to look in his eyes to see that Russand had pushed the man far enough that Phil was going to make an example of him. Hopefully, everybody else would sit back and recalibrate their stupidity after this.

Or not. He'd threatened to ask the First Lord to send a Heavy Dreadnought squadron. Not even *Dalou*'s battleships would survive for long if she did that.

"Pilot, call the time," Iveta said now, dragging Heather back to the surface from her notes and planning.

"Two minutes to Emergence," Centurion Virág replied crisply.

Iveta looked over at her with a fire in her eyes. Heather smiled. The woman had probably been looking forward to a day like this for years. Perhaps decades.

"All hands to battle stations," Heather said unnecessarily. *Urumchi* had been ready for this since they left the waypoint five hours ago. "Iveta, you have Tactical."

Heather wondered if those words would trigger an orgasm in the woman, considering what was two minutes away.

Phil had reminded everyone, time and again, that they were explorers and diplomats.

Today, Iveta got to go *Junkyard*.

"I have Tactical," Iveta repeated, almost glowing now. "Gun teams, we expect missile swarms from all corners, so maintain your coverage as backup for the corvettes. Gunner, the Type-4s will be the hammer today. Phil will tell us who he wants smashed."

"Roger that," the Gunner, Hào Boyadjiev, nodded back. "Primed and standing by."

Heather looked it all over and considered her options.

"Engineering, keep the spare generators online after we drop," she ordered.

Aft, Command Machinist Rais El-Amin just nodded at her on the screen. He wasn't surprised by the order. Not after the things they'd done.

About all he wasn't immediately prepared for right now was pushing a burning dreadnought away from a station, but only because he still thought he needed to take the bow apart first in a shipyard to move some pieces around.

He had it all mapped, though. Nobody figured Phil was kidding about needing it, one of these days.

"Stand by for Emergence," Virág called to the quiet bridge.

And then they were there.

"Science Officer, hard ping please," Iveta asked.

Leyla was already at work, but Iveta wanted to know what the folks had had for breakfast over there.

Heather watched the screen fill in with details. Striker Solo had maps he had supplied previously, so she had a rough idea. Habitable planet that was more land than ocean but not by much. A handful of big stations in orbit, one of which was a small shipyard capable of turning out frigates from scratch and repairing bigger things.

Until recently, *Pioneer*, *Dragonfly*, and *Merchant Venture* would have been somewhere in orbit, probably close to the main station. Pity that two of them were back at *Meerut* undergoing repairs.

She wasn't sure if Phil would keep them, but she'd put in a word for at least one of the missile frigates. Strip half the launchers, add some generators, and mount a couple of spare weapons out of boxes, and they'd be trouble.

Maybe a Type-3-Pulse and a pair of Pulse-Twos. Dish it out and take it.

"Heather, how's the reaction?" Phil asked from another screen. "Seems quiet."

She had to agree.

Leyla's ping was in the process of waking people up, but that might be an annoying rooster folks wanted to doze through.

Shadowbolt had come out first, with everyone stretched back from him like an arrowhead. *Ewin* ship in the van meant that this was not an invasion.

Per se.

She was still invading *Jacoby* orbit with everything unlocked.

"We might have complete surprise, Phil," she said carefully.

They'd been expecting everyone to launch everything in the tubes. Nobody had yet.

Yet.

"Let's take advantage of it, then," he said. "You take the flag for now."

"Roger that," Heather said. She switched a button to the general line. "*Aquitaine* squadron, this is Lau. I have the flag. *Shadowbolt*, lead us in."

Nine missile frigates in orbit, but no more than two in close formation anywhere, like they were all just hanging out at a bar or something.

"Leyla, where's *Pioneer*?" Heather asked.

"I think he's dry-docked, boss," the woman replied with an evil grin.

Oh, that would be priceless. He'd had to leave all his fighters behind at *Meerut*, where they'd surrendered when the alternative was being annihilated. And the ship had taken serious damage from *Viking* as well as *Hollywood* and her two consorts there at the end.

"Okay, I have missile launches finally," Leyla called.

Heather watched the screen light up as two of the frigates started launching. The others wouldn't be far behind.

"Iveta, all yours," Heather said.

TWO

I veta had to almost sit on her hands, so as to not be gesturing madly today.

Outmatched opponent (read: *mugging victim*). Dead asleep in their home harbor like they'd planned to do to her friends at *Meerut*. Nothing bigger than a frigate on her boards, when their idea of a frigate was physically barely larger than her corvettes and with only a third the engine and generator power.

Oh, yes.

Iveta studied her boards as frigates started making themselves a nuisance. She marked them all into mental quadrants and started assigning sectors.

"Heather, we have the high ground," Iveta said. "Split out a cruiser and a corvette paired this way?"

She transmitted an arrangement to her boss and watched the woman's face.

"Do it," Heather nodded.

"Squadron, this is Beridze," she called over the open line. "New sailing orders for everyone. *Forktail* and *Storm Petrel*, you stay high with us."

She got acknowledgments and watched the four *RAN* corvettes each pair up with a cruiser and move down towards the frigates below. Until those folks started forming up into teams and squadrons, they were not a serious threat.

"Science Officer, confirm *Pioneer*'s status," Iveta said now, having split things up so her flanks were secured.

Storm Petrel had a condor firebird on the bow. Big, gnarly plasma torpedo weapon.

"I have the hull in dry-dock, Tactical," Leyla replied. "No power signatures live."

Oh, Baron Fuckup, I **own** *you now.*

Iveta smiled.

"Pilot, bring us down and in along this line," she said. "*Forktail*, maintain close escort. *Storm Petrel* on the starboard high wing."

NONE of the frigates were close to the dry-dock?!?

Any ship moving to intercept her now had to cross under at least one of her four corner cruisers to get there, too.

"Station Two is starting to come alive," Leyla called. "I've got targeting scanners warming up over there."

"*Forktail*, that's your corner," Iveta called. "Gun Teams, you have that flank covered as well."

More acknowledgments. She felt like a pirate today. In all the good ways. *Hollywood* Ward and her friends would be so jealous to have missed this. Maybe that woman needed to take command of one of the newly captured ships and start flying an *RAN* flag for a while?

Weirder shit had happened, even just since they got to Balhee.

"Pilot, bring us here and hold," Iveta said, sending him a position marker. "Gunner, hold the Fours."

Optimum for the Type-4s to crush *Pioneer*. Pretty good for the condor.

Somebody had forgotten to add missile racks to the dry-dock platform. Or guns. Or they would have been firing at her by now.

Should have been.

Iveta dialed her scanner back a few notches and counted missiles. Nine frigates put out a lot of firepower, but all of it was uncoordinated and climbing out of the gravity well at her. Worst possible starting point for those ships.

Whoopsie.

None of the big guns had spoken yet, as everyone was busy killing missiles. Station Two was finally launching old, slow fighter craft that had about as much chance against her today as a snowball in hell. Thirteen of them, which suggested every single one they had, after the idiot Baron had lost his first team at *Meerut.*

"First Centurion, we're in position to do some serious damage," Iveta said now. "What are your orders?"

THREE

Phil still felt like the worst of all possible evils, even after he had woken up from his nap earlier. But this was necessary, as he'd told folks. Nobody would be interested in causing him grief after this. Unless they were actively suicidal.

He looked at the layout of the system. Amateur hour, when he'd brought stone professionals on his side. This was a rugby match between a pro, planetary team and a scratch team of drunk, middle-aged accountants. Kittens had about as much chance against him today from the way someone over there had screwed up.

"Iveta, how tough is Station Two?" he asked.

"Probably their main operational base, First Centurion," she replied instantly. "That might be where the Baron was asleep an hour ago, considering."

He nodded, pensive.

Then he hit the lock-out so he was only talking to Harinder and her folks.

"You have an evil gleam in your eyes, Phil," she said from across the table.

"I'm going to lay out a scenario for you," he replied, unable to not grin.

Jessica Keller was the benchmark that **everyone** in the *RAN* measured themselves against. By extension, his mission was also going to be held to that woman's standards.

"Go ahead," she said warily.

It was like she knew him or something.

"So the dry-dock is unarmed, and likely surprised," he said. "Station Two can fire their big beams at us but we're all really out of range of that right now, so they have missiles and fighters. That's just an ugly way to order your crews to die facing us, considering what we're up to."

"Agreed," she nodded.

"How crazy would it be to cut out *Pioneer*?" he asked.

The measure of his words were the number of heads around the room that suddenly turned this way. The enormous eyes blinking at him like little bunnies suddenly looking up at a bobcat.

The utter silence, save for reports coming in and the blowers dealing with all the sweat and adrenaline that came with battle.

Even Harinder's mouth had fallen open in utter surprise.

He wished he had a camera handy, because he knew she'd deny it later. Maybe he'd have someone pull the security tapes, then blow up a still he could hang on the wall in his office until she tore it down and burned it.

Nobody **ever** surprised Harinder Abbatelli. Flag Command Centurion. Trained by Zivkovic himself. Truly one of the best in the business, competing only with her old teacher's legend.

He smiled and nodded, then pressed a button.

"Security, Opeyemi here," she said as she came on the line.

Senior Centurion Temitope Estera Opeyemi. He'd never told her, but her eyes always reminded Phil of blueberries, they were so dark as to be almost indigo. Rare on an Anglo genotype. She was tall and elegant, but red hair kept short to fit under a helmet and paler skin than normal around *Aquitaine*. She could walk down the street on most *Fribourg* worlds and fit in.

"Got a mission for my Dragoon," Phil said in a sidelong kind of way.

He watched her hackles rise in response.

"Oh?" she asked carefully.

"Grab Xochitl Dar and take five minutes," Phil ordered. "Including *Storm Petrel* and the rest, do we have enough marines to storm the dry-dock and capture *Pioneer*? Then cut it out and sail it away?"

Phil found himself rather enjoying the looks of surprise his own people were giving him today. He'd gotten a shade nervous that he'd grown predictable, since his various foes in the Cluster had been able to surprise him too many times lately.

"You're serious," she whispered.

Phil couldn't help himself. That famous line had become something of his signature over the years, but it fully encapsulated his approach to things. Especially today.

"We're the *RAN*, Dragoon," he growled at her with a smile. "That's what we do."

"On it," she said, cutting the line and no doubt lighting a fire under various asses.

Storm Petrel was a training ship. They had a lot of excess marines, mostly to protect all the important people aboard, as well as to help get people ready for life in the navy. They were also a militant culture that trained with live steel.

He caught Markus standing close.

"I suppose you want to go play pirate?" Phil asked with a grin.

"I might be your resident expert," Markus replied tartly. "But if I get a finger blown off it doesn't count."

"Agreed," Phil nodded. "You are detached until the dragoon is done with you."

"Yee-HAW!!!" he hollered, causing several folks to flinch as the man went out the main hatch at a dead run.

Phil unlocked the squadron feed.

"Iveta, bring *Urumchi* here," he said, marking the map.

FOUR

Heather scowled. Wanted to bitch at her boss. He was, however, right. Doing this would ram home to everyone that Phil was here to negotiate trade deals and open diplomatic relations.

And if you pissed him off, you were going to get an open palm slap across the face, followed by three or four good body blows to knock you down before the steel-toed boots started stomping.

"Squadron, this is *Ground Control*, aboard *Urumchi*," she called on the main line. "I have the flag. All teams, you have been briefed. The frigates are not prepared to intercept you on this, nor should anybody really be ready to stop you short of missile fire, so when you launch shuttles, I expect every gunner to reach as far as they can killing anything out there that doesn't transmit an *RAN* transponder code."

She paused and took a sip of coffee, mostly because she'd gone dry-mouthed with the sheer audacity of what Phil was going to try today. What he had ordered her to pull off, because she was better than anybody at handling all those vectors and sounds in her head at once.

One of these days, *Junkyard* might be better, but Heather

still had nearly a decade on the woman. Old age and treachery against youth and skill, as the old saying went.

"On my mark, all vessels come about and transition to maximum acceleration," *Ground Control* called. "All marine units on high alert and stand by for tactical assault. Three. Two. One. Go. Repeat: Go!"

She leaned back and muted the line at her end enough to blow all the air out of her lungs and then sucked clean air in.

There was crazy, and then there was this whole new plateau of rude that Phil was going to take things to, a place she hadn't been since some of Keller's crazier raids back during the war.

Yeah, historians back home would write entire outcome studies on this day.

Better make it good.

FIVE
SKYCRUISER LI JING

Stunt Dude checked his fittings and blinked in surprise when Captain Xue Dao Zhiou suddenly stepped close. He'd been surrounded by her marine assault troops as everyone got ready, answering questions because he was the expert.

"I am still uncertain that this is a wise course of action, Trinidad," she said carefully. "The First Centurion assigned you to *Li Jing* as a liaison officer, not a boarding party."

He shrugged. *Stunt Dude* was short for a guy, so he looked up to the woman. At the same time, he outmassed her considerably. And his adrenaline was up.

In his head, he was already seeing things in terms of camera angles, lighting setups, and special effects rigs. Even after this long, it was all coming back.

"How many enemy vessels have you boarded and captured?" he asked in a loud enough tone that the twenty-eight men and women around him stirred and fell utterly silent.

Conflict among the gods, as it were.

"None," she bowed her head. "As you are aware, we don't take prisoners among pirates who trespass, but destroy them instead."

"Whereas I have been present when three different enemy

ships were taken by raider teams physically invading," he countered. "And I was in command, all three times. That is what a Dragoon trains for in the *Republic of Aquitaine* Navy, Captain."

He couldn't help that his voice had gotten hard by the end of that. Even as a civilian, he heard that siren call for one last joust and couldn't just walk away. Plus, he **was** an expert, and the folks with him would need that. All of them could shoot and punch. He'd spent months training with them and training them to understand that.

None of them thought like pirates. Precious few did, so he really missed *Lady Blackbeard* all the more today, but Siobhan was off having her own adventures somewhere.

He watched Dao Zhiou's eyes change now.

"If something happens to you, I will never hear the end of it from Sam," she tried now.

Low blow. Really low blow.

Still…

"She is aware of who I am," he replied. "Sam knew that when she agreed to come to *Aquitaine* with me. And on this mission. And coming to *Li Jing* was her idea. Plus, I'll be fine, because I no longer have all that craziness I had when I was younger."

"Assaulting and boarding an enemy platform during a raid and firefight is a step down?" she asked sharply.

"*Mansi*," he replied quietly, referring to that planet that had been the end goal of Phil's entire war against Buran.

Three raids to that system. Sneak in and discover what it was. Go back in order to steal a ship. Then storm the place to free hundreds of Imperial prisoners captured and left on the surface of the only inhabitable planet to work or starve.

Personally, the people in charge of that planet had gotten off easy. *Stunt Dude* might have executed them individually with swords, had he been in charge.

Dao Zhiou fell silent now. She'd heard his stories. As had the men and women around her.

The *Emperor of Fribourg*, Karl VIII herself, had pinned a medal on his chest for the actions at *Mansi*. He never, ever had to buy his own beer on any Imperial planet he ever visited, once someone realized who he was. Not after what the crew of *CS-405* had done.

Dao Zhiou could not argue with that. *Ground Control* had been there. He presumed that Markus was moving heaven and hell to be allowed to join with *Urumchi's* teams, doubly so since Heather couldn't come.

He and Markus were the experts today, because not even Dragoon Opeyemi had ever done something like this with live weapons.

Only the *Pirates* of *CS-405*.

He let his scowl speak volumes. Captain Xue nodded and stepped back.

"Good luck, Dragoon," she said, extending her blessing to the rest.

"Thank you, Captain," *Stunt Dude* replied.

And then they were alone on the flight deck.

Guardian Ma Jianhong Ping had already made it clear that he would defer to *Stunt Dude*. Trinidad had far more experience in this sort of thing, and many of these folks had begun to pick up the *RAN* way of doing things. Whoever was there first or had the greatest experience on a topic took charge immediately. Only later would rank factor in.

On *Urumchi*, Dar and Opeyemi might put Markus in charge, even though he was only a Senior Chief these days.

Same reason. Dude had stormed enemy vessels under hostile fire.

Even all the times Trinidad had done it for the cameras before the Navy, doing it for real was something more. He reached up and checked that the exterior camera on his helmet was running by the feed on one side of his faceplate.

Just another late night, low budget, pirate video shoot. With live weapons in hand.

Stunt Dude turned to Guardian Ma. The man was slender and fast. A little taller than *Stunt Dude*, but so much lighter. Sparring with him was like trying to catch a chicken.

At the same time, he was one of the officers of this ship. The equivalent of a dragoon, though well outside his experience with something this crazy. Jianhong Ping's face split into a huge grin now, lighting up everything, including his dark eyes.

"Figured she'd pull rank on you," Ma said now.

Stunt Dude nodded.

"Same," Trinidad admitted. "But she's also right. Ma, you will be second or third at all times, so pick who leads. I'll be in the middle where I can issue orders and coordinate with *RAN* teams. This will get hairy because they are only used to their own space armor, and won't immediately recognize us as friends, so we have to make sure we know who we're shooting at. Questions?"

"Why did they assign us the bridge?" someone behind him asked. They were loose enough around him now to do that, rather than politely raising a hand and waiting to be called on.

Quiet culture. Restrained, though not as bad as *Buran*.

"*Ground Control* has an expectation that a small team can move quickly," he replied. "Plus, we don't want anybody else not *RAN* doing that, because they might not handle it delicately."

"What's delicate?" that voice asked.

"We need to fly *Pioneer* out," he said. "That means we need to make sure the dry-dock doesn't damage it. Maybe have all those folks in hand so they can answer questions."

"So we're not just going to fly the entire dry-dock out?" Ma asked.

Stunt Dude felt the local gravity twitch, but it was all in his head.

"Fly?" he asked weakly. "*RAN* platforms don't have engines."

"Ah," Ma nodded. "This one should. Mobile dry-dock platforms are common around here. Not fast, but you don't have to wait for a tug."

Stunt Dude looked around menu options until he found the line he wanted.

"*Urumchi*, Lau."

"Heather, it's *Stunt Dude*," he said. "I have experts here who think that the entire platform might have engines and JumpSails. Self-portable, as it were, but powered down right now. Thoughts?"

The long pause suggested she was just as surprised as he was.

"I'll update the other teams," she finally replied. "Add that as a secondary mission parameter."

"Understood," he said, then turned back to Ma and the others. "She's giving us the option to see if we can capture the whole thing. All hands load up and stand by to launch."

Shit, could he turn this whole thing into that scene at the end where the credits rolled as the ship sailed into the darkness?

He was in Shuttle Number One. Guardian Ma was in Two.

Shortly, they would be launching to try to capture two ships, apparently.

Only been here a day, and already topping our legend?

Stunt Dude found a growling smile and checked the charge on his rifle again.

SIX

I veta had a symphony going. She wondered if it was similar to what Heather heard. Or Phil. Tones and beats telling her where everyone was headed and how soon they would get there.

The frigates had stood there like dolts for several minutes before someone finally figured out that the attacking force wasn't running away. Hell, they'd even stopped firing for a time, convinced that the invaders had been frightened off and unwilling to waste ammunition.

Iveta presumed that the Baron had been the one to see it. All of those invaders suddenly turning and running towards the platform where *Pioneer* was undergoing repairs necessary because Auke on *Viking* had kicked his ass and almost ended him.

Auke was like that. Not a true warrior in the bloodthirsty sense, but more like an offended shopkeeper. Possibly more dangerous that way, because you never expected someone who looked like that to suddenly go for your throat.

"Science Officer, what is our status?" Iveta called.

"All friendlies have launched shuttles," Leyla replied. "Optimized flight times are running close to time on target arrivals."

Iveta couldn't help her smile. *Time on target* meant that everyone would arrive at the same instant, from every direction, rather than strung out. Overwhelm someone with superior firepower localized.

Like say, rent-a-cops handling security duties on an unarmed dry-dock in homeport orbit?

Iveta had wondered about the risk, but Phil had ordered *Urumchi* and her two sidekicks close enough to the platform so that anybody over there would have started shooting. Over on the big station a quarter away around orbit, they were firing everything they had, but the range was literally astronomical, and the chances of keeping a beam coherent that far was in the realm with being struck by lightning.

Her Fours could have done some damage, but only because she would be shooting at a huge station, rather than something as small as *Urumchi*, to say nothing of the rest of the squadron.

Phil had instructed her to leave anybody alone who didn't get close. *Her* definition of close, which meant frigates even turning a bow this direction, instead of sailing broadside to her where they could keep launching missiles.

Useless missiles. And they would run out soon. Even with as many reloads as *Ewin* ships kept aboard.

Then those ships turned into mere Patrollers. Harmless Search and Rescue boats with no business in this sort of action.

"What about the fightercraft?" Iveta asked after a pause.

They would be a threat to the shuttles. At least until someone took a hammer to them.

"Holding an escort formation near Station Two," Leyla said. "No, wait, I'm getting a signal from Station Two. Speaking for the Baron."

"Route it to Phil," Heather suddenly awakened from wherever she'd gone mentally while they had waited. "He's been waiting for this call. All vessels, bring your alert up one more status, even if you think you are at the top of the chart."

One more? Iveta wasn't sure where else they could go, except that it dawned on her that Baron Russand had finally figured out what Phil was up to. Was he attempting to surrender on terms before he lost everything?

What would the First Centurion say?

SEVEN

Phil paused and put on his best scowl.

"Lag two seconds?" he confirmed with Harinder.

She nodded.

He keyed the line live.

"This is First Centurion Philip S. Kosnett of the *Republic of Aquitaine* Navy," he said heavily. "We are in pursuit of a band of pirates who attacked the moorage at *Meerut* two weeks ago. All vessels in this system are ordered to withdraw from hostilities or you will be treated the same as the pirates."

He kept the scowl and leaned back. Baron Russand would take a moment to catch up.

"Kosnett, this is Baron Russand," he finally said. "What are you DOING?"

Phil had the impression of an aging Lothario. Mid-fifties, maybe, though the black dyed hair and expert makeup around the eyes made it hard to judge. Skinny face like an ax blade, with a prominent nose and chin and almost no cheekbones.

There was panic in his eyes.

Phil refrained from pointing out the obvious. The *RAN* didn't suffer pirates or piracy, while the Balhee Cluster treated it like a fact of life. Along with Death and Taxes, as it were.

And he wasn't feeling particularly benevolent today. Hell, he'd come here to see if he could annihilate *Pioneer* and anybody else that felt like getting up in his face.

Stealing the ship instead would just be even better.

"We have traced a pirate cruiser known as *Pioneer* to *Jacoby*, Baron Russand," Phil noted. "Now we are going to deal with it, so that pirates learn not to challenge the forces of law and order. You should reconsider having any dealing with such people in the future."

Again, he didn't smile. There had been no doubts that *Pioneer* had been the Baron's flagship in the *Meerut* attack. Phil pretending that it was an idiot cousin or something out joyriding at least gave the man some level of deniability later.

If he was smart enough to take it. Phil had his doubts.

"That's my vessel, *Urumchi*!" he screamed. "You can't do this!"

Phil did smile. It was hard, cold, deadly. Tomas Kigali had taught it to him, of all people. Over the decades, lots of people had overlooked just how deadly that man was, because he flew in a squadron with Keller and d'Maine, and their legends for savagery to their enemies.

Kigali was usually flying the warship closest to the enemy at all times.

"Baron Russand, you can't stop me," Phil reminded him in a cold, methodical voice. "And the next time you try, I won't be satisfied just taking your ship. If I ever have to deal with you again, I'll bring my entire force over and destroy every ship in orbit without mercy. Just so you understand me. Do not bother replying on this channel, as I'm not even interested in taking your surrender right now."

He cut the line to make his point and turned to Harinder. She wasn't surprised. She also wasn't asking if he thought he was going too far.

"What will the *Ewin* king say?" was all she said.

"I'll ask the man when we get to *Ewinhome*," Phil nodded before cutting to the squadron line.

"All vessels, this is Kosnett," he said simply. "I expect them to finally get desperate."

EIGHT

ASSAULT SHUTTLE ONE, APPROACHING THE DRY-DOCK

Lights. Camera. Action.

Stunt Dude was back to the day they stole *Packmule* by sneaking up on it, then leaping an entire marine team across open space before the folks aboard realized that they weren't alone.

These locals knew trouble was coming, but there was nothing they could do about it.

"Team One, stand by to go to vacuum," he said on the command line.

Over on Two, Ma would be doing the same.

"Pilot, vent us to space," *Stunt Dude* ordered.

Everyone was latched down, and their assault armor came with thruster packs filled with compressed nitrogen gas. The shuttle had never been designed for hostile insertions, so they would normally take fifteen minutes to get there.

Instead, they were just shutting down life support and opening every door.

The whirlwind lasted about thirty seconds, then they were seeing stars out open doors.

He made sure his systems were good, including the camera

that would no doubt be used to take training footage. And maybe some bad video back home, one of these days.

"All raiders, check your systems and signal green," he continued.

Shit flying around might puncture something. Better to patch it now than discover you were out of air all of a sudden.

Helmets went green as he watched, including his own.

"Pilot, what is our status?"

"Approaching the bow top deck marked for assault, Centurion," the woman replied.

Everyone called him Centurion these days, except when they called him *Stunt Dude*. He could live with that.

"Everyone up and grab handholds," *Stunt Dude* ordered, finding himself a spot in the middle.

A safe spot, so he wouldn't catch too much hell from Sam for what he was about to do.

"Centurion, we are slowing down and aimed on target," the pilot called now. "Ready for you to jump."

Trinidad located the man by the front hatch and pointed. That fellow stuck his head out, then looked back and nodded.

"We're on target, sir," he said.

"Go," *Stunt Dude* said.

Packmule, coming up. All cameras rolling. Sound technicians mind your microphones.

Bodies poured out and started to thruster their way inward and down.

Down, because this dry-dock was big enough that *Urumchi* could have slipped in, with enough grease and maybe moving a few frames around. Open latticework meant that he could see *Pioneer* inside, like a pea on a pod.

Around him, more than a dozen armored suits, again, with him safely in the middle. He wouldn't have shot it that way for the vid, though, so he might have to take film from the guy up front.

Idly, he wondered if Dao Zhiou had gotten to all the rest of the team on a private line and told them to treat him like a priceless vase. Or maybe Ma had.

Somebody.

Nobody was broadcasting local scanners right now. Just eyeballs, because the shuttles had gotten them close enough to do this and had imparted enough momentum. Any weapons coming in were the responsibility of the corvettes, anyway.

He had to board the dry-dock and see if they could capture it.

Worse, steal it with *Pioneer* still docked.

Talk about frosting someone.

His lead got there a little ahead of Guardian Ma, but that looked like the two having an agreement about timing. Quickly, everyone was standing on the skin of the platform around a docking airlock meant for a shuttle or small ship.

Guardian Ma looked over at him.

"Airlocks are traps, Guardian," Centurion Mildon said. "Too easy to pick off small teams before help can arrive."

"Demolition team into the lock," Ma ordered.

Half the team was pointed inward. The other half faced out on overwatch. *Stunt Dude* was the dragoon in charge of this part of the operation, so he had no business being up front, much as it galled him. Did give him a good camera angle for watching the folks doing the actual work.

Sam would already complain. Best not to add any reasons.

"Clear the hole!" Ma called as bodies flooded back out of the airlock, followed a few seconds later by a hard thump, and then a small hurricane of air and ice crystals.

Packmule. Vent sections of the big ship to space so people cannot get to you until they suit up themselves. Hit hard. Hit fast.

Unleash maximum brutality of mind on them now, so they are much more likely to be polite later when you haven't killed them.

"First squad in," Ma called.

Eight went into the hole, including Ma. *Stunt Dude* had the rest with him outside in two larger groups.

"*Stunt Dude*, ready for you," Ma called a few moments later.

"Team Two in," *Stunt Dude* ordered.

He went in with them, but second to last.

Inside, the inner airlock hatch had been blown apart by experts with big booms in hand. The others were holding both directions of a long corridor.

Too long. What idiot designed this?

Then it dawned on him. Civilian dry-dock, not built to *RAN* standards, where you kept your frames relatively close together so that you didn't lose whole sections if you had a leak.

Or if some asshole blew open an airlock.

One of the reasons Trinidad had been good as a martial artist and actor was the ability to mentally track things in three dimensions, so he always knew where people were. And cameras.

"Forward now," he said to Ma. "Look for a right-hand corridor or frame hatch that gets us closer. Team three, stand by to make entry."

Ma and his folks moved, loping like wolves chasing deer. *Stunt Dude* followed at a more sedate pace, picking up the twenty gunners with him.

It was hard, not being at the point, but he was management now. Was this what it felt like to move up from Second Unit Director to the boss?

"We have a hatch that shows pressure on the other side," Ma said on the comm.

"Override the sensors and open it," *Stunt Dude* replied. "Stand by to rescue anyone we catch out of suits."

Every one of them had a spare emergency softsuit they could put on someone. Best way to keep someone alive, because most would be dock workers. Likely not even armed, let alone dangerous.

Deadly was flying with him today.

Ma put a device on the sensor that told the thing it was now reading pressure, and it happily opened up for him. Air began to whistle past, turning to snow as Trinidad watched. Elsewhere, other hatches would slam shut and seal, but this one hadn't noticed anything.

The winds fell off. Ma's first squad surged through. Nobody had been caught in the open. That was good. *Stunt Dude* and his groups followed.

Again, long corridor. Transverse this time, running right across the spine.

About halfway, Ma stopped and signaled.

"Bridge access, *Stunt Dude*," he said. "Currently locked."

Trinidad laughed. Like that would keep his wolves out.

"Blow it," he said, turning to the group behind him. "Seal us into pressure but maintain vacuum discipline."

It would even sound good as part of the movie, but he'd been pretty good at improvising dialogue for fight scenes in his time.

At either end of the deadly snake, teams went to work. They hadn't seen anybody yet, but that might be luck. And it might be folks smart enough to remain in their cabins since most of them were unarmed.

"Ready to breach, Centurion."

"Fire in the hole."

Boom.

There was atmosphere, so he could see the smoke. Later, the FV team would add more stuff here. Maybe some roostertails of sparks to look extra awesome on screen. Life support would be working overtime to clear it in the background, while Ma and his teams opened fire into the room with stun pistols.

Stunt Dude approved. You could be indiscriminate in firing those, because you could always apologize later.

The firefight was brief. Like the time he'd taken *Packmule*. *Stunt Dude* wondered if there had only been the captain armed here, as well. Pity nobody with camera experience had been making sure lights and angles were good, but he also doubted *Yaumgan* would want to turn this into an adventure vid.

Maybe *Dalou* or *Aditi*. He could always sell them the footage later.

"Bridge secured, Centurion," Ma called over the team line.

"Team Two in," Trinidad replied.

Again, second to last in, just so Sam would only be slightly incensed at his antics.

Bodies inside. Softsuited in case some asshole vented the space to vacuum. Otherwise unprepared. One man down with guards, so either the captain or the gunman.

"Team Three, take charge," he ordered.

Unlike the first two groups he'd commanded, this team was half made up of other specialties, including a couple of enlisted crew members qualified to sit bridge watches and fly starships. If they really could steal the whole platform, he'd ask for Flyer Hu BooLa or one of his experts to handle things.

Bodies got hauled off and processed. They'd be waking up as prisoners in about five minutes.

"Team One and Team Two, secure our perimeter against counter-attack," *Stunt Dude* ordered.

This would be when someone would do something, about the time when folks started relaxing, thinking they had won. The start of Act Two, as it were, when the villains got their shit together and struck back.

Stunt Dude had been trained in his time by some serious killers, as well as a number of pretty good screenwriters. Now, all he had to do was sit back and watch.

"Sir, they left systems unlocked in the moment," one of the group sitting said. "We have full operational control of the drydock."

Well, fuck.

"Do we have engines and JumpSails?" he asked.

"Affirmative, Centurion."

Double fuck, they might really pull this stupidity off.

"Get me a line to *Urumchi*," he said. "And cut all power feeds to *Pioneer* unless a friendly asks."

"On it, sir."

Trinidad Mildon found the captain's station and wondered how silly his dress uniform would look if he had a medal for piracy with four bars. No wait. Five. He also got credit for *Pioneer* if they did this.

"First Centurion on line three, Centurion."

"*Stunt Dude*."

"You did it?" Phil asked.

"In the process, I think," *Stunt Dude* replied. "What do you want us to do?"

"Start moving," Phil ordered. "If you can get out of the gravity well far enough, we can move you somewhere else and handle things from there. What do you need?"

"Keep everybody off my ass, Phil," he said. "When you want us in Jump, I'd like an expert or two in charge over here. My folks are good, but I need a Flyer or Pilot for that part."

"How easy is the tech?"

"Stand by."

He walked over to the man currently warming the engines up. *Yaumgan* did things much differently than anybody else, so *Stunt Dude* had asked for redneck engineers for things. At least as close as the Philosopher/Kings got. He'd found a few.

"We can do it?" he asked the man.

"Peace of cake, Centurion," the new semi-Flyer replied. "Mostly automated for civilians. Won't be fast or pretty, but we can initiate a course."

"Do it now," *Stunt Dude* said. "Up and out until we can rendezvous with a real bridge crew off *Li Jing* or *Urumchi* to handle it. Let everyone else correspond to our course from here."

"On it."

Stunt Dude returned to the captain's chair.

"You caught all that?" he asked.

"I did, Trinidad," Phil said. "Good job and tell your people thank you from me, until I can do it personally."

He cut the line so Trinidad did the same.

"Guardian Ma, what's the status with the other teams?" *Stunt Dude* asked.

He'd been so locked in here that he'd practically ignored the rest of the operation.

"*Pioneer* had a few ground combat teams still aboard, Centurion," Ma replied. "Centurion Dar took charge of that operation personally."

In other words, Xochitl was about to hand someone their asses and embarrass them in the process. That woman was scary when she got locked in on a target.

Trinidad nodded and started poking at controls until he found the ship-wide he wanted.

"Attention all hands, this is Senior Centurion Trinidad Mildon of the *Republic of Aquitaine* Navy," he said in a radio voice meant for voiceover work. "This platform has been lawfully captured and you are all prisoners of war if you surrender peacefully at this point. Otherwise, I will treat you like pirates and send hunters into the air ducts after you with orders to kill. Signal your location if you intend to surrender, and we will see about getting you off-loaded in escape pods before we leave the *Jacoby* system."

He cut the line and smiled, hoping that this was the end of the movie, rather than just the end of Act One.

NINE

ABOARD FLAGSHIP URUMCHI AT RAN
WAYPOINT TWENTY-SIX

Striker Gotzon Solo knew that he was being honored to sit at First Centurion Kosnett's right hand in the meeting of his strikers, but it felt weird.

First off, because he'd gone into *Jacoby* and led the assault force that had cut out Baron Russand's flagship and dry-dock, then sailed it right out of the system. That was likely to cause feuds later, possibly even duels, though the king tried to forbid such things.

A man's honor was the one thing that he had control over, so at times you had to step up and do silly things to protect it. Even that much iffiness was something of a revolution, because a year ago Gotzon would have assumed duels over this and blood feuds down the generations for as long as folks still talked about *The Jacoby Raid*.

Today, he wasn't so sure. Gotzon put that down to spending so much time around the aliens. *Aquitaine* folks had a hard honor, but it wasn't personal. It was wrapped up in the uniform first and the patch on the left shoulder second. Personal came much later.

Weird, but not his place to question.

Instead, Gotzon looked around and tried to figure out what the other strikers were thinking today.

Command Centurion Lau, directly across from him, was just a scary, beautiful woman. Hard as nails. Quiet, in that way that suggested she might sneak up behind you in a dark alley and cut your throat, then leave you to bleed out without ever saying a word. Not even take your wallet in the process.

At least she smiled a little when she looked up and saw him.

Gotzon let his gaze slide away.

That was even worse, as his eyes landed on Lady Kugosu, daughter of the *Dalou* Hegemon.

Initially, he'd wanted to object to including her in the top council. One, she wasn't a Striker. Two, she was a woman, but the First Centurion had a lot of women in command. Third, she was a child.

Then she had opened her mouth and eviscerated one of the fool *Dalou* people at another meeting and Gotzon had wisely kept his own counsel silently on the topic.

Fourteen-year-old girls weren't supposed to be that sharp. That dangerous. It made sense that she was sitting next to Lau.

She scowled at him as if she could read his mind, so Gotzon concentrated on thinking pleasant thoughts and turning to the man beside her.

Captain Yukimura from *Storm Petrel*. Short, dark-skinned, heavyset black man with almost no hair and calm, deadly eyes. Deadly. All of them. Had Kosnett put all the killers on that wing of the round table?

Then what did that say about this side? Him, Cruiser-Captain Khan of *Juvayni*, then a gap of two chairs before Captain Singh of *Aranyani* and the *Yaumgan* Captain, Xue.

Indeed.

Killers over there. Philosophers and diplomats along the bottom of the arc. And a pair of buffoons here?

Gotzon found himself uncomfortable for the first time in

way too long, contemplating the nature of his patriotism. Had it blinded him to things?

A year ago, he would have considered fifteen drone frigates and three cruisers enough to secure any moorage, unless and until the king decided to gather up an entire sector force to deal with one of his renegade nobles.

First Centurion Kosnett would have gone and gotten *Viking* and the other two corvettes, and maybe not even needed the Balhee Cluster forces that had been attached.

And he would have annihilated Baron Russand.

Instead, he had embarrassed the man and emasculated him in the most public way Gotzon could imagine. And Kosnett had no fear of reprisals later, because the rest of the squadron would finish off anyone even raising a fist.

Right now, Gotzon expected King Doysan to send over a small squadron to reestablish his authority, because Russand had no forces left worth mentioning.

Shit, what am I turning into that I even think these thoughts?

The First Centurion rescued him from answering that question by arriving from his personal office, with his Flag Centurion in tow. Abbatelli took the open spot next to Singh and still left that tiny, monumental gap separating Gotzon and Khan from the rest, like it was a social divide.

Had he forgotten to shower this morning?

Ewin and *Gloran* were, according to most quiet rumors, the most likely to be left behind when the effects of the *Aquitaine* arrival made themselves felt. How did Gotzon Solo stop the Principalities from utterly fading from relevance?

Kosnett sat and placed a mug of coffee just so in front of him. Much of the man gave the impression of being relaxed and unconcerned, but Gotzon watched how precisely everything was done, even when the man didn't seem to be working at it.

Was that the trick? They were so focused on their vaunted *RAN* professionalism that it infected everything they did?

Ewin didn't do that. They were all about the *flamboyant*.

Dangerous because they could overwhelm any target with missile swarms.

Until three days ago. Earlier, certainly, but three days ago Gotzon had watched a dozen missile frigates be reduced to irrelevant bystanders for the first time in his life.

Was that *Ewin*'s fate?

His?

"I want to thank everyone for joining me personally," the First Centurion said. "This is a political discussion far more than merely tactical or even strategic."

Gotzon had to agree, but he'd also had a quick meeting with the man in the aftermath of *Jacoby* to try to determine what Doysan IV would do when he heard.

When everyone realized that Russand was toothless.

When some other nation figured out that *Ewin* was defenseless as well from what *Aquitaine* could do.

Not even swarms of missile-armed fighters and frigates would save them.

Not from *Aquitaine*.

Kosnett nodded towards Gotzon. It was a friendly movement.

"I've spoken with the Striker," Kosnett continued. "We have to be five places at once, so we need to determine our movement priorities from here."

"Are you keeping *Pioneer*?" Lady Kugosu asked now, acting like a peer in a council meeting.

It was a weird feeling, realizing that a fourteen-year-old girl's opinion probably had more weight that Gotzon's. He had to stop and remind himself to also make sure she didn't make him look stupid in the process.

She was that smart, too.

"Right at the moment, I intend to sell it to Governor Dexter at *Meerut*," Kosnett smiled. "Along with the dry-dock we liberated from the pirates at *Jacoby*."

That prompted a round of chuckles around the table. And a

few smiles his way. Because *Shadowbolt* had led, that had been an officially-sanctioned mission, at least as far as most people would consider. The king might have words, but everything Gotzon had done so far had fallen under the quilt of orders that had seen him and *Shadowbolt* attached to the *Aquitaine* force for piracy patrols.

Baron Russand had already been renegade enough, before he irritated the most dangerous man in the galaxy. Now, he was a footnote waiting to be written.

"Will that turn *Meerut* into an *RAN* base?" Lady Kugosu asked as a follow-up.

"It will remain so, Lady Kugosu," Kosnett clarified. "I have a base there now, under an agreement with the system government. This will turn them into a more effective system, by allowing them to repair larger vessels as well as construct and maintain a defensive fleet sufficient against folks like renegade *Ewin* nobles."

Gotzon found it enlightening how Kosnett left unspoken the threat of *Dalou* princes going rogue when speaking to the woman. There were probably more of them than *Ewin*, if you were to line up all the wanted posters in the Cluster.

At the same time, the threat was conveyed. Politely.

He could see an *Ewin* Duke screaming obscenities and pounding his fist on the table right now, so that everyone at the table understood that the man was serious.

Kosnett didn't need to. He was that secure.

Was that it?

Gotzon tried not to gape as pieces in his mind suddenly aligned into a new formation.

Ewin was all about honor and fought duels over it. *Aquitaine*, and to a lesser extent places like *Dalou*, were all about duty.

They weren't held hostage to an inferiority complex like *Ewin* seemed to be.

Except it wasn't a complex. *Ewin* truly was inferior to the others. Not much, to be sure, because missile swarms could level any playing field. The arrival of *Aquitaine* had shown a much harsher light of truth on things.

Ewin was behind. Maybe in last place among five, with the *Zen-Mekyo Syndicates* now broken and in the process of being finished. *Gloran* might be next ahead of *Ewin*, but then it was a full step up to *Dalou* and *Aditi*, with everyone a step behind *Yaumgan*.

Kosnett had turned his way. EVERYONE had turned his way.

Gotzon didn't think he had made a sound. He did remember to close his mouth before he caught any more flies in it.

"Striker?" Kosnett asked. "You had a question?"

Gotzon willed his heart to start beating again, because it might have stopped, as painful as that moment of realization had been.

"No, uh…no, First Centurion," he managed.

"Very good," the man nodded as if nothing had just happened.

But then, Kosnett's entire life hadn't flashed before his eyes, had it?

Gotzon sucked a hard breath to the bottom of his soul and started working on figuring out how he didn't end up in a wrecker's yard in three years.

TEN

Phil wondered if Striker Solo was having a medical event of some sort, but after a second marked it down to some sort of emotional breakthrough. Or breakdown. *Ewin* gentlemen could be fragile creatures. Especially if you didn't let them gesture madly when they spoke.

After a moment, the man seemed to relax, so Phil went back to the others.

Lady Kugosu wasn't sucking on a lemon, but the poise of her mouth wasn't far off. As with the rest of her countrymen, she'd probably hoped that *Meerut* might eventually be moved into *Dalou*'s political, social, and perhaps economic orbit. With three cruiser hulls and the lagoon, plus the stations protecting it, they could be fully independent. With a functional dry-dock, they could become something of a rival to other shipyard when it came time for maintenance duties, especially a portable one that could be flown out to repair something broken down in the field.

Phil still thought that *Dalou* needed that occasional nudge, in order to not backslide later. With Lord Morninghawk getting into trade on one corner and *Meerut* on another, they had that long flank with *Ewin* perhaps opening up to commercial possibilities.

Captain Yukimura stepped up emotionally now, when it became clear that Lady Kugosu and Striker Solo had withdrawn some.

"Where do you need to have representatives, First Centurion?" the man asked.

Storm Petrel was a *Dalou* Command Cruiser. He was used to showing the flag, but usually at *Dalou* systems.

"We need to transport *Pioneer* and the dry-dock safely to *Meerut* and get them inside the lagoon," Phil began, ticking things off. "I need to get to *Ewinhome* directly and let the king know that we are not attempting to conquer or overthrow his authority in the process of smashing Russand. The Shogun needs to be updated, as does the *Aditi Consensus*. Plus messages need to be sent to the *Gloran* Emperor, and, if we're being persnickety, the Philosopher/Kings of *Yaumgan*."

"A suggestion, First Centurion?" the man asked carefully.

Captain Yukimura had to do everything carefully, when you thought about it. He had the future Emperor of *Dalou* aboard, probably scrubbing decks like any other trainee officer to make sure they understood how starships really worked.

All these years later, Phil still remembered a lecture given by a Professor named Harold Ruud, back at the Academy, entitled *Hard, Sharp, and Heavy Things*, where he brought in the sorts of gear an *Aquitaine* Legionary infantryman had to carry in the field, so officer trainees in the *RAN* Academy understood. Stuff from the man's own, personal collection. Heavy pistol. A long, steel bayonet that got attached to a rifle so you could stab someone close enough that they bled on your boots, had been the thing that stuck with Phil. Body armor heavy enough to save your life in the field, as it once had Arlo's.

Crown Prince Shingo would be well served with a similar learning experience.

Phil studied Yukimura and nodded.

"Two birds, one stone," the man said with a smiling nod. "We all head immediately to *Meerut*. There, you hire several of those reformed pirates currently flying Pickets and turn them into a galactic messenger service to deliver most of the news you need to get out. Or at least Cluster-wide. That keeps them employed and out of trouble. And gets messages where you need them to go."

"More interestingly, it also establishes *Meerut* as a potential neutral clearing house for information," Commander Singh pointed out. "Though it would be useful later on to negotiate that sort of neutrality at central *Aditi* and other places. Extraterritoriality?"

Phil considered it. That would break down certain barriers, while opening up other options long-term. *Meerut* as a true neutral would radically alter a number of equations, and they would need to be, to be allowed to carry cargo and perhaps people.

The end of piracy turning into the beginning of tourism?

"I still need to get to *Ewinhome* quickly," Phil noted.

"So you run ahead and get everyone prepped at *Meerut*, First Centurion," Captain Xue said, smiling. "We'll escort everything in, then be ready to turn around and sail with you to *Ewinhome*."

Phil nodded. It made sense, and he figured he'd get a small revolution on his hands if he tried to visit another forbidden capital without all these folks. Too many years of political isolation and economic autarky. Instead of regular port calls, they lived behind walls.

His squadron arriving at *Ellariel* had been the first such force allowed in centuries. *Aditi* was more open, but they were the exception that proved the rule. Few warships had ever been to the capital world of the *Ewin Principalities*, either.

Phil looked around and got concurrence from everyone. None wanted to be left out, but Yukimura's idea of a courier service might be the vector of the biggest revolution yet. Small, armed, and fast. Not big enough to be threats. Not weak enough to be at risk. Fast enough to communicate.

Now, he just had to figure out who he could hire to make a long run to *Ladaux* to help set that up as a regular run. He'd ask Governor Dexter and *Hollywood* Ward when he got there.

"In that case, I think we're done here," he said. "Hopefully, you all can stay and join me for a casual dinner, and we'll aim to depart in about twelve hours, once everyone has completed their maintenance."

He'd come as an explorer, but more and more he felt like an infection bringing modernity to these folks.

Whether they wanted it or not.

ELEVEN

RAIDER HOLLYWOOD, MEERUT ORBIT

Hollywood paused and looked over at McKenzie Bonham, currently handling most of the bridge functions with the ship at rest in orbit, trailing the main station by about fifteen degrees.

"Repeat that?" *Hollywood* asked.

McKenzie grinned. She liked to play the part of a ditzy blond with a big chest, but that was all a front to keep people underestimating her. It usually worked, but *Hollywood* knew better.

"*Urumchi* just came out of Jump and specifically asked for you to come aboard soonest," McKenzie repeated, grinning evilly.

"Any reason why?" *Hollywood* asked.

"Nope. Figure he's up to no good?" McKenzie asked.

"Kosnett's always up to no good," *Hollywood* reminded the woman. "But since the battle, he's done all right by us. Even when he didn't have to."

"Shall I wake up the fools on the flight deck?"

Hollywood considered it. And reconsidered it. There were no good answers. But Kosnett could have had all their heads on stakes if he'd wanted to. Still could, if one of her old enemies had finally caught up with the man.

Except…

"Yes," she decided aloud. "You and Holman handle things here while I'm gone, but don't start any wars you can't finish before I get back."

McKenzie grinned even more at that. She and Holman were fire and kerosene when they got bored, but turned into liquid nitrogen the moment someone else threatened either of them or the ship.

Hollywood rose from her chair and figured she had time for a quick shower and change before she left. She wasn't funky, but also had no idea what the First Centurion was up to. Best to look good if this was an execution.

Hollywood stepped out of the shuttle onto *Urumchi*'s flight deck and was not greeted by an honor guard. Nor a bounty hunter with a wanted poster. She figured that meant she was coming out ahead today, all things considered.

Instead, Command Flag Centurion Abbatelli was there, without bodyguards.

"Relax," the woman said. "Phil wanted to talk to you privately before the rest of the system found out and had opinions."

Oh, goody. Opinions about what?

But *Hollywood* knew the woman wouldn't talk, so she just fell in alongside her and they walked forward.

Sure enough, instead of a conference room, they entered the flag bridge, crossed through all the people pausing to watch her, and she got deposited into Kosnett's office by herself, with the big marine bodyguard Dunklin sitting just outside with a reader in hand and a sealed bulb of coffee beside him.

Kosnett rose as she entered and extended a friendly hand. She shook it.

"Please, sit," he said, gesturing her to the chair as he did the same.

"I considered drawing this out and being cryptic, but figured that would just be a pain in everybody's ass that would come back and bite mine eventually," he said with a hearty smile she didn't trust one damned bit. "Now that you've had a little time to acclimate to being an upstanding, law-abiding citizen, what do you want to do with the rest of your life, *Hollywood*?"

She blinked and stared at the man.

"Would you like some coffee while you come up with an answer?"

There was a term. *Burying the lede*. Putting the important parts farther down in a document so they might be missed.

Kosnett had just done whatever the opposite of that was.

"Coffee, yes, please," she managed.

He did something and the hatch opened. Dunklin handed her the bulb that had been beside him. She took it like it might hold the secrets of the universe and drank some.

Kosnett watched with a bemused expression on his face.

What did she want to do? She'd been in business, but that was a business already going more bankrupt by the day. *Meerut* was paying salaries and maintenance for now, but that was because Dexter had inherited a lot of spare cash when he came to power.

That would run out eventually, too. And *Meerut* probably didn't need this many ships anyway.

Did they?

"What are my options, Kosnett?" she asked, managing to sound rational even.

Kosnett smiled. That just made it worse.

"You could become one of the leaders of *Meerut's* fleet," he said. "In addition to *Dragonfly* and *Merchant Venture*, we went to *Jacoby* and captured *Pioneer*. It's a day or so behind me. That's three cruiser hulls that can be repaired, inducted, and form the basis of a pretty serious local navy if you promise to behave. I still think you should drag the five remaining platforms in from outside the lagoon and station them here, since folks know how to get around them now. Maybe leave one out to protect any warehouses you want to build in the process of getting rich with shipping."

Solid. Rational. Perfectly normal. She trusted him even less now. The man was up to something.

*Plus, he'd just **gone** to* Jacoby *and **stolen*** Pioneer? *What the hell?*

"And?" she managed, still sucking on coffee like the world was ending.

"Someone made a most interesting suggestion, just before I left to come here ahead of everybody," Kosnett said now, smile getting even bigger if that was possible. "They thought maybe we take about half the Pickets currently at moorage and start a new business with them."

"A new business?" she echoed, unable to ascertain where he was headed. "What kind of business?"

"A courier service," he said, dropping something like the other shoe. Or the executioner's ax. Hard to tell. "Neutral messengers hauling information and occasionally priority small goods on high-speed runs between the various capital systems. Hubbed out of *Meerut* for now, but probably also needing to open something of a secondary headquarters on or near *Aditi* itself one of these days, when folks get serious about business and diplomacy."

She blinked several times, but nothing changed, so *Hollywood* leaned back with her life preserver of coffee and *considered.*

She'd heard Kosnett's rants about the foolishness of autarky, but that had been the Cluster *Hollywood* had been born into and lived in until one day the whole galaxy turned upside down.

"Neutral?" she found herself musing aloud.

"*Meerut* is not affiliated with any of the five nations of the Cluster," he replied. "And I can enforce that. Plus, *Aquitaine* is not looking to found a colony here, though we might offer warm bodies to help grow your economy in the short term. I'm hoping that you'll do the same with locals from the Cluster."

"So why are you asking me this, Kosnett?" she finally pressed.

"Do you want to be the First Centurion around here, the next Governor, or go into legitimate business?"

"Have you told Milose yet?" she asked.

"No," he shook his head. "He's busy being governor and doing a good enough job that I'm not worried. At some point, he'll want to retire, which eventually means that we'll have some sort of political crisis that you will need to prepare for, long term. In the meantime, I have needs right now, and not many of the former pirate captains I'd trust to build out something like this and do it right."

"What's *right* look like?" she grimaced.

"Neutral," he said in a much harder tone, like maybe she'd already said yes and they were just dickering over details.

Maybe they were? What *did* she want to do with the rest of her life? Kosnett had laid out most of her options. The only one he'd missed was to flat retire on the money she'd previously saved and invest it, hoping that the economy of *Meerut* survived well enough for her to be comfortable.

"Neutral," she echoed.

"Beholden to no one, loyal to no one," he said. "Willing to haul messages from capital to capital, including *Meerut* in that list, so that for now only the *Meerut* courier goes to *Ellariel* or *Ewinhome*. That way they know who you are and what you are doing, so they'll be less paranoid."

"Just messages?" she noted.

"For the time being," he nodded back. "Maybe the occasional diplomat. Later, maybe you build cruise liners to haul tourists around, but I don't think anybody but *Aditi* is prepared for that yet. I can fund such a startup for a year with the money I have. After that, if it is successful, then the other players can subscribe and folks can buy me out. Or not. Maybe at that point you extend it to other systems who want to pay for that kind of access."

"This cuts across a lot of lines, Kosnett," she said.

"It does, *Hollywood*," he agreed. "That's why I started with you. The person to run something like this will have to be hard as nails. And competent on the business side. Plus able to talk to everybody and anybody. There aren't many captains around here that fit that bill."

In spite of everything, she found that she could still blush. He'd hit that nail pretty square.

Did she want a new adventure? Or did she want to make herself over into Admiral Ward, commanding *Pioneer* or *Dragonfly*? Or just lounge around the pool and sip rum drinks?

What did she want to be when she grew up?

"So how would it work?" she asked now.

"I need to dispatch messengers to *Ellariel, Aditi, Derragon,* and *Kyulle* with updates," he said, listing the other four capitals besides *Ewinhome*. "Immediately. They can fly *RAN* transponders for this first mission, like *Varmint* did, so folks will stop to listen instead of opening fire. After that, I expect that others will want to send messages to *Meerut* for me when I get back, as I don't intend to necessarily be easy to find when I'm not here, so I might hire *Varmint* or someone as my own squadron courier, so my cargo transports can continue just running around for food and resupply. Does that make sense?"

"It does," she nodded. "Do you need an answer now?"

"Only if you don't want the opportunity," he smiled. "In that case, I will throw it open for bidders, but I wanted to start with you because I trust you'll do a better job than they would."

She blushed again, but he was right.

And he had a lot of females in command positions around him, so maybe he was trying to hammer some of the more backwards places on more equality. A lot of *Gloran-*, *Dalou-*, and *Ewin*-born women had ended up as pirates because they had so few other options growing up.

Maybe she needed only female captains as couriers? At least at the start?

Shit, she **had** already said yes, at least in her head, and they *were* just working out details.

But this sounded like so much more fun than any of the others. Like the rest of the pirates, she'd been kind of lost and bereft without her old way of life.

Maybe it was finally time to start moving forward again.

"I want it," she finally said aloud. "Not sure what or when or how, but Milose will support me, I think. With you, that covers all my bases. And I can attach Esser Jones and *Varmint* to you immediately so you can go to *Ewinhome* whenever you need to."

"Good," Kosnett nodded. "Because when we stole *Pioneer*, we did so by hijacking the dry-dock platform that was repairing it. The rest of the squadron is about a day and a half behind me bringing it in."

"You did what?" she asked.

He repeated himself.

Hollywood Ward realized just how happy she was to be on Phil Kosnett's side of any issue. The other fellow was always going to lose.

EWINHOME

TWELVE

Phil watched on his screens as scanners went live. As before, he'd left *Viking* and her two escorts at *Meerut*, but this time they were in the process of putting Markus's ideas for new gravity-well scanners into action, such that *CM-507* and *Viking* might be able to sail out one of several promising, supposed blind alleys and come out somewhere else.

Meerut was no longer secret, so such places mattered less, but being able to exit the Cluster directly and make a high-speed run to *Ladaux* or *St. Legier* without transiting *Vilahana* altered a lot of equations about trade.

Not that he was looking to be more disruptive. At least not immediately. But it gave Dexter and his successors more of a chance to get rich and stable.

And that was what Phil was really about.

For now, he needed to mollify a nervous king who had just seen one of his systems crushed. Even if he would likely be happy that it had happened. Baron Russand had surrendered, apologized, and promised to travel to *Ewinhome* to make amends with Doysan IV over his previous behavior.

Losing your entire fleet would indeed cause great changes in one's recalcitrance.

Today, Phil was going to have to deal with the most fragile of the five nations. The one that was also the most dangerous right now, if only because nobody else could really handle a fleet of missile-swarming warships.

Ewin had never been dangerous to their neighbors because they were even more insular and fractious than *Dalou* and the others. Too busy feuding within their borders to gather up and threaten someone else.

Meerut had been one of the few external invasions that anyone had launched, and even that had been the act of a renegade.

"Emergence," came the call from the bridge, as all the screens suddenly came live with transponders.

True to his threat, Phil had brought *RAN Varmint* with him, flying tucked in close on one wing so nobody mistook them for a pirate. More of a pirate than they already were.

Urumchi at the center, with cruisers in pairs on each side of a planar formation, and the four corvettes in a diamond around that. *Shadowbolt* led, because Solo had put his foot down and demanded that.

Not something Phil had been willing to fight the man over. After all, in Solo's view, he was leading a fleet of friends on a tour of his own home, just as *Morninghawk* had escorted them to *Ellariel.*

"All vessels, this is Kosnett, aboard *Urumchi*," he said calmly, watching more and more ships appear on his screen. "I have the flag. All vessels will remain at this distance while we negotiate with the local authorities for permission to call on the king. Remember, they didn't know we were coming, though I'm sure Russand warned them. They also don't know how dangerous we can be, except that Russand came in a courier or a frigate, instead of his flagship. He'll have had to explain to everyone how that happened. Standing orders for now are that all ships stay at alert status three or better while we are in system. If anybody comes out of the gravity well and doesn't immediately transition, we'll be on a combat alert. Similarly, all ships be ready to jump on zero notice and meetup again at Waypoint Forty. That is all."

He cut the line and leaned back now to watch. Three fleets worth of *Ewin* vessels down below, including at least forty of their frigates, which were either drone throwers or small escort carriers, depending. Little ships that could deploy a lot of missiles, or a handful of fighters, but nothing that threatened him this far out. More Light and Heavy Cruiser hulls, again bombards or carriers, including a couple that looked like sister ships of *Pioneer*.

The interesting ship was the monster in close trailing orbit of the main station. The big station that dominated the skies above *Ewinhome* and might be big enough to appear as a permanent small moon.

The ship identified as *Meynard II*, named for the founder of the current dynasty, at least as *Ewin* did things. They were a monarchy, but did it in the Roman style, however accidentally. Kings were elected for twenty years, and then adopted their heir from a caste of Princes of the Blood. Hence, Principalities.

The ship was an Archer. A monstrous battleship-scale beast roughly the size of the old Star Controllers that *Aquitaine* used to build, before the Heavy Dreadnought design superseded them. *Athena* or *Archimedes*, or even Keller's second *Auberon*.

It combined the firepower of a Heavy Bombard with that of a Hunter Cruiser, carrying a full flight wing as well as enough missiles to shadow the sun, to quote the ancient Hellenes.

Phil could always fight in the shade if he had to, but he knew that Iveta would give her left arm to be able to tour a ship like that after the way she'd assumed command of *Pioneer* for the flight to *Meerut* and taken the ships blueprints completely apart on the way.

It was like Phil had been prepping her to face a wall of manticores or something. Or silly Persian archers.

Harinder smiled at him from across the table.

"Think they'll talk?" she asked, mostly out of curiosity.

"For now," he nodded. "Russand will have made an impression."

"But?"

"What kind of impression did he leave?" Phil asked.

That was the ninety-six Lev question.

THIRTEEN

PERSONAL QUARTERS, ALLEMAINE STATION, EWINHOME

Giscard, Baron Russand, had been given quarters several steps up from being a prisoner, though not quite commensurate with his status as a Baron and Prince of the Court.

Songbird. Gilded Cage.

He understood the need. After all, he'd been the worst of the bad boys for nearly two decades now, both before and after his father had died. He should have been named Crown Prince instead of the man who eventually became Doysan IV, but had lost that battle after a complicated, last-minute quintuple-cross that had been so masterful that he'd mostly settled those feuds without blood or duels.

One had to honor that mastery of complex subtlety. Plus Doysan had proven himself far more adroit and dangerous than Giscard had imagined at the time.

So Giscard had mostly bided his time.

And then *Aquitaine* had arrived.

Giscard was willing to admit that he'd miscalculated the threat they poised at *Meerut*. Underestimated their firepower. And their willingness to go for his throat.

Ewin Princes didn't fight like that. Ever. They dueled like gentlemen, going so far as to match hulls in orbit for single combat between cruisers.

Aquitaine had unleashed a pack of rabid dogs that had mauled him so badly Giscard still didn't know how he'd escaped. Then Kosnett had come straight from *Ellariel* and attacked *Jacoby* nearly three weeks sooner than any of his spies had suggested possible.

Pioneer had still been under repair. Worse, that son of a bitch had stolen his only dry-dock in addition to stealing his flagship.

Finally making peace with Doysan IV was a small price to pay for not being overthrown by his own king or maybe a restless cousin who saw himself as a better baron.

In the meantime, true to his word to Kosnett, Giscard had delivered a message to Doysan's Court that the man was coming here next.

That fool Doysan hadn't believed that Kosnett was that crazy. Or that powerful that he just could arrive uninvited.

Giscard had nodded politely and kept an innocent face.

The rest of the Princes would learn.

Or not.

A rap at the hatch before it opened and admitted Bollvize, his principal advisor, in the man's guise as a mere butler.

Giscard was seated at a table where he might work or dine, in his personal quarters.

Gilded cage. Songbird.

At least he was dressed well, in his good tunic, bright purple for *Jacoby*.

Bollvize was utterly imperturbable. He seemed to see this temporary incarceration as a vacation and nothing more.

"There is news, my Baron," the man said as he glided serenely to rest.

"Oh?"

"The *Republic of Aquitaine* has arrived at the outer marker and awaits the King," Bollvize noted distantly.

"What?" Giscard gawked. "Already?"

The day after tomorrow had been the earliest possible beginning of the window when Giscard had expected the man. That matched the absolute minimum sailing times between points.

"Did he just fly to *Meerut* and leave everything for his underlings?" Giscard demanded. "Did that son of a bitch give the pirates my flagship?"

He had risen before he realized it, so Giscard just began pacing. Bollvize did not appear surprised, remaining perfectly still as an obstacle to be navigated. One that talked.

"It is not yet known, sir," Bollvize replied. "I have heard the news from a contact at Court."

Read: A spy he had cultivated or bribed. Must have been good though, to find out something like this so quickly.

Giscard began to wonder if that was the secret to *Aquitaine*'s power. They just did things, instead of talking about it, negotiating, or maneuvering for advantage.

Minimum flight time, based on *Shadowbolt* or one of the other vessels accompanying Kosnett.

What if those ships really could transit JumpSpace faster?

That was a truly frightening worry. *Aquitaine* raiders had annihilated his power base. Even Giscard's pride was willing to admit that publicly. What could they do if they didn't have to fly with slower ships?

"Orders, Baron?" Bollvize asked.

"Watch everything," he said, unnecessarily, but did it anyway. "Doysan will send for me shortly, once he comes to understand that I was actually being forthright."

"For once," Bollvize nodded dryly.

Giscard opened his mouth to flay him verbally, then caught the sly grin on Bollvize's face.

Well, true, he had hardly ever dealt honestly with the man when they'd been rivals, so Giscard was willing to grant that they might not know how to deal with it from him today.

How did he maneuver that to his advantage now?

How did he get Kosnett to destroy Doysan IV and whoever was his current favorite, so that Giscard might make himself king after this?

FOURTEEN

ROYAL COURT, ALLEMAINE STATION,
EWINHOME

His Royal Highness, King Doysan IV of *Ewin*, had been awakened to a panic around the palace unlike anything since Doysan III had died of a sudden cardiac event in the arms of one of his less-well-regarded mistresses, who then had to call for help after climbing out from beneath the man's immense weight.

At least Doysan IV had kept his fighting trim over those sixteen years, even if that got harder and harder to do every year.

Now, a new catastrophe threatened.

He paced back and forth in the front room of his personal apartment aboard the palace section of the station. It had served five kings so far, but was getting long in the tooth and probably needed to be replaced at some point.

He didn't like the symbolism that came with that image, but it couldn't be helped.

At sixty-three, he was old. Worn down. Today, he felt more like the Herwind Plinket he'd been before ascending than *Doysan IV*. And it was out of his control.

He stopped pacing and turned to Jaxom Bereoa, First Minister of *Ewin*. A bureaucrat rather than a Prince. One of the men who kept the government running when the hotheads and bluebloods were too occupied with their personal feuds and affairs.

"You told me he couldn't get here this quickly," Doysan IV raged, bouncing his voice off the bulkheads.

He could do that in his private chambers. Nobody dared challenge him here. He began to pace again.

"I have not yet heard from my spies among the former Syndicalists, Your Majesty," Bereoa replied. "We had a window, and technically he arrived within it, however barely. Like you, we presumed next week at the earliest. However, I will remind you that Russand made that same assumption at *Jacoby*."

"So the aliens can fly too fast to calculate?" Doysan snarled.

"If they are not accompanied by others, perhaps," Bereoa said. "Since *Vilahana*, as I understand it, they have always been traveling with local vessels. Perhaps that normally constrains their speed. We do not know as yet."

"Find out," Doysan ordered. "What are they doing currently?"

"The fleet he brought has parked near the outermost marker, Sire," Bereoa noted. "Kosnett sent his regards and asked for an audience. Presumably to explain why he did what he did to Russand. Possibly to apologize to you for attacking one of your worlds, however rebellious they might have been."

"And maybe setting us up to destroy Central Squadrons?" Doysan snapped angrily.

"We have twice the number of vessels of any other sector fleet," Bereoa replied. "Half of them are currently protecting *Ewinhome* itself against attack. We are secure."

"Russand thought he was secure in attacking *Meerut*," Doysan stopped his pacing to focus on his First Minister. "And he thought he was safe at *Jacoby*. Both times, Kosnett corrected that failure in his planning. What is he doing here?"

"I do not know, Sire." Bereoa bowed at the waist to emphasize his point. "He is acting diplomatically, and I believe will continue to do so until he determines our course of action."

"Is he a threat to this station?" Doysan asked, finally finding the point that had him on edge this morning.

There had been no significant personal threats since Russand had been seen off so long ago.

Not until today.

Pity that Russand had been the messenger, as now Doysan had to decide how much he trusted his worst enemy to tell the truth about a terrible dragon that was coming to ravage the countryside.

"He is not a threat where he is now," Bereoa temporized, which didn't help. "Some reports suggest that the flagship is armed with beam weapons at least comparable to this station's. In addition, *Storm Petrel* is a known vessel, with a condor mount on the bow. We can expect that the others are roughly as powerful."

"Cruisers and frigates," Doysan scoffed. "Nobody in the cluster can stand before our mass of missile fire if we choose."

"Russand believed that at *Meerut*, Sire," the Minister helpfully pointed out.

"I know that, man!" Doysan raged again, returning to his pacing.

He reached the end of the chamber, finding himself facing an archaic wall hanging depicting some equally ancient battle on the surface of a planet with swords, and wondered how they'd gotten there.

Or was *Ewin* still trapped in that glorious past they had invented for themselves?

And who did he dare trust to talk to this alien commander? One of his various princes would be maneuvering to see Doysan abdicate, just so they could take power. That had a certain siren call to it, because sixty-three-years old, sixteen of them as king, had left him drained today.

Just hand over power to somebody else and retire to some palace somewhere? Let all that crap land on one of those hungry fools forever nipping at his heels for crumbs? Even Russand fell into that category.

Doysan turned back and focused on Minister Bereoa, the closest lightning rod he had when the rage built to a strike.

"You will go out and see what this Kosnett wants," Doysan ordered abruptly.

He rather liked the pale shock that overtook the man's face at those words. It proved that he could still surprise people who spent their lives trying to outguess their king.

Fuck 'em all. You want my power? Take it from me.

If you dare…

"Me, Sire?" the man squeaked.

"Yes, you," Doysan replied, stalking right over to scowl up at the man.

Doysan was about average for height. Dark as most of his subjects. Bereoa claimed Rajput blood, which supposedly explained his lighter skin and greater stature.

Doysan assumed that was just another load of horse manure.

"You," he sneered. "Everyone assumes you are the power behind my throne. Everyone expects me to die or retire soon, so they'll have to deal with you anyway, or oust you with some junior minister unprepared to replace you as they are unprepared to sit on my throne. Let that begin now."

He watched the man's face go through several seconds of unguarded emotion before he got control of it again. Doysan had seen betrayals and double-crosses form, evolve, and be discarded.

As king, he almost found himself tired enough to walk. However, he was too angry to just let someone else have the crown. Not after he'd had to carry the damned weight for sixteen years.

No, you have to take it from me.

Do your damnedest.

FIFTEEN

Phil was in his office, with just Harinder, Heather, and Fleet Ambassador Aliza Babatunde. The inner crew he trusted the most. Two years ago, nobody had appreciated just how sexist large swaths of the Balhee Cluster would turn out to be, at least at a cultural level. The *Aditi Consensus* and *Yaumgan Domain* were highly egalitarian, while the other were…*not*.

He didn't give a rat's ass what these folks thought was the correct gender balance in his crews.

"Aliza, what do we know about the man?" Phil asked her.

True to form, she pulled out a reader from a pocket and began ticking off notes.

"First Minister of *Ewinhome* is a bureaucratic position, rather than inherited," she began.

"Like some ancient, Chinese Mandarin?" Heather interrupted now.

"Something like that," Aliza agreed. "Prince is a title that connotes membership in a specific social class at the top of the local heap. Specifically, males with political power and formal titles in the aristocracy itself, from whom kings are selected, largely by a congress of said princes when the throne is empty. Kings can designate their preferred successors, but my read on their recent history over the last few centuries is that only about half ever manage to take power. Duels and feuds are relatively common, at least at that level."

"And Jaxom Bereoa is not one of them?" Phil asked, bringing things back on track.

"Correct," Aliza nodded. "Civilian, if you will. A citizen, when back home we might compare the Princes to membership in one of the Fifty Families. If you squint a little. And we were monarchical. And only about as civilized as *Ewin* usually gets credit for."

"What does it say that Doysan is sending his First Minister out?" Phil asked.

Again, something of a surprise. He didn't like surprises pulled on him.

"I don't know, Phil," Aliza said with a shrug. "He should have invited you to the station for an audience. That would have either been a big public affair, like *Ellariel,* or a private thing. This is a somewhat radical decision, from a king not known for making those sorts of waves."

"I thought so," Phil grimaced. "Still, we came here so we could tell the king what we'd done at *Jacoby,* and do whatever apologies and such were necessary to keep things calm. The last thing I need is for *Ewin* to get so pissed that they decide to invade *Meerut* with enough force to take the place. I'm sure they could, but at that point I'm pretty sure the gloves have to come off."

"How far off, Phil?" Harinder asked.

"I'd send *Varmint* to *Ladaux* with a Priority One message packet marked First Lord Only," Phil replied grimly. "Probably in Markus's hands."

"And she'd send *Kongō* and all her sister ships?" Harinder pressed.

"I might ask her for enough corvettes and Expeditionary cruisers to end the entire *Ewin* fleet as a way of life," he nodded. "The whole point of crushing Russand and *Jacoby* so hard was to tell people that I was serious, as well as capable. We need to make sure that Doysan doesn't decide that he has nothing left to lose by attacking us, either now or at *Meerut*. How do we do that?"

"Treat this Minister like the personal representative of the king," Aliza replied. "Full honors on landing. State dinner. The works. Treat him like a serious politician representing another such creature with great power, even though we know that *Ewin* is the worst governed and weakest of the five."

"They are dangerous to everyone else," Heather pointed out. "At least until we start selling Type-1-Pulse mounts to people around here. How soon until we let them copy the Type-3-Pulse or the Pulse-Two?"

"They have nothing like a Type-2 beam," Harinder said. "To say nothing of pulsing it. Their Point Gun isn't as good as our Type-1, just as their Main Gun can't match our Threes."

"You suppose *Yaumgan* has something like a pulse and hasn't told anyone yet?" Heather asked. "Maybe not bothered mounting it yet because nobody concerned them before now? They share a long, quiet border with *Ewin*, but nobody crosses that stretch without invitation because *Yaumgan* will open fire without warning."

"You ask Captain Xue quietly sometime," Phil decided. "Or ask *Stunt Dude* to make an inquiry. Not secret, but not widely advertised."

"Would *Yaumgan* weapons be better than ours?" Aliza asked, but she was a diplomat rather than a warrior.

"They would be *different*," Phil replied. "I am more interested in getting them to trade with *Aditi* and the others, if only because that opens things up to cultural exchange in ways that those quiet Philosopher/Kings haven't done in a long time."

"That still topples *Ewin*," Heather said. "Their entire military culture is built on missile swarms and fighter strikes. Without that, they are back down to badly-undergunned ships with titan bolts and Main Guns. They can't threaten anyone at that point, and everyone else could sail right in and stomp them, especially if someone like *Aditi* went ahead and built new ships along our corvette model, designed to handle those missiles while closing to killing range."

"Are we here to do that?" Aliza asked him next. "I realize you are being diplomatic, but *Ewin* Princes have always been something of bullies to their neighbors. *Yaumgan* has historically slapped them hard enough times to make a point. *Aditi* generally keeps thing quiet on their frontier. *Dalou* has firebirds that keep *Ewin* ships at a distance. What happens if *Ewin* collapses in on itself?"

Phil pondered that. He'd done little since *Jacoby*.

"I have no easy answers," he said. "But mark this, and keep it under your hats for now."

They all three nodded.

"We want *Aditi* to survive," he continued. "No secret there. *Yaumgan* will be fine, whatever we do. *Dalou* seems to have turned a corner that puts them on a path to modernize, both technologically as well as culturally. That leaves our two problem children."

"*Ewin* and the *Gloran Empire*," Heather noted.

"Exactly," Phil said. "I'm not entirely sure they can be saved, given certain cultural elements that have retarded their social and political development up to now. I'm also not sure I care if they collapse in on themselves. As Heather has noted, *Ewin* might not survive our arrival, even if we did nothing, because they always seem to be looking for an excuse to fuss at each other. If they do, we can always withdraw and make it clear to *Aditi* and *Dalou* not to meddle."

"Will they honor that?" Aliza asked.

"Yes," Phil said. "I can make them, if I have to. They've seen the diplomat. After *First* and *Second Meerut*, they've seen the warrior as well."

SIXTEEN

APPROACHING THE ALIEN FLAGSHIP, EDGE
OF THE EWINHOME SYSTEM

Jaxom Bereoa sat buckled in and watched on the monitor as the second shuttle began to approach the enemy flagship.

Could he call it enemy? Should he?

On the one hand, they had finally eliminated Giscard Russand as a threat to the *Ewin* throne. That fool was behind him on the station, behaving himself better than at any point Jaxom had notes covering, going back decades at this point.

On the other, this Kosnett fellow had also so utterly crushed the *Zen-Mekyo Syndicates* that they were all folding up shop and disappearing as fast as they could safely escape whatever law might be coming for them.

So Jaxom was approaching this with an open mind, while at the same time not extending much trust to the outsiders.

He smiled, but didn't mean it.

It didn't help that Doysan had put him on the spot to risk his life alone with the outsiders. They should have been invited to the station, where a bureaucrat like him would deal with simple things and protocol. He did not appreciate being cast in the role of principal diplomat. Doubly so when the hotheads behind him were likely plotting all manner of palace intrigue and possible insurrections while the cat was away. Setting fires that he would have to handle when he got back.

If he got back.

Some days, Jaxom wondered if he was the only adult in the room.

Today, he had ridden in one of Doysan's yacht-like shuttles to the rough midway point between the station and the outsider ships. Just inside the safe line of travel for the gravity well. From there, he'd met a shuttle from Kosnett's flagship and gone through a quick medical scan from one of Kosnett's people.

Because he was a diplomat today, instead of a bureaucrat, he had accepted the offer of a broad-spectrum shot designed to protect him against whatever germs and diseases might have grown up on *Aquitaine*. Jaxom had only accepted because so many of the other Cluster folks had apparently had the same and suffered no ill effects.

It meant that he trusted Kosnett with his life. Which Jaxom supposed he had to do, as he was about to land on the man's flagship as a representative of the King of *Ewin*, that damnable coward that had put him here.

Jaxom breathed out slowly and regained his composure before the snarl arrived anywhere near his face.

Always calm. Always discreet. Always polite.

Even when some of those idiots behind him deserved to be slapped silly.

Urumchi. The outsider flagship. It dominated the screen as the shuttle began final approach. Not as big as *Meynard II*, Doysan's own flagship, but Jaxom had quietly spoken to a few military people he trusted to know what they were talking about.

All had been impressed. More than a few had been frightened. Apparently the ship had a larger power curve than anything they'd ever seen, with only the palace station itself having a similar energy output.

And *Urumchi* was physically smaller than *Meynard II*.

What could this Kosnett fellow do if he wanted? Anything?

Could anyone stop him?

Jaxom found the unknowns the most frightening. Worse, he had to go into the field and get answers himself, rather than send someone trained in this sort of thing. He wasn't a diplomat, despite how charming and persuasive he had to appear to be between the various factions.

Was Doysan IV losing it?

Was there a worse time for such a thing to happen?

Jaxom was hard pressed to think of one.

"Approaching landing now, sir," one of the marines, faceless behind polarized visors, spoke aloud. The medic, he thought, but Jaxom had lost track of them in their identical armor.

Who wore perfectly matching uniforms? *Ewin* prided itself on individuality. Jaxom wore his best baggy pants, tucked into calf-high leather boots. Gray, because both faded into the background, especially around all the colorful peacocks of the Court.

Lighter gray tunic with the *Ewin* Rising Sun logo over his heart, orange half-ball bisected by the horizon. He hoped rising. The same image could imply setting.

Perspective was everything.

If Kosnett presaged the fall of *Ewin*, what could Jaxom do about it? Anything?

On the screen, *Urumchi* had turned into a wall. A station.

A maw that opened to swallow them whole. He could think of no other representation, caught up in his apocalyptic imagery today.

The shuttle landed. Softer than any he'd ridden before. Good pilot.

"Bay doors sealing now," the pilot's voice came over the intercom. "Stand by for full pressurization."

Jaxom unbuckled and rose. He straightened everything. Ran a hand back through his ever-thinning gray hair and wondered how soon until it receded entirely, leaving only a ring.

He watched the marines around him move into position.

"We're ready for you now, sir," someone spoke.

Jaxom nodded and moved to the hatch. He'd seen the preparations. The literal red carpet rolled out for him to walk upon. The lines of sailors and warriors in formation on either side. The small spot forward that had risen out of the deck, with stairs up.

Kosnett was obvious. Of the five up there, he was the only male other than Striker Gotzon Solo. Jaxom had been warned by both his spies and Solo that Kosnett had an upper council of capable females, though Jaxom had his doubts on the topic.

Capable females? Exercising military or diplomatic authority?

Barbarians. No other term to describe them.

The hatch opened and Jaxom descended to the deck. Across the way, all the people came to attention, a corridor of martial splendor for him to approach.

He kept his head up and shoulders back, moving with that particular glide that you got after years of dealing with men like Doysan IV and his damnable pacing.

Today, Jaxom was the only one moving. That was good. He was also the center of attention. That was bad.

Unsettling. Unnatural even, because those foolish children that made up the Princes were all about personal stature and esteem.

Still, he was representing a king who was too much of a chickenshit to do this himself. Maybe it was time for Doysan IV to retire. Move on.

Stop all your damned dithering!!!

Calm. Rational. Poised.

Jaxom reached the base of the stairs and ascended. Kosnett was big. Tall but also physically imposing, having broad shoulders that tapered down to a trim waist. Solo looked like a teenager next to the man.

The three women…

The one to Kosnett's immediate right was at least as tall as Jaxom. And had a carnivorous look in her eyes that belied her smile. The other two looked more like diplomats. That much suggested that the first was Lau, commander of the flagship. The darker-skinned one would be Babatunde. The one who looked like she had just come from *Aditi* itself was most likely Abbatelli.

"Ambassador, thank you for joining us and taking time out of your busy schedule to travel all the way out here," Kosnett said delicately, even bowing far deeper than a mere bureaucrat like Jaxom Bereoa deserved.

They were treating him like a formal representative of an unknown king. Unknown because even Jaxom didn't think Doysan rated that.

But he smiled.

"First Centurion, thank you for hosting me," Jaxom replied. "And thank you for such a welcome."

One hand back to indicate some hundred folks brought out here to salute a First Minister who was more of a babysitter than he cared to admit.

Most days.

"My principal aides," Kosnett said, indicating the three women and Solo, who was only here because he was the sole representative of *Ewin* that Doysan had sent. Again, had that been the smartest choice? Kosnett had not complained, so Solo must not have fucked up too much. "Command Centurions Heather Lau, Aliza Babatunde, and Harinder Abbatelli. Striker Solo of the *Ewin Principality* Light Bombard *Shadowbolt*."

Tall, dark, local. As he had guessed from his spies various submissions. All dangerous women. At least according to rumor. Plus Solo, who had been Doysan's golden child that week.

Jaxom nodded.

"Greetings and be welcome to *Ewinhome*," Jaxom said.

"We have prepared a quick reception, rather than dragging everything out for a long period," Kosnett said now. "Would you be amenable to moving there, that my crew can get back to work?"

The man indicated the group that had gathered to honor Jaxom. He nodded. Anything to get him out of the center of so much attention from so many people.

Kosnett and a much smaller group retired to a side chamber with Jaxom in tow. There, they settled around a table and relaxed, as if this was to be a casual conversation.

"You bring news?" Jaxom asked after drinks had been offered.

News. Ha!

"We have come from *Jacoby*, sir," Kosnett replied. "After a quick stop at *Meerut* to settle a few affairs."

Jaxom appreciate the understated way Kosnett covered *that* whole episode. That moron Russand attacking the newly-discovered pirate hideout on the day Kosnett should have been busy at *Ellariel* with those fools from the Shogunate. Then Kosnett striking *Jacoby* out of the blue and stealing the rest of Russand's forces out from under his feet.

"And what brings you to *Ewinhome*, First Centurion?" Jaxom asked.

He didn't know a damned thing about military affairs. *Ewin* hardly qualified to even understand such things, as most Princes usually needed three tries to spell organized. Kosnett could have been in the process of launching a full assault on Allemaine Station, but Jaxom supposed that they wouldn't be so calm about it.

Would they?

Was Ewin that little of a threat to the outsiders?

Calm. Smile. Absorb data and turn it into information.

"Baron Russand, whom we understand was at the time a renegade from the King's good order, attacked *Meerut* while I was elsewhere," Kosnett said.

Jaxom nodded. Fool had gotten his tail singed in the process.

"After he was driven off, half of his force was captured,"

Kosnett continued. "In order to teach the man a lesson, I went to *Jacoby* and captured the flagship that he had taken to *Meerut*. I have now come to *Ewinhome* to consult with King Doysan IV about his preferences on the matter, going forward. And to apologize for not allowing the king's own forces to handle the crime of piracy that Baron Russand engaged in while he was an outlaw. I was closer, and in a better position to control the outcome."

There. Yes. Steel fist, contained in a velvet glove.

Jaxom found himself warming to the man Kosnett. Not a fellow given to outrageous bluster and empty threats, which already put him several steps ahead of most of the fools on Allemaine Station.

"What happened to Russand's ships?" Jaxom found himself asking, already deviating from whatever script he had planned.

Kosnett hadn't offered any threats. Nor seemed particularly penitent for nailing Russand's sorry hide to a wall.

Just how dangerous were the outsiders?

"Having been captured from *pirates*, my intent is to sell the ships to the authorities at *Meerut*, where I expect that they will be impressed into service with the local gendarme," Kosnett said. "I also carry a diplomat from Governor Dexter, who will be talking to your people about the best way to repatriate those captured sailors currently being held on *Meerut* itself who wish to return."

Who wished to return? Wouldn't that be all of them? What the hell had happened?

Or had his sailors grown as tired of Russand's antics as Jaxom had?

Flee, and start a new life elsewhere?

Jaxom had to admit that such a thing had its attractions.

"I see," he temporized. "It sounds like we have much to discuss then."

"Indeed, First Minister of *Ewin*," Kosnett replied. "Having had a chance to talk earnestly first, I had hoped that we might then indulge in a brief tour of my flagship, followed by a formal, State dinner honoring you for gracing us. After that, we can begin such negotiations as you find appropriate. Alternatively, we have full Ambassadorial suites available and I can assign you a staff so that you can rest and refresh as needed. Truly, it is my hope that you will drive things at your pace. We will adapt, being visitors to your realm."

Well, shit.

Jaxom could suddenly understand those folks who might want to remain at *Meerut*, if they got to deal with folks like Kosnett. Grownups, as it were. He couldn't remember such a pleasant interaction on Allemaine Station over something so serious.

Usually it was some well-bred nincompoop screaming for something or unable to wipe his own bottom. And not all of them were even kings.

"I see," Jaxom found himself repeating the words. "Perhaps we shall get to dinner and see."

If Kosnett was going to let him drive things per his words, maybe Jaxom would see just how far they would let him go.

After all, they were certainly going to be disappointed when they met Doysan IV in the flesh.

Jaxom finally allowed himself to mean his smile.

SEVENTEEN

Heather had drawn something of a short straw, if only because the First Minister of *Ewin* was carefully being placed on a level with her socially, so that Phil would be the equal of King Doysan IV. And he'd responded better to her than to Harinder or Aliza.

Bereoa had started rather standoffish, but slowly warmed and relaxed as the tour progressed. Sergey Cummins and his strawberries, rendered down into fresh jam and spread over hot English-style muffins, had almost slain the visitor.

They were forward in the arboretum now.

"On a warship?" Bereoa asked, gaping at the trees and bushes around them. "In space?"

"Affirmative, sir," Heather smiled. "Phil took an important lesson from that famed ancient traveler, Javier Aritza, and carries seeds and bushes that he can trade or gift as he visits various places. After so many centuries, some things have evolved far from what they once were, so this helps bring it all back together."

The man stopped dead and just stared at her.

"Aritza?" he practically demanded. "*The Science Officer?*"

"One and the same," Heather nodded. "His starship was

piloted by the woman who is now the Librarian at Alexandria Station, on Ballard."

"Alive?" he gasped, feeling blood drain out of his skull. "How?"

"She is an artificial lifeform, First Minister," Heather explained. "A highly programmed Sentience that still has memories of those days. With her help, Henri Baudin founded *Aquitaine*, and her data from before the fall has helped the many nations of our galactic arm reestablish themselves."

"A machine?"

"*The Last of the Immortals*, as she calls herself," Heather said. "Are you well, First Minister?"

He'd gone white. Pale. Hyperventilating. About to fall over.

Heather grabbed him by the arm and then got under him to keep the man upright as something like true shock spasmed through his entire system.

"I need a medic," she said simply.

Several appeared and got the man seated with his head down, checking things.

Heather knelt nearby, just so they were about at eyeball level.

His head came up and a deadly serious gleam came into his eyes.

"Are you here to destroy us?" he whispered, probably seeing all this firepower around him as a sword instead of a shield.

"No," she said simply. "Near as I can tell, you folks have that business covered all by yourselves. We're trying to make sure you don't take everyone else down with you when you do."

Again, huge eyes. Shallow breaths. Shock.

The medics were good. Kept him focused. Got him breathing more normally.

Bereoa never once stopped staring at her as the folks around them worked.

After a time, he drank some cold water from a bottle and that seemed to help.

"Think we're primarily dealing with some low level

dehydration here, sir," one of her people said. "Possibly a mild reaction to the vaccine. More fluids and maybe less walking?"

"Can you stand?" Heather asked the man, since he wasn't reacting to anyone else.

Bereoa nodded hollowly.

Heather rose and held out a hand. The First Minister took it and she pulled him to his feet, though he wobbled a little.

"Let's get you to your suite, Ambassador," she said. "From there you can rest until dinner."

He nodded, still silent, still wobbly, so she held out an elbow and he took it like she was a herald. The group fanned out around her and a couple disappeared, probably getting folks ready for his early arrival.

Quickly, they shifted out of the forest and back into painted metal corridors.

Heather walked the man to his hatch, but he held onto her elbow when she tried to withdraw it.

"We need to talk," he murmured.

"Alone?" she whispered back.

"Preferably," he noted in a near-silent voice.

Heather opened the hatch and led the man in.

"I'll chat with him for a while," she announced to the staff inside. "You folks stand down for now. We'll be in the first salon."

Nods then folks withdrew in all directions. Heather put him in the big chair in a small chamber designed for casual conversations.

She moved to the nearer end of the couch and studied the First Minister.

Old enough to be her father, maybe. Receding hairline but still in pretty good shape. South Asian genotype that was so prevalent in the Cluster.

She didn't think the man was trying to seduce her, and he didn't look tough enough to survive attacking her, so she sat and watched him.

Moments passed.

"Giscard, Baron Russand, had interesting things to say about you," Bereoa began slowly.

Heather nodded. Few of them were probably polite, either. That was what you got when you listened to the loser whine.

And Russand had sounded like a loser over the comm, though they'd never bothered meeting the man in person.

What do you say after you've just thoroughly emasculated someone who brought so much false macho to the table?

"Were we terrible, conquering monsters come to sacrifice you and rape your women?" Heather asked sarcastically, eyeroll implied but not executed.

"Something like that," Bereoa said. His color was still improving. "He said that *Aquitaine* would be the death of *Ewin*."

"That's not a fight Phil will start," Heather replied automatically.

"Phil?"

"First Centurion Phil Kosnett," she continued. "My boss."

"And you do not refer to him as First Centurion at all times?" Bereoa pressed.

"I've known Phil for many years," Heather explained. "I was his first officer on *CS-405*, when we took our war directly to *Buran*. He specifically asked me to command his flagship, when the First Lord of the Fleet sent him west to explore the unknown."

"Unknown?"

"It took us several months just to make the run to the Balhee Cluster, First Minister," Heather said, wondering how she'd ended up in the diplomacy role.

Except that *Ewin* saw themselves as mighty warriors, while she thought of most of them as obnoxious peacocks. Assuming you could ever find a polite bird to compare them too.

Duels and feuds were the mark of a backwards, primitive society, though she kept that opinion to herself, especially around Gotzon Solo. He'd been competent, once he realized that all his histrionics and flamboyance didn't earn him any points with the rest of the squadron.

He hardly even waved his arms in mixed company these days.

Bereoa nodded now at his own internal conversation.

"To us, the *Fribourg Empire* and *Republic of Aquitaine* are occasionally monsters that mothers invoke to frighten children into compliance," he said, smiling by the time he was done.

Heather shared the smile. She'd heard similar things in *Aquitaine* of *Fribourg*.

"Why are you here?" he asked bluntly.

"Phil came to find out who lived in the Balhee Cluster," she replied, equally blunt. The man seemed to expect calm bluntness. *Why* she wasn't sure. But she could deliver. "Past that, we were intending to deliver ambassadors to various places and then send home maps so that merchants from *Ladaux* and other places could know where to sail and what sorts of things they should bring with them."

"You came with a warfleet," the man accused.

"And more than one person around here has opened fire anyway and only asked questions later," she snapped back pretty hard. "The *Zen-Mekyo Syndicates*, for example. Or Baron Russand. We stomped on them both to teach them some manners. And maybe teach others to talk first."

She left it at that. From where the squadron was currently anchored, an *Ewin* fleet might manage to drop out of Jump suddenly, close enough to be a threat. And every single friendly vessel was currently primed to cut loose with every beam they had if that happened.

Her people had all trained to fight the sharks, once upon a time.

Bereoa shrunk in on himself a little at her tone. Maybe she'd done that one purpose.

She studied him. He studied her.

Wasn't sexual, near as she could tell. Something though, like she was a real alien and not just someone born more than one hundred light-years away, like most of the Cluster seemed to define it.

Heather didn't feel like backing down. They'd gone beyond merely polite. They'd treated him like visiting royalty, including Sergey's homemade jam. Not many people got that.

And he'd asked her to join him, alone, here.

She waited.

He drew a breath.

"I must apologize, Command Centurion Lau," he finally said. "For many things, but first and foremost for being a creature of my culture and letting that blind me to certain truths. *Ewin* does not value females. The Princes hardly ever marry, instead keeping strings of mistresses and various half-siblings, from whom they establish connections."

"But not dynastic marriages?" she asked, more curious than offended. Though she was still insulted by that crap. Backward-ass barbarians.

"No, Command Centurion," he shook his head. "Up until now, I was not given to think highly of females, seeing them as too flighty, too emotional, too *something* to make effective political or military leaders. You have greatly changed that, though I am certain I will relapse from time to time so I will apologize in advance. I was sent because nobody at Allemaine Station was quite sure what to make of Kosnett. Or your fleet. Striker Solo's reports had been discounted, even by me, but I can see now that he was giving me a clean and honest assessment of things. I just didn't want to believe it."

Heather nodded. Gotzon Solo wasn't a fuckup. He had even turned into a pretty good squadron mate, once he and Khan got put on a wing together and got competitive over looking better obeying orders.

Once she'd torn a strip of hide off both of them for not being in a position she'd ordered, then offered to send both of them home to be replaced by some other ship. A frigate, perhaps. Or a system patroller that could at least follow orders.

She supposed that Solo might have conveyed things to his Court that might not have been believed.

Until now.

"We come as friends," she offered. "Phil's here to trade and make more trade. We'd like the Five Nations of the Cluster to stop sniping at each other and start trading with each other, so that our own merchants have safe places to visit and more goods they can haul home."

Phil's dream, not hers, but she'd heard it enough times to repeat it verbatim in her sleep.

Although Heather still harbored hopes that First Lord Whughy, an old squadron mate from *The Expedition*, might promote her to First Centurion one of these days and send her off to fabled Earth, just to see what it looked like today.

Still uninhabitable, but that had happened a long time ago.

"Please do not take this the wrong way, Command Centurion," Bereoa said now. "What would have happened if an *Ewin* fleet were to launch an attack against your force here?"

"I was having that exact conversation with Phil this morning," she said carefully. "He mentioned ending the entire *Ewin* fleet as an entity if that happened, though he might have to send home for a true warfleet to hunt down every last vessel, instead of using only the exploration vessels he commands today. What we have with us could probably take the forces in orbit around *Ewinhome*, though."

The man's face went completely slack. Skin pale. Eyes huge again.

"You're serious," he said, shocked apparently out of his wits for a second time.

"We are cautious and prepared, First Minister," Heather corrected him. "We're here to talk, but have more than enough firepower to destroy a threat. Any threat."

He blinked rapidly and began to breathe normally again.

"And with that, I think this is a good time for me to depart," she continued. "That way you can check in with your folks and have time to prepare for dinner. Our Head Chef believes in cooking as the highest possible form of love, so they have been preparing all day for something special. I'm rather looking forward to it."

"Love, Command Centurion?" Bereoa asked as she opened the hatch from the salon and nodded to the staff waiting outside.

"That's right, First Minister," she nodded.

Time to go talk to Phil.

EIGHTEEN

RAN FLAGSHIP URUMCHI

Kohahu sat some ways down from the *Ewin* First Minister, along a long, fancy table where the various captains and command centurions were seated for the formal dinner Kosnett had proclaimed. At first, she'd been surprised that all the commanders would be present at once, anchored on the edge of the *Ewin* home system, but Captain Yukimura had explained to her what Tactical Officers did and how even he had adopted some of the model on his own bridge.

The warfleet around her was primed to unleash unmitigated violence at the slightest provocation. And she had met Iveta Beridze enough times to understand what that woman would do if threatened.

So she could be relaxed some. Captain Yukimura had specifically brought her and Crown Prince Shingo, both of whom had rocked the *Ewin* First Minister to his core when he got introduced.

"Lady Kohahu Kugosu, daughter of the Shogun?" he had gaped at her.

She had smiled and turned to introduce the young-if-slightly-older trainee officer who had been trailing in her wake.

"And this is Crown Prince Shingo of *Dalou*," she had smiled.

"But…"

She'd never heard what he intended to say at that point, because others had rushed into the social chasm and kept things moving smoothly.

Kohahu had come to appreciate that about Kosnett. He had an excellent staff, particularly compared to the cast of stodgy elders that had accumulated around her father, before he had started thinning them out and retiring some for younger men.

And hopefully women at some point. Lady Morninghawk had been an Imperial Inspector before she met Makara Omarov. Now, she was helping found a new House.

And Kohahu was seated across from Captain Yukimura with the Crown Prince on her right. Backwards from what etiquette might have demanded, but an accurate reflection of their relative statuses in the Hegemony itself.

She turned to the young man as the soup bowls were being withdrawn for whatever the next course was. Master of the Wardroom Rei Bottenberg had limited themselves somewhat, but gotten rather good at working with the flavor and spice palates of both *Aquitaine* and Balhee, somehow creating a fusion of all the regional tastes into a thing that everyone could eat and nobody risked discomfort.

And the First Centurion refused to allow Kohahu to offer Bottenberg a job working for the Shogunate. She might have to find a way to send trainee master chefs to *Urumchi* at some point.

Even her father didn't eat this well that often. Granted, he held to the warrior mentality of simple food and uncomplicated presentation, but Kohahu had watched what someone like Bottenberg had been able to achieve when they set their mind to it.

Even the First Minister, down the table, was appreciative of the excellence of his repast.

Shingo had not yet learned to relax around her. Nor had she worked too hard to induce it.

Not yet.

If she was to ascend to the Shogunate, she would rule. If he was to be her spouse, then the fusion of the Shogunate and the Imperial House would be a new thing in *Dalou* space. Much like Bottenberg had achieved with their cooking.

"How do you find dinner?" she asked the man, the noise of conversation and service drowning out most eavesdroppers.

Across the way, Yukimura paid attention, but he was charged with protecting both of them, and Kohahu supposed that such a task included from each other.

"Excellent," Shingo said carefully. "Comparable to the best meals at the palace, before I joined the fleet."

Kohahu nodded. She had eaten well as a favored guest of the Captain, but also understood that they were eating better than normal because she and the Crown Prince were aboard. And that the regular crew ate hardly better than the average folk at home.

She studied the man now. Because they were seated, he was much taller, as so much of his height was in his torso, compared to her legs.

"What do you think of *Ewin*?" he asked her, nodding in the direction of the First Minister, currently being fêted by Kosnett and his senior staff comparable to how they had treated her.

State dinner. A thing of pomp and performance designed to honor the recipient. The First Minister of *Ewin* did not rate such a thing, being the functional equivalent of one of the Shogun's ministers, or the Premier of the Emperor's Court. A bureaucrat.

Still, she understood what Kosnett was doing. And approved.

"I think that what Kosnett does today will still raise tides that will wash on our shores when you and I take our places in the hall of power," she replied carefully.

Still, he caught the reference. His eyes widened a bit.

They had not spoken of her future, the few times that they had been allowed to speak in unsupervised circumstances. Only his. As the son of the Emperor, he would ascend, one of these days.

Emperor Osamu had disrupted things greatly, but Kosnett and her father, along with Lord Morninghawk, had managed to contain most of it before any great damage was done.

Still, her father had warned her that many things were left undone. Might remain undone for a generation.

Until he was replaced by another Shogun. And Shingo became emperor of *Dalou*.

"What are your dreams, Lady Kugosu?" Shingo asked with exquisite care now.

Previously, she had been unprepared to have a conversation such as this, but she had spent several weeks in Shingo's company. He was bright and diligent. Polite and hardworking, to the point that even Captain Yukimura had privately expressed surprise.

Young princes with the promise of future power often tended to be spoiled.

Was it because she was female, and thus initially raised with an expectation that she would be married strategically, that she had not developed such an attitude? Her older sister was a bookworm. Her younger an artist in every sense of the word.

Kohahu had chosen the dojo floor as her expression. As her place of focus.

She continued to study Shingo. He was taller than her. Broader in the shoulders, so he significantly outweighed her, but she was still solid and blocky, compared to her willowy sisters that both took after their mother.

"Other Houses maneuver themselves quietly for dynastic marriages," Kohahu replied. "I have two sisters so three such might look to ally themselves directly with the Shogun and seek to place one of their own at the pinnacle."

He watched her rather than speaking immediately. That was one of the things she found the most interesting about the man. He wasn't completely reticent, but stopped and considered his words with care. Many others would blurt things, but she supposed that he had grown up in just as circumscribed circumstances as she had. And had learned to keep his own counsel well.

There was a new light there that hadn't been in his eyes previously. A realization of where she was going. Or threatening to go.

She had spent several weeks studying the man. And had read a number of intelligence reports compiled over the last decade. And spoken to Yukimura himself in evasive terms.

"Have you identified a promising candidate House for the Shogunate?" he asked so quietly she practically had to read his lips.

She wondered if Yukimura was doing the same. Others around them might, but were far enough away that they might miss details for the happy noise of conversation.

"I have narrowed it down to a few," she replied, softening her face to suggest warmth rather than mercenary hardness. "Some are obvious, given old alliances. A few…revolutionary in nature."

He blinked as he processed her words and drew a conclusion that seemed to unsettle him significantly, though he never moved. Never twitched.

Never gave any show of the emotional jolt that she'd seen course through his unguarded eyes, gone in a blink.

Crown Prince Shingo had, however, stopped breathing for several heartbeats. He began again with almost a rasp.

"That is truly an interesting revelation, Lady Kugosu," Shingo said carefully. Diffidently. "Would the older powers of the Hegemony even countenance it?"

With those words, she added another gold star next to the man's name in her mental dossier. Smart enough to understand that the many Damyo—the Great Houses of the Hegemony— might not accept a marriage that directly allied Shogunate Kugosu with the Imperial Yosan.

At the same time, it would cause many of the smaller Houses, small because they'd been on the losing side of the Civil War that originally saw the Shogunate created, to be drawn closer into her orbit as Hegemon of *Dalou*.

If she could take such a thing and hold it. Wield it. And this young man might accept the strange fusion that sought to bridge the ancient gap that saw *Dalou* split into two parts that were each much weaker than the combined whole might achieve.

They might seal the breach that had formed in the Hegemony.

What might that future bring?

Lord Morninghawk had warned her and her father both that Kosnett was a revolution that might bring the *Dalou Hegemony* down. Even unintentionally.

An avalanche gaining speed as he ground madly down the mountainside, destroying anything in its path not strong enough to resist. And Morninghawk had been correct that *Dalou* as it had been would not survive.

What about *Dalou*-yet-to-be?

But Shingo had asked a question. A cogent one, deserving of a well-considered answer.

"Lord Morninghawk saw the need to remake *Dalou*, Lord Yosan," she said, using his other title, instead of calling him a Crown Prince. "To strengthen it in the face of revolutionary pressures. It is entirely possible that other Houses might express their displeasure. Thus, such a task would need to be given great thought, as it would require terrible commitment to achieve."

As in, are you man enough to be merely the husband of a Shogun, even as you ascend to become Emperor of *Dalou*? The visible factor, rather than the powerful one?

He leaned back some now. Not breaking the conversation but perhaps taking a moment to consider the full implications of what she had put in front of him.

Kugosu allied to Yosan via marriage might start another civil war. Who would join? Who would seek to overturn?

Shingo had two younger sisters. If Kohahu established a precedent, would they become greater pawns in the political maneuvering, were an enemy House intent on overthrowing Kugosu and throwing down Shingo as emperor?

How big and bloody might it get, if they didn't approach it with the care of cutting diamonds?

"That is a most interesting consideration, Lady Kugosu," Shingo finally said, ceding her the field of battle for now, as she had expected.

She might have just completely overthrown everything the young man had spent his nineteen years learning and preparing for.

How big did they want to dream?

NINETEEN

ROYAL COURT, ALLEMAINE STATION, EWINHOME

Giscard had been seated on a couch reading when the hatch opened and admitted Bollvize. He looked up as the man glided across the entry chamber to this corner and came to rest.

"News?" Giscard asked bluntly.

It would achieve nothing to unleash his pique on Bollvize. The man was immune. And not a prince, so he didn't take things as personally. That had served them both over the years.

"Jaxom Bereoa was sent out by Doysan to meet the outlanders," Bollvize replied, looming over him. "Apparently, rather than a brief meeting to set up an audience, Kosnett is treating the trip as a full state visit, including a formal dinner that includes representatives of the Hegemon of *Dalou* as well as the Crown Prince himself."

Giscard blinked, trying to process this new information.

The Crown Prince of *Dalou* was traveling with this fleet? How the hell was that possible? The man was a prisoner of the Sunflower Palace. Everybody knew that.

Worse, it was possible that they might find a bribe sufficient to make Bereoa switch sides. It wouldn't take much, as the man had a known disdain for the Princes of *Ewin*.

Would he be setting things up for his own favorite to be named king in some palace coup?

Giscard wasn't entirely certain if there was a designated Crown Prince currently. Doysan IV could be mercurial, and Giscard seemed to remember that the last one had overstepped and been demoted over something.

"If Doysan got rid of the last heir, where does that leave betting in the Court?" Giscard asked now, tossing his book reader to one side and rising to pace.

Bollvize moved just enough to watch and be out of the way, like he did.

"Bertrand Farouk isn't fully outlaw, but that's because he retired quietly to his estates when Doysan got angry enough," Bollvize replied. "Duke Godfrey Kalidoona might be your most formidable opponent at present. He's currently Prince of the Eastern Squadron."

And technically the man Giscard had mutinied against when he went mostly rogue this most recent time.

The Central Squadron, stationed mostly out of *Ewinhome* itself, was the most powerful. Eastern Squadron, facing *Dalou*, was second, declining to Southern Squadron across from *Dalou* and Western peering over the moat at quiet *Yaumgan* itself.

"Michelle Agrimond is still in control of Central Squadron, yes?" Giscard asked.

"That is correct," Bollvize nodded.

Agrimond was an old drinking buddy of Doysan IV who had been elevated to supreme authority over the war fleets by the man. Agrimond was also usually too busy attempting to set some new record with the number of mistresses he could sustain, usually keeping three in every port.

He was not a threat to overthrow Doysan. At the same time, he would be too focused on Kosnett to do anything on Allemaine Station itself.

"I need you to arrange a private-enough audience for me

with Doysan," Giscard said. "Preferably while Bereoa is stupidly too far away to advise our drunken lout of a king."

"Time to whisper things in the king's ear?" Bollvize asked hungrily.

"If I don't, Kosnett's the next most likely person to," Giscard replied. "How fucked are we if he turns Bereoa?"

Even a hard killer like Bollvize could shudder with fright at what might happen if Kosnett successfully demanded that Baron Russand be punished.

Shit had just gotten ugly around here.

TWENTY

ROYAL COURT, ALLEMAINE STATION,
EWINHOME

Doysan didn't like the peon who was today's messenger, but managed—barely—not to scream in the fool's face. This stranger hadn't ordered Bereoa off the station, leaving behind incompetents to wait on their king.

"Russand?" Doysan demanded.

"Aye, My Liege," the man said. "Claims to have remembered something important that he is unwilling to share with any ears but yours."

Doysan stewed. His right hand found the goblet of brandy he'd been using to calm his nerves as he waited for his First Minister to return.

"Fine," Doysan grumbled. "But have him searched before he is admitted. I beat that son of a diseased camel once, and he has had sixteen years to think of how he might repay the effort."

The courtier bowed and withdrew, leaving Doysan alone with the half-empty bottle that he poured into his cup and slurped at.

It had been full earlier, but Doysan didn't handle the waiting well. And the cryptic messages from Bereoa hadn't helped.

Why was this alien treating Bereoa like an ambassador? He was merely a bureaucrat, a messenger. Nobody important.

Not a Prince of *Ewin*.

Or was Bereoa maneuvering? Seeking to enlist Kosnett to elevate his own preference to replace Doysan IV?

It was one thing to retire and be done. It was something entirely else to be shoved off the stage by common-blooded peons who thought they knew better than you did how to run things.

Doysan studied the bottle. He didn't remember it being empty. It had just been full, damn it!

He rose, staggered a bit, then righted the ship of state and made his careful way to the rack of more bottles by the sideboard. As king, he had an enormous selection of things to drink.

The next bottle was also brandy, but in a blue-labeled bottle.

Blue felt pretty.

He made his way back to the table where he'd been sitting and filled the empty cup again.

"Enter!" he bellowed angrily when someone rapped at the hatch, disturbing his peace and quiet.

Couldn't they see he just wanted to be alone to drink???

An aide entered. Not Bereoa. He was off doing something or other.

"Baron Russand, My Liege," the man announced, then stepped to one side, just inside the door, and Doysan had to deal with that punk again.

Still, he'd been chastened right proper. Kosnett had kicked his stupid ass twice now.

Turned the man into the laughingstock of *Ewin*. That had to sting, since the aliens wouldn't settle for a proper duel to handle things like that.

No, they were more likely to just blow your silly head off and be done with it. Look at what they'd done to *Jacoby*. The only reason Russand had escaped with his life had been the unwillingness of his mistress to sleep on an empty ship in dry-dock, so the Baron had gone over to her.

Probably saved his life. Might not have done the fucker any favors, though.

"Sit," Doysan commanded. "Someone get this man a cup!"

Russand took the other chair. A gold goblet appeared, matching Doysan's but not as nice.

Never as nice. He was king, after all, and the rest of you are just peons around here. Keep that in mind!

Still, magnanimous in victory, or something like that. He poured Russand some excellent brandy and stared at the man.

They hadn't been this close physically since Giscard's own half-sister had sold his ass down the line, sixteen years ago.

Doysan smiled at the memory. She'd even hung around the palace for a time, before retiring off to…somewhere.

When was the last time he'd thought about Ellevain?

Years.

He made a note to see whatever had happened to the woman.

Doysan steadied his hand and his gaze.

"What the hell do you want now, Giscard?" he asked irritably, feeling all the energy from the brandy light a hot fire under his ass.

It had been ages since anyone had really dared challenge him. Even Giscard had been an annoying fly not worth the effort to bring to heel for the last several years.

Giscard smiled and seemed to shrink in on himself a little before he spoke.

That was good. Suggested that the pompous buffoon had finally learned his place in things.

"I heard that you sent your First Minister out to visit Kosnett's flagship, Your Majesty," the man said in a polite, almost simpering voice.

Like he should.

"That's right," Doysan replied. "See what the barbarians are about before we let them get too close down here. After all, they tore you a new asshole pretty easily."

Doysan liked that flash of raw hatred that he saw in Russand's eyes. They weren't alone, so the fool would get utterly stomped on by any of the bodyguards around here that Doysan considered just more furniture.

Still, it was nice to taunt the man to his face for once.

"And I am given to understand that Bertrand Farouk is no longer favored at Court?" Russand continued, still not rising to the bait.

Maybe he finally had admitted defeat after all. That would be nice.

"That shit Duke slunk home with his tail between his legs," Doysan growled. "Serves him right, too."

"Huh," Russand said, nodding and taking a long draught of brandy, as if in thought.

"What?" Doysan demanded.

"Just odd, Your Majesty, but I'm obviously not an insider when it comes to the depth of your political maneuverings," Russand admitted.

"What are you talking about?" Doysan asked loudly, taking another drink and finding the mug empty.

He refilled it and drank some more.

"I was of the opinion that Farouk and Bereoa were close allies," Russand said. "At least at the time. It surprises me that you sent him out to negotiate the possible fate of *Ewin* by himself. That's all. Again, what do I know?"

Doysan paused in his next drink, even as Russand had another.

Bereoa and Farouk *had* been allies. True. At least of convenience. As most were. Heir-designate and First Minister. Had anything happened to Doysan IV, the Duke would have immediately stepped in. Maybe even managed to hold it.

Not now. Too many others had piled on when Doysan had broken that punk and sent him packing to his estates.

That was before Kosnett. Before *Aquitaine* and *Dalou* and *Meerut*.

Before shit got real.

Doysan took a gulp and refilled his mug. Russand was obviously spoiling to be brought back into royal favor. He was transparent that way.

Still, maybe he had made a bit of sense there. Bereoa hadn't seemed pleased to be sent out there. Would this be the man's chance to get rid of his king once and for all and maybe use Kosnett's power to control who took the throne next?

Maybe make himself king? The dukes and barons wouldn't stand for it, but they'd also all just watched Kosnett's fleet end Baron Russand as a threat to anything except the virginity of a young redhead.

Was that rat planning to upend the whole system? Overthrow his king and just take charge himself?

Everybody laughed at *Ewin*. That was, until they were facing a missile swarm.

That was when they stopped laughing.

Except that Baron Russand had been the one who had stopped laughing. Twice now. *Meerut* and then *Jacoby*.

"I am king around here, Russand," Doysan finally managed when he realized that everything had gone too quiet.

"I am acutely aware of that, Your Majesty," Russand replied. "My continued existence relies entirely on your forbearance at my previous behavior and forgiveness. The outsiders have changed everything and I begin to wonder if they aren't a threat to *Ewin* itself. After all, they broke the Syndicates. Convinced *Aditi* to hand them a fleet to hunt pirates. Got *Yaumgan* to join them, which the philosophers have never done. Even traveled to *Ellariel* as guests of the Shogun for the first time in history. Now, they come to *Ewinhome*. What threats do they bring to the Principalities, as you never summoned them? Kosnett just presumptively chose to bring a warfleet to your doorstep, after making an example of *Jacoby*. Do we have anything that could stop him from simply conquering *Ewin*?"

Doysan went cold all over, in spite of the abundance of brandy that had been keeping him warm ere now.

That Russand had stumbled onto the nightmare that kept him awake at night didn't take much imagination. *Ewin* had never been a significant threat to their neighbors, if only because holding an entire fleet together that long without duels or feuds causing things to unravel had tamed every King of *Ewin* yet.

Pirates notwithstanding, *Ewin* was not a threat.

But how much of a danger were the outlanders? Worse, could Kosnett convince *Dalou*, *Aditi*, and *Yaumgan* to team up and invade *Ewin*? Was that what was parked on his very doorstep? A war squadron capable of savaging Central Squadron before they could react? Were there other fleets even now preparing to pounce on his borders and strip his power away?

He'd considered attacking them, just for the audacity of arriving here uninvited.

Had they been counting on that? Russand had attacked without warning. And lost badly.

Was Doysan IV their next intended victim?

"I can see that you are a busy man, Your Majesty," Baron Russand spoke now. "With your permission, I will withdraw, though I thank you for taking the time to hear my concerns for your well-being and that of the kingdom."

"Yes," Doysan nodded absently. "Thank you. You have given me much to consider and useful counsel."

The man smiled as he rose, then bowed deeply before backing away and exiting.

"Get me Duke Agrimond!" Doysan bellowed as Russand left.

TWENTY-ONE

Harman looked up to see if anyone else in the room had heard the obscenity that he had muttered under his breath, but they were all focused elsewhere. Or ignoring anything he had to say until he issued orders. As Senior Chief, he was in charge down here in Cryptography right now.

Centurion Fabre was asleep, in the middle of her night. Her boss, Senior Centurion Ekmekçi, was with the rest of the bigshots having dinner, or maybe after-dinner drinks at this point. Hard to tell without opening a comm and asking, and given the company, Harman didn't think that was a smart move on his part.

Instead, he read the message on his screen again. Sure enough, pretty much what he'd seen on the first pass, after he'd managed to crack the cryptographic signals that the station and the ships in orbit were using.

He wasn't supposed to do things like that without orders, and everyone here was friendly, but Cerere Fabre understood that Harman had something of a compulsion there and let him be, most of the time. Didn't help that he was old enough to be her father. She treated him like the weird uncle that showed up at family events with exotic stories that were probably only half of the time utter bullshit.

The other half, he'd left out some of the more outrageous truths because nobody would believe him.

Cerere was asleep. *Junkyard* had the bridge, the flag, and tactical. That woman was just looking for a victim to maul.

Harman read the message a third time and wondered if she'd get her wish shortly.

"Jacob," he said, causing the nearest sailor to start and blink in his direction.

Comm and Crypto were generally quiet, unless you were elbows deep in blood or something. Currently, there were only four of them on duty because standing orders called for four. Computers could have handled most of it, and did, leaving the humans not a lot to do.

"Chief?" the kid asked.

Nineteen and lucked into a spot on the flagship because he had a mind for patterns and language. Necessary when you did crypto. Fantastic with math. Lousy with girls. Kinda like somebody else Harman knew.

"I need to go chat with an officer," Harman said blandly, shutting his terminal down and locking it for now. "Anything happens, you wake the Centurion immediately. Questions?"

"No, sir," the kid shook his head.

Harman rose and flipped a coin mentally, ending up headed to the bridge for now. Flag bridge might have been smarter, but *Junkyard* had the flag, and would know what to do.

Shit was about to get ugly around here.

Urumchi's bridge was huge. Well-lit.

Harman preferred the dim semi-darkness of the cryptography section, where they kept things quiet and worked in the shadows. Physically as well as metaphorically.

Junkyard speared him with deadly eyes as he entered and made his way towards her. Looking around, most of the B-Team on duty today, with a few C-Team kids earning points and training.

He stepped close enough to make this personal and came to rest. *Junkyard* just watched.

"Permission to hijack your screen and show you a message that was intercepted and decrypted?" he asked.

"Decrypted by whom?" she challenged.

It was like she knew him or something. He wondered if Centurion Fabre had warned the woman.

Harman grimaced. Technically, he could be put on a punishment duty for hacking into *Shadowbolt's* systems and stealing all their codes in order to begin calculating how *Ewin* code patterns were generated. Maybe stripped of a stripe.

Or tossed in the brig, depending on how pissed the Command Centurion was that day.

"Pixies," he replied somewhat evasively. "The information contained is more important than the bucket it came in."

"Is it now, Senior Chief Abadjiev?" she asked.

Harman shrugged. Might be worth losing the stripe, if he was reading things right.

"Yes, sir," he finally said.

She pivoted her screen to face him.

"Go ahead," *Junkyard* ordered.

Harman started typing. Did a few things that he probably wasn't supposed to, but wasn't that the story of his life?

He flipped the screen back around to face her and came to parade rest, preparatory for getting in trouble.

Senior Centurion Iveta Beridze read while he watched.

Her eyes got big when she got to the interesting bits, same as his had. Different profanity, but close enough for government work.

She locked eyes like Type-4 beams on him now.

"This order was issued seven minutes ago," she said in an accusatory voice.

"*Ewin* never struck me as particularly well organized, sir,"

Harman offered. "Probably took them two minutes to get it routed."

"And one for you to crack it, plus a few to walk here?" she asked.

"I might have forgotten more about code work than those amateurs on the station or in *Ewin*'s fleet ever knew, sir," Harman replied, trying to keep a lid on his emotions.

Sensitive spot. It had gotten him a career. And in trouble a few times. Centurion Fabre was a better boss than many he'd had.

"Why didn't you wake Fabre up?" *Junkyard* asked now. "Or alert flag bridge?"

"She's been pulling stupid long hours keeping squadron communications secure," Harman said. "And everybody else is having dinner right now, so you have the flag and tactical. Figured I should save time. That flagship over there might have a competent communications department. Weirder shit has happened."

"Do you want credit for this?" she asked.

"Not if I have to answer how I did it, sir," Harman replied. "First Centurion might not be feeling benevolent. *Ground Control*, either."

"Understood," *Junkyard* replied. "You return to duty and go ahead and wake Cerere up. That will give her time to get coffee ahead of everyone else."

"We expecting trouble?" Harman asked. "Those are just maneuver orders for the flagship squadron and instructions to scale up their alert level."

"There's nobody else around here for them to fight, Senior Chief," she nodded. "Unless they're about to crack down the middle and go full civil war, which I doubt."

"Understood, sir," Harman said.

He undid what he'd done to her station and withdrew.

As he reached the hatch, she started barking orders that left him cold. And warm.

Harman didn't think he'd saved the day, but every extra minute helped in shit like this.

"Squadron, this is Beridze, aboard *Urumchi*. I have the flag. All vessels to Alert Status Two and stand by for imminent combat operations."

TWENTY-TWO

Phil had been enjoying cake for dessert and some decaf coffee when Markus suddenly perked up, as though listening to something in his earpiece. Then the man rose, checked the room once to place everyone, and made sure to walk around to the side that put First Minister Bereoa on Phil's far side.

"Iveta just took us to Two and warned everyone to stand by for combat operations," Markus murmured in his ear.

Phil couldn't help jerking around to stare at the man. Markus just nodded.

Phil did the math and decided that dessert was over.

The First Minister was still relaxed and sipping some port. Everyone else at the table had stiffened and were poised for trouble.

Both hands now flat on the table, Phil pushed his chair back. Heather was up before he was. Most of the table joined him.

Bereoa looked at him owlishly.

"First Centurion?" he asked, suddenly aware that he was the only person still seated.

"There have been developments, First Minister," Phil replied diplomatically. "Normally, I would leave some of my folks here to continue to chat, but I might suggest you join me aft on my flag bridge for now as we see what happened."

"What happened?" the man echoed, keeping his port and rising.

Not that Phil blamed him. It was good port.

"My bridge just brought the ship to alert," Phil said as folks began scattering to duty stations. "And suggested imminent combat. Is there anything you might wish to convey at this point?"

He didn't mean to come off combative himself, but at the same time, Iveta wouldn't do something like this without a damned good reason.

She might be crazy and violent, but always under control and in the guise of echoing her hero, Jessica Keller.

"Nothing, First Centurion," Bereoa replied. "I'm as surprised as you are."

Phil nodded. That felt right. Something had happened on Allemaine Station.

Harinder moved to escort Bereoa. Heather started jogging with her folks. Phil had to fight the urge to join her.

Flag bridge was awake and alert when he got there. Markus had a mug of coffee that probably had more than caffeine in it, given his read.

"Bring the projector live and get me *Junkyard*," Phil ordered.

Harinder saw Bereoa seated at the main table, off to one side where Xochitl Dar just happened to be close and Markus also ready to pile on.

"Bridge," Iveta said as she came live. "Routing a message thread to you now, First Centurion."

Phil waited calmly as his personal screen came live. She had the flag until he or Heather overrode it. That was fine. He wouldn't have put her there if he didn't trust the woman.

Phil read what appeared to be top secret orders from the Prince in charge of the Central Squadron to stop one step short of a mass launch. Maneuvering orders that would put *Meynard*

II and a full squadron of escorts—both cruisers and frigates—right at the top of the gravity well, where they could suddenly move to Jump.

Like, say, pouncing on the *Aquitaine* squadron ninety degrees around the orbital path and pointed forward, where bow-mounted weapons couldn't bear. That might have mattered on a Heavy Dreadnought, but *Urumchi* had full arc on her beam weapons. Only *Storm Petrel* was really at a disadvantage that way.

"Where did we get this information, Iveta?" Phil asked.

"Pixies, First Centurion," she replied, grinning on the screen.

"Pixies?" he confirmed, just to make sure he'd understood her.

Junkyard nodded.

Pixies, indeed.

"First Minister, I am routing you some information that apparently *pixies* delivered while we were at dinner," Phil said, watching the man's face as he did.

Bereoa looked down. Paled so badly he turned nearly Anglo, looked up with eyes as huge as saucers.

"None of that was anything I was aware of or ordered, First Centurion," he rasped weakly.

Phil started to say something when the main hatch opened and Striker Solo was admitted, also looking a little lost.

"Flight deck wouldn't let him return to *Shadowbolt*, boss," Markus said, stepping close.

"Good," Phil nodded.

He waved the man to join them at the big table, and pointed to the chair directly opposite Bereoa. Cardinal points. It made a nice symmetry.

"What are your orders, First Centurion?" Solo asked as he sat, obviously realizing that he was stuck on *Urumchi* for now.

"Contact your first officer on an encrypted channel and check in," Phil said. "And don't use your code Lima-Six, as apparently it's been cracked."

"But that's our most secure key, First Centurion," Solo gasped.

"Not anymore," Phil smiled savagely.

Pixies, indeed.

"First Minister," Phil said now, rotating back to that unfortunate. "Why would your Central Squadron be preparing to launch an attack at this moment?"

Solo gasped. Harinder was reading messages faster than Phil was, but that was her job.

"I am at a loss, First Centurion," Bereoa replied carefully. "If I could contact the Palace, I might ask."

Phil nodded to Harinder.

"On an open channel for now," he ordered her. Then he picked out Iveta's image on a screen. "What's the squadron status?"

"Ten seconds from opening fire, Phil," she replied. "Thirty seconds from a tactical Jump."

"What's *Meynard II* doing?" he asked.

"Stand by," she said. "Leyla just took over."

Good. He needed his Science Officer right now. Especially if her people had managed to crack the top code the enemy fleet was currently using. Hell, he might be reading and reacting faster than they did, give Solo's opinion of some of his brother officers and their ability to handle complex things like cryptography.

Inside the enemy's decision curve, moving before they could. It was a nice place to be.

"Iveta, plot a Jump that puts us exactly one hundred and eighty degrees across orbit of *Ewinhome*," he ordered. "Same distance. Stand by for my orders to execute it."

Her image froze, so she was passing it along to everyone else. She was in charge until he took back the flag.

Phil didn't feel like he had enough information yet to start acting, but he could react for now.

"Radio silence from Allemaine Station," Harinder said. "Lag is about three seconds at this distance."

Phil nodded. They might be asleep. They might also be playing possum.

They might be about to launch themselves across intervening space to unleash every missile they had at short range.

Phil had been taught to fight dirty by the sharks of *Buran*, thank you very much.

"Bridge, how deep is Allemaine Station in the gravity well if I decided I needed to hit him with the Fours?" Phil asked aloud now, catching the gasps from Bereoa and Solo.

Not Harinder. She'd probably already figured that part out. She thought even faster than he did, once he gave her a direction to aim.

"Outer edge of coherence, First Centurion," someone replied. Sounded like Gunner Boyadjiev. "Better if we executed an Expeditionary Slingshot in the process."

Yes. Phil had been part of a few of those, back in the day. Come out of Jump at high speed, running down the gravity well until it forced you into RealSpace, usually with Kigali in the van and both d'Maine and Aeliaes leading *Vanguard* and Keller in to rend and ravage. Always, Kigali closer to the enemy.

Drop down and hammer the shit out of someone who thought he was deep enough while rebuilding your Jump Matrix, then ride gravity up and out the back.

But for the time *CS-405* had overheated her JumpSails and lost them deep behind enemy lines, a fantastic way to surprise someone.

"I will take it under advisement," Phil replied. "For now, plot a second hop after we land the first time, like valence shell jumps, just in case I have to remonstrate with someone for ill-chosen manners."

He smiled at Solo and Bereoa. This was something of a performance, though both men were currently trapped aboard *Urumchi*. There was no way in hell he was launching one or more shuttles right now, when he might have to jump to safety from an attack.

They'd just have to live with it. With him.

Those two men were both a little pale and sickly. But *Ewin* should have known better by now. *Meerut* and *Jacoby* were supposed to have been lessons to learn from, not insults to be avenged.

Because Phil could up the scale of things radically if he had to. It would be nice to not have to play that card.

"Flag, I have redshift on *Meynard II* and her escort team," Leyla came on the line now. "They are starting to climb to position, but doing an ugly, ragged job of it. Like the order caught everybody off-guard and they had to wake folks up. If we're supposed to be surprised, they must think we're punks."

Not the most diplomatic thing to say, considering his company. At the same time, Phil had chosen all of his people because they spoke their minds when they thought he needed to hear something. He had a thick skin. Some of the old First Fleet Lords he'd served under had indeed been martinets that way.

Most of them had been retired by First Lord Kasum for people willing to fight. For good or ill.

"*Aquitaine* squadron, this is Kosnett, aboard *Urumchi*. I have the flag," he said now, after flipping to the wide—and hopefully still fully encrypted—channel, pixies notwithstanding. "Stand by to execute Jump number one, then keep your generators running, in case we need to maneuver like sharks today. I'm not sure what *Ewin*'s Central Squadron thinks it is up to, but do not open fire first. You may return any hostile fire as you see fit until I jerk your chains back, however."

He was watching Bereoa gasp and breathe heavy. The man had been a gracious guest and had apparently latched onto Heather as something of a truth object. Someone he would talk to without all the obfuscations.

But right now he was a bystander.

An unintended hostage.

"First Minister, I would like to apologize in advance," Phil said sincerely, watching the man turn his way. "If combat is imminent, there will be no way to get you safely home, short of putting you in a hardsuit, activating an emergency beacon, and literally shoving you out an airlock. And if *Ewin* is about to attack us, I doubt that they would pause to identify who it was before opening fire. For now, I hope you won't mind being my guest while we sort things out here. If the worst occurs, I can outrun any messages to one of your nearby worlds and drop you off there, where you could presumably get safe transport back to *Ewinhome*."

Bereoa nodded. Solo was glum, but Phil presumed that the man was assuming he'd be blamed for whatever happened today, one way or another. And have to watch from the stands if combat broke out.

The air in here felt like that long moment before lightning leapt into the air and broke the sound barrier. Charged and ominous. Murmurs around him as his team locked in with every vessel in the formation and passed information back and forth.

"*Meynard II* just lit all her targeting systems," Leyla Ekmekçi said over the main line. "Stand by for missile launch."

Several seconds lag for light speed, Phil couldn't imagine what they thought they would accomplish against him with missiles. Everything would be burned out and coasting ballistically by the time it arrived, to the point that he could just maneuver around them without actually firing.

Odd. He'd say *out of character*, but *Ewin* gentlemen seemed to be defined by their macho, rather than their brains. Bantam roosters in a yard, for something to compare them to.

"We have launch!" Leyla called. "*Meynard* is unleashing a shitstorm. I have no—**REPEAT NO**—inbound tracking at this time."

"Who the hell are they firing at?" Phil demanded.

"Stand by," Leyla replied. "Target appears to be the Heavy

Bombard *Gallivant*. Below them in the gravity well and looks like they caught him asleep."

"WHAT?!?" First Minister Bereoa demanded.

"Confirm that, Leyla," Phil ordered.

"Confirmed," she replied a moment later. "*Meynard II* and her squadron just unloaded a shitstorm on *Gallivant* and her escorts. I have counter-missile fire from *Gallivant*, but no locks. Looks like they are starting to run."

"Where to?" Phil demanded. "What's the best escape route for *Gallivant* right now?"

"If I had to guess, I'd say about where we were planning to jump to, First Centurion," she called. "Not that far off it, and it would put us in front of them and above, like a cork in the bottle."

"Shit," Phil said. "Is anybody even looking at us?"

"Negative, sir."

Phil flipped a switch, eyeballing Bereoa hard.

"Squadron, this is Kosnett," he said. "Stand down and prepare for a jump straight backwards two light-seconds farther out from the planet. This isn't our fight, and I see no reason to get involved in it until someone else sorts out what the hell is going on. All vessels signal your readiness to jump."

He muted the line and studied Bereoa. That man had gone to what looked like pure rage, instead of being frightened.

"What am I missing here, First Minister?" Phil asked.

"*Gallivant* is allied with Duke Bertrand Farouk," the man replied. "Until recently, Heir Designate to Doysan IV. There was a falling out and I thought we had sorted it all out. That idiot king must have gotten drunk and decided to do something extravagant."

"He known for that sort of thing?" Phil pressed. If the man was feeling open to truth telling, Phil wasn't about to stop him.

Bereoa's shoulders slumped and he sighed.

"More than is good for any of us," Bereoa said. "Someone must have gotten to him."

"Gotten to him?" Phil asked.

"Drunk and listening to someone with an axe to grind or a knife to stick in somebody else's back," Bereoa said, grimacing. "It is a weak spot with the man. He tends to follow the advice of the last person to talk to him, so I usually make it a point to be me. I can't do that from here. Someone did."

"While the cat's away?"

"Something like that, yes," Bereoa said.

Phil noted that all his boards had gone green.

"Flag bridge, I have multiple launches down there," Leyla said. "Looks like everybody just woke up, turned on their targeting sensors, and opened up with everything they had. There are a dozen or so headed this way, even, but far out of range."

"Squadron, execute your Jump," Phil ordered. "We'll back away and see how it all turns out."

TWENTY-THREE

PERSONAL QUARTERS, ALLEMAINE STATION, EWINHOME

Giscard smiled as he watched the screen. Bollvize had smuggled in a monitor tapped into the military channel. Passive only, but it allowed one to watch everything that was happening.

All hell had just broken loose in orbit around him. It was lovely to watch. Doubly so as he was reasonably safe aboard the station. Others might launch a few missiles this way, but Doysan's abject paranoia would keep even his worst enemies safe inside.

Like, say, renegade Barons with an eye to the main chance.

"What am I seeing?" Bollvize asked, sitting next to him at the table and watching.

"*Gallivant* looks like they were caught dead asleep by a mass launch," Giscard noted. Bollvize was many things, but not a sailor. "To the extent that they have had to launch their own missiles defensively, targeting incoming missiles just so they didn't get overwhelmed. Right now, they are low in orbit, so they have to run if they want to survive. Oh, yes, there! Now, forces nominally loyal to Kalidoona are getting into action, firing back at *Meynard II* just to force him to the defensive. And this group, under Agrimond's command, have really just been transferred here from the Western Squadron, so they aren't sure if this is all some sort of bizarre triple-cross, so it looks like they are about to laager up hard and sail off to a corner until somebody they do trust tells them what the hell is going on."

"And that's not Prince Agrimond?" Bollvize asked.

"Not today, it seems," Giscard laughed harshly.

"Who would they trust?" Bollvize asked.

"That's the best part," Giscard snickered. "The First Minister might be able to talk sense to them, but he's trapped aboard the enemy flagship, and Kosnett just jumped backwards almost to the point that he doesn't show up on local scanners. Jaxom Bereoa has to go with him."

"So we're in good shape?" Bollvize asked.

"For now, yes," Giscard smiled. "I might have lost my fleet, but everyone else might be in the process of forcing each other into dry-dock as well. If that happens, nobody can go to *Jacoby* and do anything to me."

"If you can't have it, nobody can?" Bollvize asked with his own grin.

"Damned right, man," Giscard nodded. "That drunk thinks me neutered by Kosnett. Pity that he didn't think about that before attacking Farouk and his allies, right here in local orbit. Maybe I'll get lucky and they'll destroy each other."

"What about Kosnett, though?" Bollvize asked.

Again, fantastic in the board room or dark alley, but lousy with stellar combat.

"He's made it clear he doesn't want to get involved, which is stupid," Giscard laughed and laughed and laughed. "He could probably sail right down to the station and destroy anything that got in the way before launching those damned combat teams to physically assault the place, like he did my dry-dock. Poof. Just like that, Doysan IV wouldn't be king anymore. And Farouk is out. Agrimond goes down with Doysan. Kalidoona might be able to rally forces from the Eastern Squadron, but *Dalou* is still twitchy and he won't want to turn his back on the Hegemony to sail here and proclaim himself king. Especially if *Meerut* is a thorn in everybody's side."

"So that just leaves you?" Bollvize asked innocently.

"Who else is here to take charge, when it all falls apart?" Giscard smiled.

TWENTY-FOUR

Heather was in her station, but only watching at this point. Iveta was patiently scanning everything, waiting for an opportunity to hurt someone.

Anyone.

Phil was probably dealing with his two strays from *Ewin*. That left her to do things with the squadron.

"Boss, I got Khan on line, being a pain and asking for you," Leyla said over the quiet chatter of the bridge crew being poised for action with nobody to shoot.

It was almost like those long moments before a team of sharks would jump out of the night sky and shred you with their weird weapons.

Heather looked over at Leyla. The woman had a grouchy expression on her face. Must have been dealing with Khan earlier and the man had finally escalated enough to irritate her.

He could be like that.

"I'll take it," she said.

"Channel nine." Leyla nodded and went back to her work.

Without close enemies, the Science Officer had the most to do right now.

Heather keyed in a privacy field around her station and switched channels.

Cruiser-Captain Adham Khan, commander of the battlecruiser *Juvayni*. Short for a man, shorter than her by a handspan even, though it did not come across as small. Compact like a coiled spring. As dark as anybody she'd met from the Cluster, but not as dark as the African Diaspora. Van Dyke, trimmed precisely on the sides but growing almost long enough to become a goatee.

As always, dressed in a uniform that combined black leather pants and tunic, bronze-colored chain mail with a few plates, and tall, leather boots. Starkly primitive, at first glance, but it had the feel of something rather more anachronistic. Probably intended to contrast with the simple cloth uniforms everyone else wore around here.

Pseudo-space-barbarian, as it were.

Top notch commander and small unit tactician, but Heather had never been able to determine if he'd been assigned to this force as a reward from his emperor or a punishment. The *Gloran Empire* was better run than *Ewin*, but that was a low bar to clear. More strictly hierarchical, perhaps, but the man at the top was just as moody and mercurial as Doysan IV, from what she'd heard.

Just maintained a firmer grip on the leash.

"Cruiser-Captain," Heather nodded to the man. "You had questions?"

She didn't say *suggestions*. Anything he offered would be some form of charging in and going for somebody's throat. Teeth or blade or claws was really the only distinction he might make, if it came to that.

"Why have we not attacked them, Command Centurion?" Khan asked, right off the bat.

It was like the man was predictable or something.

At least right up until the moment combat actually began, then he got as twisted and wily as a snake.

"Because nobody has attacked us," Heather stated baldly. "I don't count those few missiles that might get here by tomorrow, because even *Juvayni* could handle them."

That deflated the man a little. Did he demand that those were a significant threat and admit that he was scared of them, or scoff at such a pitiful offering?

After this long, Heather had also learned which buttons to push on the man.

"We could crush them!" He was off on the next track, like Bereoa seeing all this firepower as a sword instead of a shield.

She wondered if she could plot this entire conversation in her head ahead of time and replay it for him sometime. *Gloran* wasn't as big on dueling as *Ewin*, but doing so might piss the man off.

Whether that anger would cause him to sulk or would show him weak spots he needed to address was a question for a trained psychologist with a lot of time and unearthly amounts of patience.

"They're doing a fine job themselves," Heather replied. "For starting all this, *Meynard II* has already taken two near hits that have done internal damage. *Gallivant* is hurt as well. The Hunter-class carrier *Freewind* has lost half their flight wing but managed to keep the main ship from being hurt. Several frigates have suffered significant-enough damage that normally I would expect them to strike their colors, but instead appear to be limping off, presumably to retire to whatever home base they think safe, since *Ewinhome* is a battlefield."

"All the more reason to attack!" Khan cried. "We could finish them off."

Heather let her scowl descend into a full-on glower so intense that Khan shut his mouth. Must have reminded him of some teacher with a similar look when he was a child or something.

"We're not here to fight *Ewin*, *Juvayni*," she said flatly. "If anything, I expect orders from the First Centurion shortly to fully withdraw from the system to someplace where we might be able to drop off *Ewin's* First Minister safely, before going on and doing *whatever the First Centurion orders us to do.*"

That got through. Being aggressive was one thing. Getting out of hand in front of his peers and superiors was something entirely else.

Gloran saw themselves as warriors instead of shopkeepers. Which was funny, because most of the *Republic of Aquitaine* Navy would probably better identify as shopkeepers instead of honor-crazed berserkers like *Ewin* or Charge-Madly-Into-Battle-At-Any-Costs types like *Gloran.* That latter might perfectly describe Khan.

Khan subsided.

Then the man perked right back up again.

"If we are done with *Ewinhome* then, would it be a good time for the squadron to visit *Derragon*?" he asked, naming the *Gloran Empire's* homeworld.

"I'm certain that the First Centurion will let us know, Cruiser-Captain," she said with a hard finality in her voice. "Any other questions?"

"No, ma'am," he replied, dutifully chagrined.

She cut the line and only then rolled her eyes at the entire situation.

Phil had warned her that *Ewin* was a fragile place. She hoped that their mere presence hadn't caused them to fall out over each other and start the civil war that her *Aditi* friends had warned her was always just around the corner.

Every new king, it seemed, had to take power after at least some level of bullshit, though Heather's read of *Ewin* history suggested that the wars on the scale of Caesar or Octavian were rare. Those had lasted generations, and really hadn't stopped so much as paused briefly, like coals burning down until someone tossed fresh wood onto the fire.

The *Ewin Principalities* weren't really organized enough to even handle a civil war properly. All the shit happening below her in closer orbit looked more like a brawl, or maybe a food fight, than anything meaningful.

As long as nobody fired anything at her, Iveta wouldn't need to kick in anybody's teeth today.

Today.

TWENTY-FIVE

ROYAL COURT, ALLEMAINE STATION, EWINHOME

Doysan missed the old days, when he might be standing on the bridge of a mighty vessel like *Meynard II*, named for the real Founder of the modern dynasty, and sail into the teeth of a storm.

He was wondering if he needed to cashier the fool in command right now and find someone competent to take over. That idiot hadn't even launched his fighter squadrons until after *Freewind* had done the same, settling for just filling the skies with missiles instead of taking control like the fleet flagship that it was.

With such surprise, *Gallivant* should have been utterly overwhelmed. Instead, that cruiser had managed to limp to cover behind his frigates and slingshot down and under the planet, picking off chasing missiles but leaving *Meynard II* on the opposite side of the planet.

Doysan looked up from the screen to snarl at Agrimond, Prince of the Central Squadron and an old drinking buddy who had been promoted to command the fleets when Doysan settled into his rule.

The man had changed. Even drunk, Doysan was a little disgusted at what he saw.

Granted, Michelle Agrimond had a string of mistresses, but Doysan saw how fat the man had gotten. Perhaps the sudden call to action tonight had caught him off-guard and he hadn't had time to be laced into a corset he must have normally worn, to be straining this badly at his tunic? Something, because he hadn't remembered to put on the toupee he frequently wore like a dead muskrat glued to his head.

Thankfully, the alcohol fumes that followed him in here covered up whatever smells the man might have added.

"I thought you said that your forces could crush Farouk's ships," Doysan snarled at the man.

Michelle started to snarl back, then remembered where he was. And that there was somebody who could give him orders. He slammed his jaws shut so hard that they clacked.

"When this is done, that striker will be removed," Agrimond replied tersely. "What about Solo?"

It took Doysan's alcohol-riddled brain a moment to place the question.

"*Shadowbolt?*" he screeched. "What of him?"

"He has chosen to remain with the outlander fleet instead of assisting us."

"I wasn't aware that you were in such sad shape that a light missile bombard might turn the tables, Prince Agrimond," Doysan sneered now. "*Meynard* should be the match of all the other cruisers out there, so you tell me. And many of those have chosen to remain loyal. Although I'm beginning to wonder about that, as well."

Agrimond grew pale at those words, which had the unfortunate effect of showing off just how much makeup he was wearing tonight, and where the edges of it were.

"Besides," Doysan continued. "If we invited the outlanders down into this fracas, haven't you, of all people, assured me that they might prove invincible?"

"Not I," Agrimond cried. "We can take any force that threatens *Ewinhome.*"

"You can't even take down a Heavy Bombard, Agrimond," Doysan snarled. "Even now, *Gallivant* is escaping, where he will no doubt sail back to his duke and I'll be facing insurrections on all sides tomorrow!"

"We shall destroy him," Agrimond assured him.

"Then do so!" King Doysan IV bellowed.

At least Michelle Agrimond had the smarts to immediately flee the room, leaving Doysan alone with his worthless courtiers and bodyguards.

He looked around now.

"Somebody get me another bottle of brandy and a glass!"

TWENTY-SIX

Phil studied the big, three-dimensional display of near-*Ewinhome* space from his spot at the head of the table. Harinder was still opposite him as always. He had Bereoa on his left and Solo on his right. Heather, Iveta, and Leyla had joined them, after the squadron had hopped several more times randomly around the ring of local space.

"What's the final score?" he asked tiredly.

It was the middle of the night, personal time. For him and most of his people. They'd already had a full day, which had then turned into being passive observers of a long battle for...*something*. Even Phil wasn't sure.

"Whoever got the job handling Tactical for *Meynard II* must have a rich and powerful uncle," Iveta said disdainfully. "Because I'm not sure he could spell incompetent if you gave him three tries."

Phil was a little shocked. Iveta was widely known as one of the Jessica Keller clones that a whole generation of the *RAN* had turned out. One of the best of them, too. However, that was a pretty savage assessment. Unfortunately, probably pretty accurate, too.

"How bad?" he asked his Science Officer now.

"*Meynard II* got hammered," Leyla replied. "Somebody else was paying attention to those loading and firing cycles, because they caught the flagship with nothing in the racks that could even be fired defensively to stop incoming trackers. The ship got a hard broadside that might be enough to take them out of action for six months. I'd have to be closer to be sure, but it didn't look good."

"What about *Gallivant* and *Freewind?*" he continued.

"The former got it almost as bad as *Meynard*," Heather spoke up now. "They were running most of the time, however, so had more opportunity to kill missiles. And someone on that side wisely tasked a frigate with doing nothing but defensive counterfire, to the extent that only a few missiles got through. None of *Gallivant's* escorts were hurt, but their flagship got overloaded twice before they jumped. Again, we weren't close enough for a good scan to be sure, but I'm comfortable saying they need a month or more in repair dock."

"*Freewind* suffered no damage," Iveta took up the thread. "That is, the ship. They only recovered two of their twelve fighters before they also fled, heading in an entirely different direction from *Gallivant.*"

"Where?" Phil asked.

"Functionally, west and east," Leyla said. "We're not sure what's those directions, though. Or who."

Phil noted that she was staring at Bereoa when she spoke. Something got through, because he had been sipping some tea and put his cup down now and cleared his throat.

"The warship *Gallivant* is generally considered part of Duke Bertrand Farouk's Court in the Western Region," the man said. "The Duke was, until about six months ago, Heir Designate to the *Ewin* throne, before a rough falling-out with Doysan. Possibly over a mistress, but I've never been able to get the full truth out of anyone."

"And *Freewind?*" Phil asked.

"East suggests that they might be headed to *Elox*," Bereoa

said with a grimace. "That's the home port of the Eastern Squadron under the command of Duke Godfrey Kalidoona, Prince of the Eastern Squadron, nominally facing the *Dalou Hegemony*."

Phil nodded.

As with *Dalou*, a civil war in the *Ewin Principalities* had been one of his worst case scenarios. On the other hand, *Ewin* seemed to always be on the verge of such a thing anyway, so it might not make that big a difference. Missile swarms made them dangerous, but if they were busy feuding with each other, they wouldn't be bothering neighbors while he was trying to conduct diplomacy.

It was a little mean to think that they might not matter in the grand scheme of things, but it also likely gave Governor Milose an extra year or three to build up his economy and defensive forces before another fool like Baron Russand tried his luck at the lagoon.

Phil's next message home to the First Lord was certainly going to be asking for a wing of the older 400-series corvettes that might be home-based at *Meerut* for a time, before eventually being sold to the ex-pirates for one Lev each.

All he needed now was enough firepower to keep folks at bay while trade eventually replaced rivalry and autarky.

"Are we looking at Duke Farouk, Duke Kalidoona, and King Doysan IV all turning on each other?" Phil asked the man, mostly ignoring the grimace of real pain that came over Gotzon Solo's face.

"It is possible," Bereoa replied with an equal grimace.

What good was it to be a hero of *Ewin*, if that got rendered irrelevant overnight? Or worse, if your enemies were suddenly in power and making decisions? Would *Shadowbolt* have to flee and become an outlaw like Baron Russand had?

Russand.

Shit.

"First Minister," Phil said sharply. "What is the status of Baron Russand on the station?"

Bereoa looked confused for a moment, then enlightenment dawned.

"Not a prisoner," the man replied. "But also not a valued guest, either. However, I have found him to be a wily and dangerous foe in negotiations."

"Good enough to put a stick in and stir things with Doysan?" Phil asked. "Especially if you weren't around to stop him? Maybe get back at everyone by dragging them down to his level?"

"I would not put it past the man," Bereoa replied.

Phil turned to his Science Officer now.

"Leyla, what's the status of the vessels still in orbit of *Ewinhome*?" he asked.

"More than half need at least some level of dry-dock," she said. "As of ten minutes ago, they were all on the sort of high alert that shoots first and asks questions later. At the same time, we've been counting missiles and fighters. Just about everybody is out of things to throw at each other until they go through a full reloading cycle. Considering that they rely on missiles from themselves or their flight wings as their primary striking power, *Shadowbolt* might be the most dangerous *Ewin* ship in the system."

And *Shadowbolt* was a light bombard, still surrounded by half a dozen heavier cruisers and battleships.

It was the exact opposite of Expeditionary logic as laid down originally by that pirate Bedrov. The man had designed ships with nothing that required ammunition, even to the extent of ending the reliance on primary beams that had been the backbone of the fleet for more than a century, to say nothing of missiles.

Pulse weapons had rendered strike fighters irrelevant, because they couldn't hit you as hard as Bedrov-style ships could hit back.

"Ladies and gentlemen, I want to point something out, in case anybody missed it," Phil said now. "Everything *Ewin* does relies on significant logistics trains, even as short as they might be in the Balhee Cluster. One major fleet action and most of those ships, below us or fleeing, are reduced to one or two titan bolts and a handful of Main Guns. They can win a single battle with missiles. They cannot, however, pursue a fleeing enemy. And if an enemy survives those incoming swarms, they themselves have to flee because they cannot hurt anybody right now. I'm sure there are folks in the squadron that wouldn't mind if we went in and did to *Ewinhome* what we did at *Meerut* or *Jacoby*. Namely, crush them because we have a technological edge that is today insurmountable. I choose not to, and route anybody to me if they have complaints. I can always send them back to their own capitals with their tails between their legs."

Because none of them would be *RAN*. The shopkeepers weren't firebreathers. Even the firebreathers like *Junkyard*. They all had a switch they could turn on and off as needed.

That was why he'd hired them in the first place.

"First Minister, I cannot in good conscience return you to Allemaine Station under these circumstances," Phil continued humbly. "As my Science Officer has noted, they might shoot first. They might even be your enemies, such that someone might apologize later for the terrible misunderstanding, but only after they've murdered you in cold blood. At the same time, my presence here can be seen as a provocation. And others might blame me for starting all this, even though I've never fired a shot and you and Striker Solo can testify to that later. I need to leave. Now. I must, unfortunately, kidnap you for a time as well. What system would be best for us to drop you off, that you can return here later in safety?"

Phil had been staring into the man's eyes, so he was privy to the incredible range of emotions and calculations that went on. Bereoa had risen as high as he had purely on his brains and competence, where men like Gotzon Solo or Baron Russand had been born into a class and had allies and relatives that put them into positions of authority.

"This feels like someone mixed a drunk Doysan IV with a conniving chiseler like Giscard Russand," Bereoa replied after a time. "I might not be safe immediately on Allemaine Station, even if I could return tonight. As you noted, accidents happen. Especially at times of high tension. Could I ask you to transport me to *Elox*, First Centurion?"

Phil nodded. That would be where he'd have wanted to go, if the circumstances were reversed. After Central, the Eastern Squadron was the most powerful. Possibly even more ships, but spread over a larger sector, as they had to cover the approaches to *Dalou* space. And a newly-proclaimed ex-pirate kingdom on their left corner.

Was this the beginning of the long-rumored Next *Ewin* Civil War?

Did he care?

"We can do that," Phil said. "Normally, I'd detach *Shadowbolt* or one of my corvettes to make that run, but I am not sure I trust our reception there, either, given that *Freewind* will be carrying rumors."

"Could we outrun them?" Bereoa asked, but the light in his eyes said he knew the answer already.

"*Urumchi* could," Phil replied. "Is it that important?"

"It might be, First Centurion."

ELOX

TWENTY-SEVEN

Heather understood the logic, but that wasn't the same as liking what Phil was doing. At least she'd convinced him to bring along *CB-502* on this run.

They would arrive at least a day ahead of the rest of the squadron at *Elox*, to whatever reception might be waiting. According to First Minister Bereoa, she should be getting there faster than *Freewind* and his escorts could.

She was more likely to trust Leyla's concurrence on that topic, though.

It wasn't that Bereoa was a bad guest. If anything, he'd turned most polite, once he realized that he was stuck aboard *Urumchi* until they got him where they were going. It was that she was pretty much the one person he'd picked to be his special friend on this trip.

That went back to the beginning of this stupid adventure over *Ewinhome*, when the man had looked at the choices of her, Harinder, and Aliza, then decided to glom on to her side for the tour.

Heather didn't think the man was hitting on her, though she also was ignoring any subtext that wasn't purely political. As Command Centurion, that was her prerogative.

He felt old to her. Which was a rude thing to say, since she was approaching forty-two and he was only about a decade and a half older. But they were years without first-rate medical available. Too much drinking, not enough exercising.

Brains, but the shell wasn't anything to write home about. Still, they'd enjoyed a few conversations in a wardroom lounge. Again, historical and diplomatic, rather than personal.

Ewin men tended to be chauvinistic pigs, even when they didn't realize it. Strings of mistresses but never wives, for the ones at the top of the political pyramid. There were no prominent women in *Ewin* history. Or *Ewin* today. Only men.

"Pilot, what's our count?" she asked, looking around the room at faces.

Not yet her A-Team of people, but that was happening shortly as folks came on duty.

"Seventy-four minutes to emergence, Command Centurion," Bozhidar Virág replied.

She contrasted the two, Bozhidar and Jaxom Bereoa, in her mind. Centurion Virág was tall, dark, and somewhat slender. First Minister Bereoa wasn't as tall, or as dark, or as slender. Hawklike face.

Both men were sharp, but Bereoa had a full generation of political cunning that Bozhidar lacked at present.

Maybe that was it. Bereoa was an operator, and currently operating on her. Maybe that was why he got her hackles up occasionally.

Other than that, he'd been a model guest. And they were a few hours from him being somebody else's problem.

If she honestly believed that Phil might gather everybody up and withdraw to *Meerut* for a time while *Ewin* worked out its problems.

The *Ewin Principalities* had centuries of unresolved issues. That wasn't changing tomorrow.

"Security, locate First Minister Bereoa for me," she called, letting the systems route things to whoever had that desk today.

"Forward observatory, Command Centurion," a man's voice replied too fast for having to actually look for him, so they were watching the man. "Shall I alert him?"

"Negative," Heather said. She turned and located Iveta, already perked up and watching. "You have the bridge for now. Poke me if I'm not back in fifty minutes or seated at Phil's table aft."

"Got it," Iveta said.

Heather unbuckled and rose, exiting and heading forward to the bow of the great gray lady that was *Urumchi*.

The forward observatory was literally the space where the Bubble Gun would have fired, had they included it in this design, a wide oculus covered over with transparent steel that let you see where the ship was sailing.

JumpSpace was usually just a gray haze with a few darker spots indicating gravity wells, so she wasn't sure what Bereoa was looking at. At the same time, she had questions, and nobody else would have better answers than the First Minister of *Ewin*.

Heather transited the Ambassadorial spaces and located the marine guarding/watching the First Minister. That woman nodded and did something that almost made her fade into invisibility as Heather walked by.

She made noise as she approached, so Bereoa glanced over a shoulder and smiled.

"Enjoying what view there is," he offered. "I so rarely travel, and when I do it is usually aboard a flagship like *Meynard II* because Doysan IV is on some promenade to show the flag."

Heather nodded. Old ground, trod several times. She probably knew more about *Ewin* history and culture than she'd ever wanted, but she also knew that folks like Aliza and her various Ambassadors would find that information priceless later.

Assuming *Aquitaine* managed to open some sort of formal diplomatic relations with whoever sat in the *Ewin* throne in a year.

Maybe that was it. Phil had worked to keep everyone else

stable, but here, he seemed to be in the process of throwing up his hands and backing safely away, like you might do with a hissing cat. Or a rabid chipmunk.

Certainly *Ewin* didn't qualify as a barking dog. At least not to *Urumchi* escorted by *CB-502*.

"What do you expect to happen when you arrive?" Heather asked, taking a spot on the man's left and watching the weirdness of JumpSpace roll by.

Elox's star was growing more prominent by the minute, but they wouldn't get all that close.

"I have no idea, Command Centurion," he said with an ambivalent tone. "Had I been on Allemaine, I might have short-circuited whatever stupidities were about to occur. At the same time, I have spent the last few days contemplating the longer arc of recent history, and I'm not sure that anybody could have stopped this."

"Why is that, First Minister?" Heather perked up. More priceless observations to record, from a topic expert of the first water.

"Before *Aquitaine* arrived at *Vilahana*, things were relatively stable," he said. "Not great, but not out of control."

"So we did it?" she pressed.

"No, *Ewin* is always a chaotic place," he shook his head as he spoke. "You just showed that the past could no longer hold. The forces had been building for a while, but entropy and *ennui* are powerful forces themselves. *Ewin* cannot threaten *Aquitaine*. Not like *Dalou* or *Aditi*, to say nothing of the philosophers on my western shore."

"So a probable civil war was already in the cards?" she asked.

He nodded, contemplative.

"Doysan has been in power for sixteen years," he continued. "He's old and tired, and a new generation of turks has come along that see the old farts and don't understand why they are in charge. And *Ewin* rarely has bloodless, polite, formal hand-offs of power between kings."

"So you think Doysan's time is done?" Heather turned halfway to look at the man now.

Jaxom Bereoa was something of the power behind the throne, if only because the bureaucrats actually ran things for the Princes. Without the First Minister, what things weren't getting done?

Or was there a new First Minister at *Ewinhome* already, moving into Bereoa's old office and redecorating?

Was the whole structure of the government in the process of collapsing, and the fight in *Ewinhome*'s sky just the most visible signal of generational change?

Bereoa shrugged. Grimaced. Sucked in a noisy breath and let it go.

"Change is coming, Command Centurion," he finally said, gesturing outward with both hands to encompass the whole of *Urumchi* and everything that Phil Kosnett brought to the table, merely by being here.

"Good or bad?" she asked.

"If Duke Kalidoona is feeling anxious or unruly, he could probably grab up a portion or more of the fleet at anchor above *Elox* and sail it directly to *Ewinhome*," the man replied. "As your staff have noted, most of the important ships are damaged. Some extensively, including *Meynard II*. Had you attacked, most of them would have also been unarmed and you could have brushed them completely aside. By now, they have reloaded and gotten at least somewhat dangerous. On the other hand, given a week, how many might have moved to the repair yards or shut themselves partially down to repair things? If Kalidoona strikes immediately, does he catch Central Squadron off-guard and capture the entire system? Does he proclaim himself King of *Ewin*?"

"Will he listen to you?" Heather pressed.

She was surprised that the man shrugged. She was still used to the obvious bravado of Gotzon Solo when you asked him a question like that. Absolute certainty, even when it was unwarranted.

But she supposed that Bereoa was used to those folks as well, and understood how much of it was false and hollow. Hopefully, she and her officers had shown the man other ways to behave in public.

Not that *Ewin* would change overnight, but they might actually grow up, one of these days.

Maybe.

Or fall completely apart and have to deal with *Dalou* and *Aditi* perhaps making common cause to straighten them out. Again, all it would take would be a force of ships equipped with pulse weapons, and *Ewin's* dangerous fleet stopped being a problem.

"We shall find out in a few hours, Command Centurion," First Minister Bereoa said.

"What outcome would you prefer?" There, the ninety-six Lev question.

"I'm still not sure," he said.

Heather managed to keep her mouth from falling open, but only barely. If this man was ambivalent to the outcome, would it come down to the strongest personality in the room? In the fleet?

Was she looking at the start of a full-scale war when they arrived?

TWENTY-EIGHT

PERSONAL QUARTERS, ALLEMAINE STATION, EWINHOME

Giscard was pleased with his new quarters. Doysan had taken a new liking to him and upgraded his suite to be commensurate with his rank as a planetary baron. It was nice, having available mistresses again.

He'd been denied even professionals while he'd been something of a prisoner.

Now, he had space. Not that he'd brought sufficient staff with him to fill it, but he had rooms and rooms he could wander into when the mood struck. Giscard considered pretending to take up painting or something, just to have a hobby room he could dedicate to it.

He was in the dining area this afternoon, enjoying a quick snack of meat and cheese that the kitchen had delivered, along with several bottles of nice wine. Giscard could just call someone and they would fall all over themselves to serve him.

It was almost like he was home on *Jacoby* again.

But being on *Ewinhome* was better, because Doysan was old, tired, and cranky. Worse, that fool Bereoa had been captured by the outlanders and hauled off, leaving a terrible, gaping wound in the government that Giscard had been able to quietly manipulate.

Bollvize appeared at the doorway now, smiling serenely in a manner that would have a smart man clutching at his coin purse and checking that he had thick enough armor to turn a knife.

"Grab a goblet and join me," Giscard gestured to the shelf.

He might be Baron, but Bollvize was the master manipulator who had *adjusted* things around here. Giscard frequently repeated things Bollvize told him verbatim. It helped that Doysan was the one listening.

Thus, better quarters. Better everything, really.

Giscard's joy was so infectious that Bollvize's feral smile relaxed. The man poured himself a glass and seemed to relent some.

"It must be good," Giscard prompted after his man had had a hardy gulp.

Doysan's favorites got some fantastic wine to drink.

"There has been something of a purge," Bollvize grinned.

"Do tell."

"A number of folks who were originally promoted or rewarded based on their connections to Farouk," Bollvize said. "Your reminder to Doysan prompted him to clean house. Bereoa wasn't here to stop the man, so more than two score have been sent packing to the planet below. Some fired. Some demoted. Three transferred to the distant corners of the land. Four are currently rotting in jail while the king gets around to assigning them punishments, as he has already adjudicated them guilty."

"Terrible," Giscard replied. "Whatever shall we do?"

"Doysan needs friends now," Bollvize said. "Men who will rally to his cause when other dukes and barons are busy thinking only of themselves."

"We can't have that," Giscard said.

Then he paused. Sobered for a moment, though he'd not had much to drink before now.

He considered the whole situation. It had played out just as he and Bollvize had envisioned, though Giscard had never imagined he would catch that many fish in his net when suggesting a house cleaning around the Court.

Bollvize noted his mood and quieted to watch.

"I am at an interesting intersection, Bollvize," Giscard noted aloud. "On the one hand, I am finally paying Doysan back for some of the insults he has heaped on my soul and reputation over the years."

"And on the other?"

"We could probably bring him down right now," Giscard smiled cruelly. "Central Squadron has been hobbled and shattered by his ill-executed ambush of *Gallivant* and the others. It will likely require new commanders considerable time to rebuild the cohesion that they had as recently as a month ago."

Bollvize nodded. They had walked this ground before.

"However, if we do break Doysan, have we just made it easier for Farouk or Kalidoona to sweep in and depose the man? Neither has any love for me, so my situation will not improve with a change of crowns. Even if I maneuvered myself to replace Doysan today, I couldn't hold it."

"I'm not positive that any man could hold it, my Baron," Bollvize replied quietly. "Your orders were chaos, not revolution. I have exacted a terrible vengeance for you there. Doysan totters, even as we speak."

Giscard nodded.

"He must pay for everything he did to me," Giscard growled angrily. "For all the betrayals and double-dealing. For all the times he insulted my house and my honor. I want him brought low. And I want him to know, at the very end, who did it to him."

"And then?"

"And then *Aquitaine* looms over everything and everyone," Giscard said. "What they did to *Jacoby* they could have just as easily done here, had they swooped in there at the end when *Meynard* lay prostrate and *Gallivant* and the others were fleeing. Nothing and no one could have stood before them."

"Where does that leave us?"

"*Ewinhome* cannot be held, so we shouldn't try," Giscard decided. "Doysan will see his weakness soon, but there is nothing at all he can do about it. Not if both Farouk and Kalidoona are rallying their followers to come here. At best, it turns into a free-for-all to see who can get to the king first, and they will lay utter waste to anything and anyone that gets in their way."

"We should be elsewhere on that day?" Bollvize asked now.

"Indeed," Giscard nodded. "We should be gone as soon as we possibly can, because *Aquitaine* has already proven that they can fly faster than anyone appreciates. They might have gone somewhere, and found themselves a pretender to the throne they could install. That force could hold *Ewinhome* for as long as they wanted, a breakwater against which everyone else will simply shatter their teeth."

"Perhaps we need to go rally allies for Doysan in his hour of need?" Bollvize asked brightly.

Giscard blinked at the man, then saw the sarcasm in his eyes.

"Yes," Giscard agreed. "Lovely and intriguing idea. *Jacoby* has little that they can offer. A few frigates and no more. But I can also play the martyr for other barons. They generally have no more love for Doysan than they do for whatever duke rules their sector. And I can tell anyone who will listen what *Aquitaine* will do if given the choice. They broke my fleets at *Meerut* and *Jacoby*. As soon as they arrived at *Ewinhome*, Central Squadron came apart and we can show them pictures of the betrayals that left the flagship in near ruins."

"Private passage to someplace other than *Jacoby* will be the easiest to arrange," Bollvize perked up. "If you told the king you were headed to visit Baron Valéry Garnier or Baron Pascal Daniau, in order to rally them to the cause at the head of a returning fleet, he might be amenable."

"When does he normally start drinking these days?" Giscard asked.

"It is more that he rarely stops, my Baron," Bollvize chuckled. "The man has tripled his consumption lately under the stress and weight of his crown."

"Excellent news."

"And you do not desire to supplant him?" Bollvize asked sharply.

"You and I will go after the fool who deposes Doysan," Giscard said. "The Principalities are in serious danger of collapsing because of *Aquitaine*, but we will have clean hands when it comes time to blame the man who holds the crown next. And we can rebuild."

"You do not expect *Aquitaine* to conquer?" Bollvize asked.

"He would have been able to crush Central Squadron and take this very station days ago, Bollvize," Giscard said. "Remember *Jacoby*. He'll be happy to deal with me when I am king in a few years, but let some other fool have to deal with this mess for now. You get us to Garnier or Daniau so that our heads aren't on the chopping block next to that fat drunkard's."

TWENTY-NINE

Phil watched the screens come live with information as *Urumchi* dropped out of JumpSpace. As at *Ewinhome*, he'd made a point of coming out long, well away from the spots where defenders might be poised to ward off an attack.

Bereoa had joined him on the flag bridge, looking far more philosophical than he had previously. There was a note from Heather that she had gossip and updates, but they were ready for combat right now, and other things could wait.

"*CB-502*, this is Kosnett aboard *Urumchi*. I have the flag. All hands to battle stations," he said, as if they hadn't plotted this carefully on their one drop out into RealSpace, back in the darkness a few hours ago. At this short of a hop, both ships had emerged within a few seconds of each other. And ready to shoot first. "I am transmitting a message packet to the Squadron Base in orbit of *Elox* itself. Lag is nearly four seconds at present, so stand by to see who is awake over there."

He muted the line and glanced over at Bereoa as transponder signals began to be processed and identified.

"Is this more or less than you were expecting?" Phil asked.

The man shrugged. Almost phlegmatically.

"It almost looks like they are at rest on a weekend morning," he offered. "We may have gotten lucky and outrun the news getting here."

"Not sure that qualifies as luck, First Minister," Phil offered. "But you'll at least be back among friends shortly."

"No," Bereoa said so sharply that even Harinder looked up. "I have been among friends for several days, First Centurion. Your crew has gone well beyond basic courtesy in seeing to my needs and making me feel welcome. I am simply sorry that I wasn't able to show you true *Ewin* culture on your visit to my homeworld, though I suppose what you saw is what outsiders think of us."

Phil nodded diplomatically, rather than reply to that.

"Thank you, First Minister," he said. "As always, I am here to open diplomatic and trade routes. If the Balhee Cluster has grown a bit insular over the centuries, perhaps we can do things in a soft way, rather than as a bull in a porcelain shop."

Bereoa even smiled at that, but they both recognized the difference between *aspirational* and *actual* right now.

"We're being hailed," Harinder broke in. "*Ewin* warship identifying itself as *Utron Heavy* with a battleship designation from their transponder."

"Good," Bereoa said. "That's Kalidoona's flagship. Heavier in main combat than an Archer like *Meynard II*."

"Science Officer, give me a single hard ping of *Utron Heavy* and escorts," Phil ordered. "I want to know what we're facing, if they get frisky."

He shifted to Harinder now.

"Video?" he asked.

"Not on their original message, but that was a standard challenge by an officer of the deck sort of thing," she replied. "I'm guessing the Striker is currently stuffing his feet into boots as he races to his bridge."

"Good enough," Phil said. He keyed the recorder and fixed his hard glare at the camera. "This is *Republic of Aquitaine* First Centurion Philip S. Kosnett, aboard *RAN Urumchi*. I have diplomatic and political messages for Duke Kalidoona, Prince of the Eastern Squadron. I also am traveling with First Minister of *Ewin* Jaxom Bereoa. Reply on this channel, please."

And transmit.

"Leyla?" he asked on her line.

"Standard hexagonal pillar design, Phil," she replied. "Boom that sits inside the aft section like *Buran* does it or the locals. Forward section has one titan bolt and three Main Guns, like *Meynard II*, but the Energiya Module has six more titan bolts and nine Main Guns in a one-two-one pattern. Awful lot of missile launchers, but it looks like they only carry a single squadron of twelve to fifteen fighters. Someone designed that ship to wade into battle and punch someone. Pretty decent design, too."

As with Iveta, high praise.

"Comparable rating?" he asked.

"Maybe the old *Warspite*-class," she said. "Back before Third War Fleet went with all Expeditionary hulls. I served on her when I was a pup."

Warspite. The standard dreadnought design when he'd been a young Centurion. Missiles and Primaries, with Type-3 and a lot of shielding. Not a match for *Urumchi* one-on-one, but still a tough ship. Phil had been in smaller ships for most of his career, originally culminating in the old *Founder*-class Heavy Cruiser *Cyrus*, before Pet Naoumov had promoted him to the Academy and assigned him the homework of preparing for this mission.

"*Utron Heavy* is awake," Harinder said. "Stand by. I have a decreasing lag as they blueshift towards us. Still inside the gravity well, so they're not jumping, but moving up with three cruisers and nine smaller ships. Frigates and destroyers both. Call it their battle group."

Phil nodded. *Urumchi* and *CB-502* were no match, but other folks had taken what he'd done at *Meerut* and *Jacoby* to heart and were throwing the kitchen sink in. Hopefully, they wanted to talk. He was getting tired of folks shooting first.

Jacoby was supposed to cure people of that stupidity, not encourage it.

"*RAN Urumchi*, this is Striker Corvin Zechiel, aboard *Utron Heavy*," a man said as he appeared. "What is the nature of your messages, over?"

Long lag. The result of sitting this far away, but Phil would rather be safe than sorry.

"There have been developments at *Ewinhome*, Striker Zechiel," Phil said. "It would be easiest if you or one of your senior officers came aboard *Urumchi*, as I'd rather not broadcast things to the entire system at this moment. From there, you can brief the Prince."

Even encrypted, someone might read it. Like those pixies had done at *Ewinhome* that got him clear of the fight before it even began.

This time, the lag was even longer. Phil presumed that he had his Prince on a separate line and was asking for orders.

Phil didn't want Bereoa knowing how badly their codes were compromised, so he opened his keyboard and sent a quick text message to Harinder.

*** Can we intercept messages from HQ to* Utron Heavy*? ***

She read the note and nodded. Good, she'd handle it and he would just get messages in the clear, probably as fast or faster than Striker Zechiel might.

Never let a technological edge go unexploited. Especially if it might help bring peace to the Cluster faster.

"Flag, this is the Science Officer," Leyla said now. "Blueshift has ended. Repeat: ended. *Utron Heavy* battle group is coming to rest at a higher elevation and laagering up defensively. Other forces are maneuvering for the corners, but it doesn't look like anyone is about to swoop and pounce on a corner."

Phil really appreciated having folks who knew what to look for, and went ahead and took charge of things. Made his life so much easier.

Phil watched the amazement take shape on Bereoa's face.

"Sir?" he prompted the visitor, making sure he was locally muted.

"Command Centurion Lau has used a particular term more than once to describe you folk," the man said slowly. Carefully. Diplomatically. "*Professionalism*. The highest standard."

Phil nodded as he considered a diplomatic response.

"We see ourselves as professionals, First Minister," he replied. "This is a job and we strive to do it better than anybody else, anywhere in the galaxy."

Bereoa looked for a moment like he'd sucked on a lemon.

"And the *Ewin Principalities* do not have a similar concept," he said with a sad shake of his head. "They have other standards. Crispness of formation is not high. And while they are prepared to fight or duel one another at the drop of a hat, you are prepared to defend yourself, extricate yourself, and only rend someone's throat if you have no other choice."

Phil smiled. The man might have learned some things over the last few days, even as Phil and his people were picking his brain.

"Kosnett, this is Zechiel," the return message finally came. "If you are not prepared to come aboard *Utron Heavy* for discussions, we propose a rendezvous at these coordinates and I will join you on *Urumchi* for now."

Delicately phrased. A threat without a threat, as the spot was inside the gravity well of the planet to the point that JumpSails wouldn't work well.

Except that everybody forgot the key technology underlying. The JumpDrive itself just bounced you up and out. If you were too close to planet, the warping of space caused you to go somewhat randomly and haphazardly, even as your warp matrix collapsed and had to be rebuilt.

Urumchi and *CB-502* could flee to safety, and meet up elsewhere if this turned out to be yet another ambush.

And the rest of the squadron was about a day and a half behind him if he needed them to crack heads together again.

"Thank you, Striker Zechiel," Phil transmitted. "I appreciate that we are not following the usual protocols, but my message is that important and you will need to transmit it directly to the Prince in short order, once I convince you."

He cut to an inside line.

"Heather, you know the drill," he said. "Get us there, keep us safe, and you and *Junkyard* trade off Tactical and Flag as one of you needs to sleep. I think we're good for a few hours so one of you might nap immediately."

"I'll send Iveta now," she replied. "If they get stupid later, I'll want her there to bloody somebody's nose."

Phil nodded and smiled at Bereoa. Gotzon Solo wasn't here, so anything that happened would be limited to the First Minister's stories later, for good or ill. Except that Phil expected things to be pretty good when this was all done.

Duke Kalidoona, Prince of the Eastern Squadron notwithstanding.

They were all walking tightropes right now.

THIRTY

Iveta reviewed Leyla's scan logs again. *Meynard II* was a Space Control Ship, using the old *RAN* designations for flagships like *Athena*. *Utron Heavy* was a battleship like *Fribourg* might have built them in the old days. Lots of guns facing forward. Launch tubes for a fighter squadron. Missiles racks on all sides, ready to kick arrows out in a hurry.

Anything less than *Urumchi* and *CB-502*, and she might be concerned. As it was, she had already assigned a few engineers the task of taking that design over there apart and finding her the weak spots, in case she needed to hammer a volley of Type-4 heavy beams into them. The Pulse-Twos would keep local space clear for long enough.

"Helm, I don't require utter precision on those coordinates," she said as they sat at the inner edge of the gravity well and waited for the other shuttle to arrive. "Drifting is fine, as long as we always have a reinforced shield facing a cruiser or heavier ship. And a course plotted that gets us to safety."

"Aye, sir," the woman acknowledged.

With *Utron Heavy* minding their manners, Iveta was watching the store for now. All the senior officers were having a quick nap or break, but were less than fifty steps away in an alarm.

Downtime, if you could sleep.

She'd skipped the concept of a nap and dragged Markus back to her cabin, where she'd made him scrub her back in the shower then snuggle on the bed briefly. Taking the body to a euphoric state while the mind continued to process.

One battleship. Three cruiser hulls. Nine smaller escorts. Anywhere else, a serious threat. Here, they were mostly just platforms for launching smaller things that did all the work.

"Science station, confirm the readings of Cruiser Three," Iveta called to the Chief currently on duty.

"One is a Hunter, like *Pioneer*, Tactical," he replied without looking up. "A strike carrier like Keller's *Auberon*. Two is a Heavy Bombard, like *Dragonfly*. Three appears to be more of a standard Heavy Cruiser design. Transponder identifies as *Paradise*. Titan bolt and three Main Guns on the boom like everyone else, but they have three more titan bolts and six Main Guns on the aft section, plus a number of Point Guns for defense and maybe only a handful of missile racks. Nothing like the others."

"Waddle into combat flanking or leading *Utron Heavy*?" Iveta asked.

"That'd be my assessment, Tactical," he replied. "Two of the destroyers also seem to be built for close combat, while the rest are just platforms."

"Excellent work, Sciences," Iveta nodded. "How soon until the shuttle arrives?"

"They are broadcasting three minutes to lock," he said.

"Keep a sharp eye for blueshift from *Utron Heavy*, *Paradise*, or those two destroyers," Iveta ordered. "If they move this way, I want to know immediately. Override any conversation to tell me."

"Aye, sir."

Iveta leaned back and watched. She didn't expect trouble,

but she hadn't expected *Ewinhome* to come unraveled while they watched, either.

Were the *Ewin Principalities* all just a house of cards?

They'd find out shortly.

THIRTY-ONE
FLAGSHIP URUMCHI, ELOX ORBIT

Jaxom stood to one side and watched through the big window as Zechiel's shuttle landed and the bay closed up. Striker Corvin Zechiel wasn't someone he knew personally, but by general reputation. Commander of Kalidoona's flagship. *Aditi* would have considered him an admiral. *Aquitaine's* equivalent rank was apparently Fleet Centurion, similar to Aliza Babatunde, Kosnett's lead ambassador who he had spent several meetings with on the flight here.

It was a completely different way of looking at the universe. Professionalism, as Kosnett and Lau had both indicated, was the highest form of duty. After several days in their company, Jaxom was beginning to think that pure luck had included Gotzon Solo in the mission when Kosnett and *Aditi* had first asked.

Back home, Striker Solo had a reputation as something of a quiet commander, rather than one of the flamboyant ones. Sending him off had gotten him out of Doysan's hair because his introversion was irritating a few folks.

And yet, Lau considered him loud and abrasive, to the point that she admitted to chewing him out for being too extravagant to fly with them.

But Solo had learned. Got high marks from Lau and others now for his professionalism. That gave Jaxom hope that maybe others could learn.

He hesitated to say *grow up*, but in the back of his mind, there was a strong element of that. *Ewin* seemed more and more to be permanently trapped in a sort of teenage rebellious phase, compared to the others.

And now one of the most successful strikers of the day was about to arrive and have to deal with Kosnett's quiet intent, without any warning.

Jaxom had his work cut out for him.

The bay pressurized, and Kosnett himself led a small group out, with Jaxom inside the ring of bodyguards. Red carpet, as he had gotten, because Kosnett was serious about his duty.

The hatch opened and a trooper emerged, coming to the bottom of the steps and turning to one side as a protector. Striker Zechiel emerged next. Stepped down. Came to rest in front of Kosnett.

The comparison between the two men was striking. Zechiel was much shorter. Maybe only Lau's height, but gave the impression of ranginess from how slender he was. Eyes, skin, and hair were all a darker hue than you normally had around *Ewin*, making him look more like he belonged in the *Aditi Consensus*.

The head nodded to Kosnett then located Jaxom in the group, eyes inquisitive.

Jaxom nodded and stepped closer. The combat force troopers bristled, but that was automatic on their part.

"Striker, I am First Minister Jaxom Bereoa, come here directly from *Ewinhome* on the fastest ship available," he said.

"King Doysan?" he asked, hinting at the obviousness of the man finally keeling over.

"Alive when I left, but facing a serious rebellion," Jaxom said. "Possibly a revolution as well. It is my expectation that the Hunter *Freewind* is probably about twelve hours behind me now, in spite of a head start. We have much to discuss. First Centurion Kosnett is along as a witness, rather than a participant."

Zechiel looked up at the much taller man.

"Truth?" he asked.

"That is correct, Striker," Kosnett said. "Normally, I would make this a formal visit, but the First Minister has convinced me that you would not be offended if we were to delay such a thing to a later date, that we might handle the current situation quickly. I do intend to return for such a thing later, though."

Kosnett even bowed slightly to the man, which caught Zechiel off guard. Obviously, the striker thought of Kosnett as a Prince of a Squadron. They did not bow to their subordinates. Except that Kosnett had promoted the man to a position of authority and importance.

That would help, with what was coming.

"Lead on, then, good sirs," Zechiel replied. "I find myself looking forward to your news."

Kosnett's dangerous, petite combat trooper Dar led them. *Urumchi*'s ambassadorial flight bay was close to the forward quarters, with the expectation of important people needing to come and go. The main bay was well aft.

Here, it meant that they were not far from a meeting room with sumptuous fittings, as though intended to host Doysan IV.

After a week in their company, Jaxom understood that many of them considered it ornate, bordering on tacky, while Doysan might be insulted to find it so plain.

Professionals versus unruly children, as it were.

Zechiel got sat at the head of the table, which again surprised the man. Kosnett was directly across from Jaxom on Zechiel's left, which meant that Jaxom was acting as First Minister for Zechiel, and by extension Prince Kalidoona.

That realization settled into his eyes like a ghostly shawl cast over his shoulders.

"We had gone to *Ewinhome* after a quick mission to *Jacoby* to remonstrate with Baron Russand," Kosnett began. "That gentleman's fleet is now neutralized and he will no longer threaten his neighbors."

"Neutralized, sir?" Zechiel asked.

"All three of his cruisers, as well as his dry-dock, are now orbiting *Meerut*, where they are being repaired prior to being inducted into *Meerut's* defensive fleet, Striker," Kosnett smiled.

Jaxom watched that surprise get layered over everything else. It was unpleasant, the first time you processed it.

"Go on," Striker Zechiel managed.

"As I said, we arrived at *Ewinhome* to meet with King Doysan and explain our actions," Kosnett continued. "Rather than inviting us aboard his station, the King sent his First Minister out to this ship for consultation."

Zechiel's head *snapped* around to look at Jaxom now. That man understood just how insulting such behavior was. And maybe had a better grasp of why Kosnett was remaining clear out here, rather than just sailing right up to *Utron Heavy* to chat.

"Just so," Jaxom took up the thread now. "Kosnett gave me full honors on my arrival, including a formal dinner and tour of his ship. While we were having dessert, something happened. I will let the First Centurion explain, because the two of you are sailors, and have a better technical understanding."

Jaxom heard his own words and wondered at them. Any admission of weakness back home was an invitation to be insulted. Humiliated.

Kosnett's folks acknowledged that other people might be better experts and deferred directly to such knowledge. Without recrimination.

So alien to *Ewin* trains of thought.

"Sir?" Zechiel turned his attention back to Kosnett.

"While we had them under observation from the outer boundary marker, the flagship *Meynard II* began maneuvering in an aggressive manner, along with their battle group," Kosnett said. "*Urumchi* and our squadron came to high alert, but we were not the target. Instead, *Meynard II* launched an ambush attack against the Heavy Bombard *Gallivant*, which I was later informed showed primary loyalty to Duke Bertrand Farouk, apparently the former Crown Prince."

"The dogs," Zechiel muttered under his breath.

Jaxom commiserated. The old Jaxom. The one that had watched the battle unfold. This new person he'd started to become over the last several days saw it with different eyes. *Aquitaine* eyes, as it were.

"From there, it became something of a free-for-all in lower orbit, with ships attacking each other almost randomly," Kosnett continued. "The Hunter *Freewind* and escorts also came under attack and fled. At the end of the battle, First Minister Bereoa concluded that they were probably going to limp here as quickly as they could. At the same time, it was too risky to try to return the First Minister to the station, so I offered to transport him here as rapidly as possible, so that Duke Kalidoona, Prince of the Eastern Squadron, was prepared, both politically as well as militarily."

"Are we at risk here?" Zechiel asked immediately.

"I doubt it," Kosnett shook his head. "We'll provide full scan logs of the state of the remaining ships when we left *Ewinhome*, but most of the cruisers required some level of repair. Additionally, the rest of my force is about a day and a half behind me. That includes five cruiser hulls and four more escorts, currently representative of the entire Balhee Cluster. Anyone launching an assault while I'm here gets to deal with us, before they get to your current defensive fleets."

"This is not your fight, Kosnett," Zechiel warned.

"The next time someone walks up and just opens fire on my flagship without a damned good reason, I intend to order my command staff to make an *example* of them, *Striker*," Kosnett growled back.

Jaxom considered what this man had done to Russand at

Jacoby, stealing his flagship and the dry-dock it was parked in. And the reports of that first battle at *Meerut* that had broken the backs of the pirate rebels.

Heather Lau had suggested that nobody had really pissed her or Philip Kosnett off even yet. That suggested a whole extra layer of meanness that the man might unleash if provoked.

Truly frightening to consider.

Zechiel fell silent. A quick glance over and Jaxom nodded. Kosnett was both serious and capable.

Utron Heavy, according to Command Centurion Lau, with all Zechiel's current escorts, might be a threat to *Urumchi* and the corvette flying escort. The rest of Kosnett's force could clear the skies of *Elox* when they arrived.

It was Iveta Beridze's calm assurance of that latter point that really frightened Jaxom. There was no bravado about that woman, false or otherwise. The crew called her *Junkyard* to her face, apparently short for *The Junkyard Bitch*. And it was a term of affection. From killers.

"Striker," Jaxom interceded now. "Prince Kalidoona needs to be made aware of these circumstances. That was why I asked the First Centurion to bring me here, instead of one of the closer bases where I might simply be able to return to *Ewinhome* aboard a military transport or warship. You must be prepared."

"What do you expect Prince Kalidoona to do?" Zechiel turned his attention and pique away from Kosnett now.

"He has many options, but I suspect that *Freewind* will arrive with a story calculated to inflame a greater war than we already face."

"Greater?" Zechiel asked.

"*Gallivant* and his escorts escaped," Jaxom reminded him. "That means that they likely race to inform Farouk that Doysan has become openly hostile. Farouk must respond. Normally, forces he might call upon in the West are not sufficient to overcome *Ewinhome*'s defenders, but now a major battle has seriously damaged many of them. Others have fled to points unknown. *Ewinhome* when we left was down to perhaps a third of the combat capability it had before, according to Kosnett's staff. I have seen their reports. Such will be made available to you and the Prince."

Striker Zechiel turned back to Kosnett now. Studied him closer.

"What is *Aquitaine* intending?" he asked bluntly.

Kosnett shrugged.

"If my presence makes things worse, I might simply withdraw to *Meerut*. Possibly *Ellariel* or even *Aditi*," he said, ticking off the three major port calls prior to *Jacoby* or *Ewinhome*. "At some point, I have invitations to visit *Derragon* and *Kyulle*. *Ewinhome* came up because Baron Russand forced my hand, else they might have been much later on my itinerary. In fact, in the hopes of giving you two space to sort out what you think needs to be an *Ewin* response, I will withdraw for now and get some paperwork done. If you have questions, First Minister Bereoa has staff that know how to reach me. Good day."

And just like that, the big man rose, nodded, and walked out.

Jaxom was almost as surprised as Striker Zechiel, especially when all of Kosnett's staff and troopers that had accompanied him withdrew as well, leaving only the one who had come with Zechiel.

"He's serious?" the man asked now. "This isn't all just some calculated bluff?"

"Quite serious, Striker," Jaxom replied. "He could have stomped on the survivors after the battle, according to his people. Eliminated the shattered remains of Central Squadron in one day. Instead, he left. They get to pick up the pieces, if they want to. I asked for him to bring me here, because Kalidoona might have to get involved."

"Why?"

"Baron Russand returned to the fold after Kosnett eliminated *Jacoby* as a threat, Striker," Jaxom explained. "I suspect that he saw the opportunity to provoke Doysan into striking at enemies that had been imaginary until that first shot was fired. And so he did. Farouk will not take that insult lightly. How would Kalidoona react if informed that Doysan's fleet had attacked *Freewind* unprovoked?"

"He would likely organize a force to go to *Ewinhome* and challenge someone to a duel," Zechiel replied, as if that was the most normal thing in the universe.

For children, perhaps. Not mature adults. And that was the demarcation that Kosnett's people made with dealing with the peoples of the Balhee Cluster, sad as it was. *Ewin* did not rate with the rest, because they didn't act like grownups.

"And if the person was Doysan himself?" Jaxom asked. "Then what?"

The light finally dawned in the man's eyes.

"Does the Prince have to overthrow the King?" Zechiel asked in a quieter voice.

"Have to?" Jaxom asked. "No. Should he? That is a conversation that should be had with cooler heads than will prevail when *Freewind* arrives. Something that Kalidoona needs to look at, while in possession of everything that I have been provided by Kosnett, as well as everything I have myself seen in the last several days."

"Is *Aquitaine* an ally, then?" he asked.

"Kosnett is not yet our enemy, despite all the provocations heaped at the man's feet," Jaxom corrected him. "That might yet change, depending on our actions, but I think it would be one of the most foolish and costly mistakes that we could make."

"Why is that?"

"Because Kosnett hasn't threatened to annihilate anybody else that I am aware of," Jaxom said. "Only the *Ewin* fleet has gotten that warning. And after spending days with them, they are not bluffing, either."

"And Duke Kalidoona?" Zechiel asked.

"Convince the man to be nice to Kosnett," Jaxom warned.

He didn't have to add, "Or else."

THIRTY-TWO

DATE OF THE REPUBLIC DECEMBER 19, 411
APPROACHING ELOX PRIME STATION

Heather was surprised as the shuttle rode inward, but at the same time, this event was the decorum that they should have received when they arrived at *Ewinhome* originally. Phil had withdrawn from the room to let the two locals hash it out. A few hours later *Freewind* had dropped out of Jump and probably nearly swallowed their tongues when they realized that *Urumchi* was already there.

One of these days, folks around here were finally going to realize that their JumpSails were about as far behind *Aquitaine* as their weapons tech.

Whatever had transpired in the conference room after Phil left, it had been good, because Striker Zechiel had left about two hours later, much more polite and friendly than he had been when he'd arrived.

What had surprised Heather was that Bereoa hadn't boarded the same shuttle and left as well. That would have solved just about all of her problems, because at that point they could have flown back out to the point where the rest of the team was due to arrive in a few more hours, and waited.

Then left, and let the Princes at *Ewin* deal with their own litter box filled with stinky, runny shit. Because that was what they had right now.

And it wasn't her problem, except that she hadn't managed to offload Jaxom Bereoa yet.

Duke Kalidoona, Prince of the Eastern Squadron, had invited them to his palace station headquarters fortress orbiting the planet *Elox*, directly above the capital city of the same name below.

Phil had decided to ride over in one of his gunships instead of a simple administrative shuttle, and had ordered her to join him.

Granted, that left Iveta in charge if something happened, but that just meant that Phil was serious about smashing somebody's nose in and then maybe curb-stomping them afterwards. His standing orders had prettied that order up, but not much.

Bereoa was aboard. Phil. Aliza. Command Diplomatic Centurion Nicolae *Nicu* Torosian, who had possibly drawn the short straw of the ambassadors. Except that the man looked like most of *Ewin* in being somewhat swarthy, but not as dark as folks from the *Aditi Consensus*. What Nicolae did have was a deep understanding of tough guy syndrome, as Aliza classified *Ewin* culture, and the ability to imitate it expertly.

Watching the man talk and move was like standing too close to Gotzon Solo or being in a modernization of Shakespeare in the park. Possibly *Hamlet*. Hopefully with a better ending.

She had her doubts.

"First Centurion, stand by to dock," the call came from the flight deck.

Urumchi had stayed a little high in orbit. *CB-502* had drifted down until the Type-3-Pulse were just in range of the station, if needed. The Fours already had sufficient reach.

Phil put away the tablet he was reading and looked around. Dar was armed, but she was also a weapon. She had apparently been talked out of bringing along a couple of her new trainees from *Dalou* on this mission.

Phil hadn't wanted the extra grumpiness from the locals. Heather agreed.

Bereoa made eye contact.

"You will be unique, Command Centurion," he reminded her. "They are not prepared for a female in command. Let alone a competent one. Let alone a killer."

Heather half-smiled and half-grimaced. He meant well, and had thrown himself headlong into the job of being an ambassador for *Ewin* to *Aquitaine*, when he didn't need to.

She supposed that he was looking for allies as things were coming apart.

She rose. Joined in the mob by the hatch as Dar prepared to open it.

There was always a risk in a situation like this. Ill-met strangers, as it were. The hatch opened and the first face Heather saw in the mob over there was Striker Zechiel, so she relaxed a little.

Him being here didn't say great things, but him not here might have said bad things. The gunship was inside the stations shields and had orders to fire everything they had directly into the hull if attacked.

Personally, she thought that Phil was letting the macho paranoia of the Princes dictate things a little, but he'd also given that order in front of Bereoa, so the First Minister was aware that Phil didn't have many nerves left for anyone to get on if they felt like getting stupid.

She wasn't much better, but Heather's job was just to fly Phil's flagship, so in many ways her place in history would be more like Denis Jež.

She could live with that. There was always a chance that the new First Lord would promote her to a fourth and maybe fifth stripe one of these days. Then she might explore all the way to *Lost Earth*.

She'd take a heavy dreadnought, though. *Urumchi* was just polite enough that folks didn't immediately behave.

Dar emerged. Heather followed Bereoa, with Phil and Aliza and Nicu behind her.

Godfrey, Duke Kalidoona, was obvious when she got out into the dock. Not only was he the best dressed, in gold and blue, but the man was huge. Not just tall, but big. Phil, scaled up another ten percent taller and wider. Start of a pot belly going, but not as bad as it might have been.

Bear, without all the fur.

Dark skin like most of the locals, but not as red as *Aquitaine* tended to be. Black, straight hair. Bereoa, two sizes larger.

And he wore a sword on his hip. Saber, rather than something big, but one hell of a personal statement. Probably for the best that Xochitl Dar didn't have a pair of her samurai with her today.

Striker Zechiel stood next to the Duke, along with a handful of other strikers and men who looked like sailors. A few bureaucrats like Bereoa stood back some. Out of the limelight of the Princes, as demanded by *Ewin* culture.

She was accustomed enough to it not to roll her eyes where anyone might see.

It was their reaction to her that nearly got Heather to growl at them. Disdain she was prepared for. Outright lust was something new. Did these jackasses see her as some sort of Amazon war goddess?

In that case, she'd need to bring Iveta down sometime, and let them try to impress her with their… *tactical acumen.*

Heather moved to one side and glowered at the men ogling her. It wasn't a bad body. She was in better shape at forty-two than just about any point since she'd first been commissioned.

Obviously, these punks only ever saw mistresses and occasionally wives. Never a peer. Certainly not their superior. Probably not dressed much, either.

Since Phil was just the messenger, this whole thing had been hastily arranged, and Phil had put his foot down at formality, like he did.

The two mobs slowly merged instead, like differently-colored lumps of dough stuck together. Heather was across from Zechiel when Phil and Bereoa lined up corners on the Duke.

"Duke Kalidoona, I am pleased to introduce you to First Centurion Philip S. Kosnett, Governor-Plenipotentiary from the *Republic of Aquitaine*," Bereoa said, maybe spooning it on a little thick in his obvious attempt to put the two men on an equal footing. Dukes could be touchy boys when their honor was involved. "And the Striker of his flagship, Command Centurion Heather Lau."

She didn't like the gasps from everyone but Zechiel, but she supposed that one had already gotten enough over himself. From the looks the rest of the men were giving her, Heather seriously considered announcing that she was a lesbian, but figured that would just make them try even harder, if they thought that *only they* had the magical penis that could *cure* her.

Oh yes, she had a good understanding of *Ewin* noblemen.

"Duke Kalidoona," she murmured, nodding politely to the man.

Equals, as they both commanded fleets. Hers might be smaller in terms of overall tonnage, but once everyone got here, she'd be willing to *explain* to these gentlemen that usually it was what you did with what you had, rather than pure size.

"Come," Kalidoona gestured. "As agreed to earlier, we have a quick reception and drinks prepared through here. Striker Zechiel has already briefed me and sent along the First Minister's reports. Striker Thardson of *Freewind* did as well."

He gestured to one of the men around him. Heather had never met the commander of *Freewind*, and not much about him stood out, except that he was another one of the peacocks around here trying to look both intimidating and apparently sexy enough to attract her eye.

Which just explained what fools they were.

Still, the first mob turned and surged away. The second mob

floated more in its wake, with Zechiel and Kalidoona both remaining close enough to chat.

Heather tuned most of it out as Phil, Aliza, and Nicu started their various sales pitches. She wanted to see if anything about the Eastern Squadron was going to be a problem for her force from a military standpoint. Iveta would have lists of questions when she got back.

The whole group eventually ended up in a suite that might have been designed and built to hold cocktail parties. She got a fresh bottle of juice from Markus and passed on the food.

The space itself was awkward. Other people would have lined the bookshelves with actual books, but this space had a few plants and a lot of what she took to be trophies from the way they were displayed. Strange pieces, some as large as her, others tiny enough to fit in her hand, each with a date and a quick description. After reading several, she presumed battles, where the person looking would have the depth of local historical knowledge to understand what was being celebrated.

She didn't. And didn't really care. She was here to make these people deal with a woman in command. On her terms. Phil was here because that was his mission. Aliza and Nicu because it began and ended with diplomacy.

Heather Lau handled diplomacy by other means…

"Are you enjoying things, Command Centurion?" Striker Zechiel stepped close but not too close, a glass of something fizzy and purple in one hand.

"Well enough," she answered. "*Ewin's* internal struggles are really not our business, Striker. We just happened to be in the wrong place at the wrong time, and needed to transport Jaxom Bereoa someplace where he could help sort things out."

"And then?" he asked.

"And then we depart, Striker," she replied, turning away from something that might have been a gauge off a generator to look more at him. "Once the rest of our fleet arrives, I expect that's what we'll do."

"You will not stay and help fight?" Zechiel asked.

As if fighting was the *sine qua non* of flying a starship. She supposed that for these men, it might be.

"Not our battle, Striker," she said. "Not our war. At the end of the day, not even our culture, other than the fact that we're here now and Phil wants to establish the ties that will allow trade, both within the Cluster as well as with the nations of the arm."

"Will *Fribourg* really come peacefully as well?" he asked.

"I'm reasonably confident in Centurion Weigand," Heather replied with a cold smile.

"Who?" She had him confused now. *Far* better than hitting on her.

"*RAN* Centurion Casey *zu* Weigand," Heather said. "You probably know her better as Emperor Karl VIII of *Fribourg*, but she once sailed with the *Aquitaine* fleet as an officer. I served in the same squadron with her, when I was Phil's First Officer in the war against *Buran*. She's still a penpal with the First Centurion, and sent him a birthday present both last year and this."

Heather figured she might be enjoying herself a little too much, but these men really did irritate her with their casual chauvinism. And their assumption at this social level that women existed as objects of pleasure and breeding, rather than peers.

Zechiel looked like she'd just punched him in the nose. Not that she hadn't considered it. Bereoa had been a consummate gentleman for the last week. She'd forgotten that Gotzon Solo was quiet and polite among his kind, rather than loud and macho like the rest of them.

And she'd broken Solo of some of his more egregious habits over enough months. Now, he was only occasionally annoying.

Zechiel was studying her, but for once it didn't look like he was mentally undressing her as he did.

"After the various battles at *Meerut,* as well as *Jacoby,*

Urumchi and your fleet could turn the tide in any war, couldn't they?" he asked now, voice dropped to a level where she was the only one who might hear.

"Likely," Heather replied. "We've spent the last century fighting for our lives. First against *Fribourg*. Later *Buran*. We're probably more than a century ahead of you technologically."

"Then I don't understand why you haven't just conquered the Cluster," he said, earnestness now evident.

Because that's what you did with power, wasn't it? Bullied people?

Heather finally realized what it was about *Ewin* that made her so angry. These people were bullies, plain and simple. Teenage punks who had never grown up and had real jobs with real concerns, because—along with power—they inherited commoner servants who were tasked with holding things together when egos like Doysan IV or Giscard Russand broke shit.

Like Jaxom Bereoa, who was still trying to thread a needle to stop the latest civil war.

That man at least understood that this one might end *Ewin* as an independent power, if they fell apart at the moment when everyone else was suddenly investing in better warships.

"We came looking for new friends, Zechiel," Heather replied after a moment to grind off some of the sharper things she might have muttered. "*Fribourg* is an ally now. As are most of the rest of the nations of the galactic arm around us. Eventually, the pieces that made up *Buran* will settle down and start trading as well, but we share no border with them. Instead, we sought to explore our open western frontier. You folks happened to be halfway to the next arm, so we started here."

"But you intend to visit the west from here?" he asked, still lost.

Warrior, not explorer. Almost a foreign language to the man. Heather wondered if he was literate, or just well-bred enough to be trained to command.

It was rude to think of them as barbarians, but she wasn't convinced that it was wrong.

"Eventually, I'd like to orbit *Earth*," Heather admitted. "See where we came from."

His eyes glazed over a bit at that. Probably had to stop and remember what Earth was. Certainly hadn't had a semester class specifically focused on that last war, the one that had destroyed everything.

"I don't understand," Zechiel finally said, which might have been the first honest words out of his mouth since he'd boarded her ship.

"There is an ancient **Earth** saying," Heather replied. "You catch more flies with honey than vinegar."

She might have explained what that meant, but Jaxom appeared right then and intruded into the tableau while it was still frozen.

"Come," he said, oblivious to the tension. "Prince Kalidoona would like to gather the players."

Heather expected Zechiel to go. He flew the man's flagship, after all, but Jaxom gestured for her as well.

She raised an eyebrow at the man, but allowed him to take her by the elbow and lead her back to the main group like a formal herald, weird as that was.

Still, she supposed it made sense. Kilo for kilo, she commanded the deadliest vessel in the system. Possibly in the entire Cluster, at least until *Yaumgan* upgunned their Eight Immortals at some point.

If they did.

The First Minister of *Ewin* led her out of the cocktail party, leaving most of the guests behind, and to a much smaller room.

Where the future of the *Ewin Principalities* would likely be decided.

THIRTY-THREE

DATE OF THE REPUBLIC DECEMBER 19, 411
ELOX PRIME STATION

Phil found a spot off to one side, rather than on the far end of the long table facing Duke Kalidoona. Heather was immediately to his right, like she chose when given the option. Aliza and Nicu were across and separated, so they had folks on either side to chat with. Others scattered around, with Kalidoona at the high end of the table.

The group seemed about three to one strikers over bureaucrats in the stripe of Minister Bereoa.

Duke Godfrey Kalidoona smiled this way. Phil gave him the sort of haughty neutrality that would draw a hard, bright line in the sand.

"My friends, I have had a chance to hear from many of the key witnesses, in their own words," Kalidoona began in an expansive voice as big as he was. "Doysan has, I believe, finally descended into madness, as many of us long expected would happen. It behooves us to do something about it, especially if, as many suspect, Giscard Russand has wormed his way into the King's graces and poisoned the well against the King's loyal subjects."

It had the feel of a well-prepared address. If nothing else,

201

Kalidoona had a good speechwriter on staff. Phil held his peace and watched, utterly unwilling to be drawn into something.

"As the same message was delivered by both *Freewind* and *Urumchi*, I believe that we can trust the veracity of things," Kalidoona continued, possibly sticking to a script. Or maybe he was just naturally gifted as a public speaker. "Put simply, we have an impossible situation on our hands."

Phil let his face descend a little into a glower at the suggestion that he might be involved.

"Prince Kalidoona, a question?" Heather asked now, causing every single head in the room to snap around almost painfully. Phil was not an exception, because he hadn't expected her to say or do anything.

He knew how much of an introvert she was, much of the time.

"Yes, Lady Lau?" Kalidoona smiled at her.

"That's *Command Centurion* Lau, Duke Kalidoona," she snapped right back in his teeth. "*Republic of Aquitaine* Navy."

Even a Duke could appear chagrined. Might have never met a woman with the guts to talk back to him.

"My apologies, Command Centurion," he said with a quick bob of his head. "Your question?"

"For what reason did you think that the *RAN* should be present, if this is a planning meeting?" she asked bluntly.

Blunter than Phil would have done it, but they had played Good Cop/Bad Cop before. His half of the role was obvious from where she was going. Aliza and Nicu were remaining distinctly silent, but they were diplomats and this had suddenly turned into a military conference.

"Madame?" Kalidoona asked, a bit muddled now.

Phil assumed that the man had been following somebody's script, and nobody had taken Heather Lau into account. More the fools them.

"This is an internal problem facing the *Ewin Principalities*, Prince of the Eastern Squadron," Heather said slowly, enunciating every syllable distinctly as she did. "*Aquitaine* has no business being involved. Certainly not if you are in the process of discussing the possibility of forcing Doysan IV to retire so that someone else can become King of *Ewin*."

"You would not help?" Kalidoona asked, possibly a bit wounded by his tone.

Thwarted by a woman for the first time? Phil knew Heather's general opinions on *Ewin* culture. His weren't much different. But she was setting herself up to take all the heat now, leaving Phil with clean hands later.

Whatever that required from her personally.

"That would cast us in the role of king-makers," Heather replied. "Others might see us as meddling in *Ewin* affairs to overthrow a ruler we perhaps didn't like, and then hesitate to deal honestly with the *RAN* in the future. Nobody wants to invite that camel into the tent, after all."

Phil could tell which people around the room knew the aphorism by the smiles or blank faces around the table. Mostly the bureaucrats smiled. They could explain it to the warriors later.

It was telling when Kalidoona turned to First Minister Bereoa. Some message passed, but Phil couldn't read the subtext. Looked like Bereoa had won the exchange, though, so perhaps the man had warned the Duke that Kosnett wasn't about to fall all over himself to help depose Doysan.

It was also educational to watch Duke Godfrey Kalidoona recalibrate things on the fly. Not many folks could react that quickly when all their plans got tossed out the airlock. That was the sort of thing that separated the true First Centurions from the old First Fleet Lords who were more often well-connected than well-educated.

"What about Russand?" Bereoa asked.

"What about the baron?" Phil responded. "It was my understanding that his military power had been largely eliminated with the losses to his fleet. His piracy and banditry have been curbed."

"Not if, as I suppose, he is the one responsible for the sudden shift in *Ewin's* behavior," Bereoa replied.

"If *your king* is suddenly taking advice from the man, I'm not sure he still qualifies as an outlaw, First Minister," Phil said distinctly.

"We cannot know for certain, First Centurion," Bereoa replied. "However, the orders declaring the man an outlaw have not, to the best of my knowledge, been rescinded. As I would have been the one to prepare them, I feel confident in that assessment. Doysan was holding him until he figured out what to do about Russand."

"You think we should accompany you to *Ewinhome* in order to arrest the baron?" Phil asked now, feeling his own bluntness come into play.

It was one thing to be asked to help. It was something else to be maneuvered into action as part of a civil war.

"He may have convinced others of the rightness of his cause," Kalidoona suddenly found a track again, "but that does not justify ordering an attack on friendly vessels in orbit and part of Central Squadron. That is also a crime to be investigated. If we can assume Russand had some hand in it, that opens the way for you to assist us in a law enforcement action not dissimilar to your mission to hunt down the pirates of the *Zen-Mekyo Syndicates*."

Heather had leaned back and crossed her arms. Not defensively. From her body language, it was to keep from pounding her fist on the table or maybe punching somebody.

Disgust and negation.

And yet, Kalidoona and Bereoa had points, if Phil was feeling charitable. If Russand was behind all this, taking the man down probably helped *Ewin* survive this current crisis. Whether the next one caused the edifice to tumble or the one after that was a matter for bookies and speculators.

"What's in it for me?" Phil asked simply.

He smiled, but that was the way all the faces around him slid into shock, Heather's included.

"First Centurion?" Bereoa finally managed.

"Why should we indulge in this level of speculative action, which I might add, may result in you deposing your king?" Phil asked. "Possibly illegally, depending on how your laws of succession work? What does *Aquitaine* gain from acting now, instead of simply sailing away, having delivered the message and the messenger to where they might be of greatest use?"

Bedlam. A dozen voices raised in concern or explanation, stepping on one another to the point that cacophony was the result. It only ended when Duke Kalidoona slammed an open palm down on the table.

Even he seemed a bit shocked at the result, as he took a moment to brush back his hair and settle himself.

"Doysan is trying to provoke a revolution," he said firmly.

"He's *your* king," Heather spoke sharply. "The word you are looking for is probably *purge*."

Again, heads snapped around. Bereoa had been right. They saw her as a beautiful woman rather than a better commander than any of them. And maybe as good a diplomat as Bereoa or Aliza Babatunde.

"Purge, yes," Kalidoona agreed. "He has caused friendly warships to open fire on each other without apparently provocation. That must be investigated, even if he is king. If Russand had a hand in it, then it becomes a crime."

"So challenge the man to a duel," Heather said, almost sounding like a sneer.

The grumbles she got back were telling. Many obviously wanted to. Phil wondered if the man was personally dangerous enough to frighten off such challenges. He'd never met Russand in the flesh to judge.

Just stolen his entire war fleet.

"If it were that easy, I might, Command Centurion,"

Kalidoona replied in a cold, crisp voice. "Let me be blunt. I need to take a fleet to *Ewinhome* to demand answers. Russand likely has to provide them. Or Doysan. Your fleet's assistance would be appreciated in this, because I cannot leave my entire border unguarded at this moment. Is that clear enough?"

"Then perhaps it would be to your benefit to arrange a truce or peace treaty with the *Dalou Hegemony*, ensuring your rear flank while you were gone," Phil said.

He waited a long moment for heads to turn his way in confusion before he dropped the other shoe.

"The Crown Prince of *Dalou* and the daughter of the Shogun himself—a young woman who is his personal representative with my squadron—will be arriving shortly," Phil smiled. "I'm sure you can have a fruitful chat with them then."

More bedlam, but a good kind. Shock, utter and sincere. Cries of surprise and outrage.

Because Phil saw an opening.

THIRTY-FOUR

COMMAND CRUISER STORM PETREL

K ohahu looked around.

They were in a formal salon today. Her, as the Shogun's Personal Representative, since she had filled the role that Inspector Sobol had previously held. Shingo, in formal dress uniform rather than robes, on her right. She would be the one speaking.

Kohahu hadn't believed the message from Kosnett, delivered as soon as *Storm Petrel* had arrived in the *Elox* system then conveyed to her personally by Captain Yukimura.

Still, she had demanded that her father send her with Kosnett and *Storm Petrel* as his personal representative. She couldn't blame Kosnett for taking advantage of that.

Kohahu had spent her time on this long mission fruitfully, meeting with Yukimura's staff and watching Officer Trainee Shingo Yosan learn his trade from professionals. And this many men were better prepared to deal with her formally.

She just had the rest of the Hegemony to convince, so that she could ascend to the Shogunate when her father deemed his time sufficient.

Captain Yukimura was elsewhere, in the process of meeting with the group that Kosnett brought from *Elox Station*. Other than bodyguards and aides quietly arranged around the edge of the large room, she and Shingo were alone.

He glanced at her, started to say something, stopped.

Kohahu felt like the older of the two, but she supposed that she had been raised as part of the Shogunate itself, while the Imperial House had been reduced to isolated figureheads centuries ago and only now were in the process of trying to assert any of their ancient prerogatives. He had been sheltered his entire life.

"What questions can I help you with?" she asked the man quietly.

"I can see the shape of the thing you seek to build," he whispered back. "I do not see how it can be brought to fruition."

Kohahu nodded. She frequently felt the same way. Both of them were quietly railing against fates that sought to starkly limit their potential.

Didn't that largely describe *Dalou* culture? Rules and customs with the force of a law deeper than anything written on a tablet? A daughter could not become a Shogun. A Crown Prince could not be anything but a songbird in a pretty cage.

"We establish the image in their mind by acting without visible doubt or hesitation," Kohahu instructed this man who was five years older than her physically, and still a babe in the woods politically. "Once they accept this vision, they will shift their thinking. Kosnett and *Aditi* have both shown the others worlds where women lead. Where a person's limits are drawn by themselves, and not by the society around you. Yosan does not have to be weak, but you must assert that you are one of the Great Houses to remind the others. Eventually, they will acknowledge that."

"And if they don't?" Shingo asked.

"Then we make them," Kohahu nodded.

Further speech was cut off by the outer hatch opening. Yukimura entered first, in a dress uniform matching Shingo's to the point that the man had removed most of his ribbons and awards. Standing together, you would only have rank insignia and age to identify them. Yes, Yukimura understood how to ingratiate himself with powerful players while still maintaining his authority as Captain of this vessel.

Kosnett followed. As with Yukimura, he wore a toned-down dress uniform. Epaulets and cuffs, but no awards. Interestingly, Heather Lau accompanied the two men in similar attire.

Kohahu saw that as Kosnett reminding *Ewin* that women could command warships.

She and Shingo had been seated at the conference table, but they rose now to greet the visitors as Duke Kalidoona and others entered. Kohahu was dressed in baggy pants and tunic that were similar to what she wore on the dojo floor when training every morning. Crimson, trimmed in gold, itself a uniform, but not one she expected *Ewin* gentlemen to understand.

Few had ever met directly with representatives of *Dalou*, much less the Shogunate or the Imperial House. Let alone together.

Kalidoona was as big as she had been warned. One of the tallest men she had ever met. Heavy but smooth in his step, so a man who was not a stranger to personal training. Others followed in the Duke's wake, the flashier two looking like strikers and the quiet two looking like advisors, one of whom she thought was *Ewin*'s First Minister.

Quickly, everyone got seated and introduced. She had been right in her assessments, other than she had not met Jaxom Bereoa personally. Circumstances had not allowed it prior to this.

What might she have accomplished, had she been aboard *Urumchi* during the flight to *Elox*? Was it time to transfer to Kosnett's ship now, having established herself with the main players on *Storm Petrel*?

Wheels within wheels.

Kosnett spoke first. It was Yukimura's ship, but Kalidoona's system. Kosnett was the man bringing them all together.

The Prince of the Eastern Squadron looked to Shingo, but she understood. They did not treat women even as well as *Dalou* might, low as that bar might be to clear. She would have to deal with their chauvinism when she was Shogun.

"Prince Kalidoona, let us revert to that previous conversation," Kosnett said delicately. "Your intention to travel with a significant force to *Ewinhome* shortly, for reasons related to the internal politics of the Principalities. As you noted this morning, doing so risked leaving your entire frontier open to raids or attacks by outsiders. I currently command the largest force of such outsiders operating near *Ewin*. And the pirates have largely been broken, although I expect it will take years for that issue to fully abate. Luckily, we have access to significant players from *Dalou*, with whom you could negotiate better understandings of things."

He left it at that, but Kohahu had already felt the gravitational pull of the Balhee Cluster shift under her feet. Kosnett had begun to cause yet another star nation to rethink everything that they stood for, because he was not beholden to the old ways. And he didn't care if people refused to embrace the future that was coming.

Morninghawk had warned all of them. Luckily, she had listened.

Kalidoona looked like he might have just sucked a lemon dry. Kohahu wondered if he had been expecting another middle-aged woman like Samnang Sobol, and nobody had warned him that Lady Kugosu would be fifteen soon.

"I speak for the Shogun," she said in a calm, cutting voice her father had taught her on the dojo floor. It worked equally well in his inner council. "Crown Prince Shingo will be Emperor, on some hopefully distant day when his revered Father is no longer with us. We acknowledge various treaties that the Hegemony has executed with the Principalities of *Ewin*. Each of those established clear borders, Prince Kalidoona, and very little trade crosses them. At present. Has the time come to review them, and perhaps seek greater friendships across the gulf of stars and cultures that separate us?"

Inwardly, she quailed just a bit, watching many of the faces around her blink in momentary shock at her bold words, but Command Centurion Lau smiled. Kohahu drew strength from that.

Heather Lau was a dangerous player, one who was often underappreciated. Kohahu could see modeling herself on such a woman. It was indeed time to transfer to *Urumchi*.

Prince Kalidoona sputtered. The First Minister stepped into the gap.

"The *Ewin Principalities* face an internal issue, Lady Kohahu," the man said smoothly. "Our present hope is to remind everyone of those very borders and ask that they be treated today like impregnable fortresses that stop misunderstanding from crossing and possibly causing future issues, once the present is satisfactorily resolved."

"How do we build trust?" she asked, aiming her question at both men now.

Kosnett didn't snicker, but the laughter in his eyes was almost as good as Heather's smile for her resolve. *Ewin* warships and strikers, like Baron Russand who had started all this, tended to be even less reliable than the pirates, across just about any spectrum you wished to measure.

Kalidoona started to speak, but the First Minister leaned in.

"You travel with the First Centurion as a personal representative of the Shogun, correct?" he asked.

"That is correct, First Minister," Kohahu replied. "One day, I will take his seat as Shogun."

Quiet and not so quiet gasps filled the room. She'd never spoke those words out loud where they would become public. She had committed herself now.

Kohahu wondered how many new enemies she had just created, just among the Great Lords back home who might otherwise have been allies. Each would have been seeking to find her an acceptable husband that they expected would take her Father's power.

She had other ideas. Best that the galaxy come to understand that. Shingo nodded when faces turned to him, and Kohahu saw new calculations take shape.

Kugosu, married to Yosan, sealing the ancient chasm that had split *Dalou* asunder. The rise of a new thing. Perhaps they would take the phoenix as the symbol of their new, *joint* reign.

Kosnett rescued the *Ewin* gentlemen now.

"Lady Kugosu, I propose that King Doysan IV, via his representative in Prince Kalidoona of the Eastern Squadron, sign a new memorandum of understanding with both the Shogun and the Imperial House, via their agents," Kosnett offered, his quiet voice forcing everyone else to silence, lest they miss something critical. "Already, we have language that I think serves all players. It was negotiated at *Meerut* to provide a safe harbor for merchants willing to make that long journey, as well as setting rules for formal port calls, wherein warships of various nations could arrive as tourists, with an expectation that they could pay market rate for supplies and behave themselves like welcome visitors. These are the sorts of things that *Aquitaine* and *Fribourg* originally signed, when Jessica Keller convinced Emperor Karl VII to end that long war."

Kosnett had warned her that he was going to go big with this meeting. To push an agenda. At the same time, it was his agenda. And *Aquitaine*'s.

Peace. And trade.

"As I understand it, First Centurion, trade between *Aquitaine* and *Fribourg* has grown from almost nothing a generation ago to a significant portion of both your economies?" she asked dutifully, reminding everyone here that she understood the scope of the man's plans.

Kohahu had been studying everything she could lay her hands on from *Urumchi* on *Aquitaine*'s history. And they had been more than happy to assist her. Ulterior motives, but they were up front about breaking *Dalou* of their ancient beliefs that women should be subservient to men.

Just look at Phil's senior officers. All of them were female, because they had been the best people he'd been able to find for the job. Not gifted him by strategic marriages.

Or peace treaties with hostile neighbors.

She speared Kalidoona with her gaze now, prodding the man to speak. He licked his lips briefly, as though suddenly finding himself out of his depth.

The perils of being *Born Important*. Sometimes, the people who had to work their asses off to be taken seriously ended up better prepared.

Like now.

She already knew that Kosnett and Heather would both wait all day for the man to speak. She and Shingo would as well.

"How did you come to be traveling with the First Centurion?" Prince Kalidoona asked carefully now.

It sounded irrelevant and unrelated to the thing Kosnett had just dropped on the table like a bombshell, but only at first glance.

He wanted to know who she was.

"When Makara Omarov was made Lord Morninghawk by the Shogun and Emperor, the Imperial Inspector who had been accompanying them became Lady Morninghawk," Kohahu said slowly. Distinctly. "His vessel, the Heavy Escort *Morninghawk* itself, was detached from this force, as he is in the process of creating a new colony at *Urwel*, where he intends to trade with *Belamel* on the *Aditi* side of the border, as well as your sector capital at *Toulouse*. Thus, Kosnett was without a cruiser flying the *Dalou* flag, as well as an escort on his front line. Those were two tasks which *Morninghawk* managed with such grace that many of Kosnett's enemies will long have nightmares. I determined that the Shogun needed to replace that one vessel with two, *Forktail* and this *Storm Petrel*. Further, that I should accompany them to make sure that his orders and expectations were met. We represent the *Dalou Hegemony*, after all, so we should be exemplary at it."

She paused and watched the tall man think. Rethink. Recalibrate from seeing a bright child before him to a hard woman in a young body. He had lust there, but that was the typical sexism of such men. Even if he was trained martially, Kohahu was confident that she could kick his ass so utterly that he never forgot it, while not accidentally killing him in the process.

Accidentally.

"What does friendship give us?" he asked, bulling ahead even though he was uncertain.

The First Minister was carefully smiling, but remaining silent.

"At this moment, I could send a message to our nearest border station, to be relayed along the entire front, to remind all vessels that we are at peace with the *Ewin Principalities*, Prince Kalidoona," she said. "Signed in the Shogun's name. Any commanders who might have otherwise considered sneaking across will think thrice, if they understood that such an action will have them cashiered in disgrace and possibly exiled. What does such forbearance earn us in return?"

It was educational, watching the man refrain from making demands. Her orders to sector capitals could easily go the other way as well, letting everyone know that the border forces had been withdrawn and grown distracted.

How much *Ewin* shipping could be captured or annihilated while Kalidoona was at *Ewinhome* dealing with a rogue king?

"*Urwel?*" the tall man asked now. "I believe I heard you say that one of your lords was establishing a new colony at *Urwel?* And that he intended to trade with both *Toulouse* and *Belamel?*"

"That is correct," she nodded. "Lord Morninghawk, the hero of *Meerut* who was awarded the Republic Cross by First Centurion Kosnett at *Ellariel* not long ago."

"Just trade?" the man pressed in a disbelieving voice.

"Kosnett believes that trade alone will be sufficient to break down most of the ancient barriers and prejudices, Prince Kalidoona," Kohahu said boldly. "We believe that he is correct. And that it will render the pirates of *Zen-Mekyo* so irrelevant that they fade away and we enter an era where ships become independent transports hauling goods between worlds. Minus all the smuggling, which suggests that taxes on goods will be paid, thus enhancing treasuries as well."

Money. No government ever had as much as they wanted. But smugglers didn't pay taxes.

How much richer might trade make you, Prince of Ewin?

She managed not to smile when Kalidoona turned to the First Minister seated beside him.

"You advise kings, Bereoa," the tall man said. "What advice would you have?"

"I have not read the text of what Kosnett proposes, my Prince," the Minister replied. "But I have spent significant time working with him and his senior staff. I would approach such a thing with an open mind, confident that the results are intended to benefit the most people."

Kohahu's dour face hid a wealth of unfortunate giggles entirely inappropriate to an Imperial Agent, but perfectly cromulent for a fourteen-year-old girl watching these pompous fools realize how badly outmaneuvered they had been. And by how many players.

Bereoa had seen the truth of *Aquitaine*. The benefits aiding most people would accrue to those middle classes that birthed merchants and provided educated bureaucrats.

Dalou had much the same problems with inherited aristocracy as *Ewin*, but Samnang Sobol had been an example of what they could achieve, climbing the ranks of the bureaucracy to become an Inspector. Kohahu didn't begrudge the woman becoming Lady Morninghawk. Makara Omarov was an impressive man, made of far sterner stuff than almost anybody had given him credit for.

And he had saved her when the Emperor set foot on *Ellariel-jo*, boldly stepping into the line of fire as befit a Heavy Escort.

And the *Hero of Meerut*.

Ewin's Princes were likely the one group that would not benefit from broad trade, because they were likely to lose significant control of the economy and politics of the Principalities.

Thus was Kosnett seeding the ground with the thing that could **replace** *Ewin*.

She wondered if Bereoa was the only other native of the Balhee Cluster besides her in this room who understood that. His smile promised a wealth of interesting conversations.

Kohahu decided to gamble. It was a small one. But a single stone could cause an avalanche.

"Prince Kalidoona, First Minister Bereoa, I propose that we adjourn this meeting for a time," she said. "That way both of us can review Kosnett's proposed treaty language and perhaps come to an understanding of a future path for our two nations. It is a bit late in ship's day here, so we could reconvene sometime after breakfast to chat?"

Bereoa wanted to immediately accept such an offer, but all eyes turned to Kalidoona now. His ego would drive things. His honor, as Prince of the Eastern Squadron.

However, she could always send a message home that would light the border on fire if the man really pissed her off right now.

Interestingly, Kalidoona turned to Kosnett, then Heather Lau, as if seeking a sign. Kohahu didn't understand the body language, but Heather's nod seemed to break the stasis more than Kosnett's did.

"I agree, Lady Kugosu," Kalidoona finally said with a firm nod. "Let us retire and review things. I will contact my staff and let them know I will remain aboard *Urumchi* with Kosnett for tonight, and we will return on the morrow."

Kohahu nodded. If this worked, it might just pave her way to the Shogunate, one of these days.

THIRTY-FIVE

FLAGSHIP URUMCHI, ELOX ORBIT

Jaxom had gotten Kalidoona tucked into one of Kosnett's amazing Ambassadorial suites with his staff. Nicu Torosian had joined the man as an advisor and potential future ambassador, while Jaxom had inquired with his security trooper and been led to a lounge where Command Centurion Lau was currently having a glass of wine with a few junior officers.

She had been warned that he was coming, as she waved him close. The guests at her table took the opportunity to withdraw.

He found himself alone at her high table, standing across from the woman with his minder off to one side. Jaxom didn't see himself as a threat to the woman, but doubtless others had a lower opinion of him.

"You had questions, First Minister?" she asked as a steward left with his drink order.

"Please, call me Jaxom," he said. "This is informal and unofficial, Command Centurion."

"Then call me Heather," she replied. "What can I help you with, Jaxom?"

Her body language had shifted subtly. Harsher. More reserved.

He supposed that she thought he was about to proposition

her. Granted, she was a most interesting woman, but not his type. Far too intelligent. His father had warned him about sleeping with smart women.

Most men aren't prepared to deal with a smarter woman. The princes were easily emasculated in such settings.

"At the end, Kalidoona looked to you, when Lady Kugosu suggested a break," he said. "I find that difficult to square with the circumstances and wished to better understand, lest I make a mistake later."

Her face changed. Relaxed some. Her stance became more laconic, for lack of a better word.

"I have been thinking about it as well, Jaxom," she replied. "I doubt that Kalidoona has ever had to deal with, as you put it, a competent woman. A commander. A killer. I was his first. Lady Kugosu thus becomes his second, only because I haven't had a chance to sic Iveta on the man."

Jaxom shuddered in spite of himself. First Officer Beridze was dangerous on axes that Jaxom had never considered before now. They called her *The Junkyard Bitch* for a reason, he had learned. As a term of respect.

"So you provide him a pattern against which to measure Kohahu Kugosu?" Jaxom asked, perhaps seeing better.

"She has it in her," Heather replied. "Don't ever mistake that woman for anything less than the hard-minded daughter of a *Dalou* Shogun."

"She claims that she will ascend someday," Jaxom noted carefully. "And the body language between her and the Crown Prince suggested an alliance of some sort."

Heather paused and took a drink of her wine. The steward brought his, so he joined her, aware that she might choose to ignore his question. That might be an answer all by itself.

"I would not be surprised if someday Kugosu and Yosan eventually had a more formal alliance," she said, leaving it at that.

Still, it took his breath away. *Dalou* had always been split into two rough parts. Allies of the Shogun. Allies of the Imperial House. *Ewin* commerce raiders had been able to exploit that gap. *Ewin* bribes had helped fund renegade *Dalou* noblemen hiding in semi-exile, either on *Ewin* worlds or at one of those numerous illegal colonies that dotted the neutral zone Lady Kugosu had threatened to set afire, however obliquely.

A unified *Dalou* was a much more significant threat to the Principalities.

"Can they manage it?" he asked, voice a little hoarse now.

"She seems to think so, Jaxom," Heather replied. "I would not want to bet against her on the topic. Or any topic, for that matter."

Nor would he. Young she might be. That just suggested that she could grow more dangerous as an opponent as she got older. As Shogun, she might be a terrible foe along *Ewin*'s longest border.

"Thank you," he said, nodding his head and drinking more of his wine. He set the glass down half empty and leaned back. "You have given me much to consider, Command…Heather."

She seemed a bit surprised at his abruptness.

"Leaving so soon?" she asked in a surprised voice.

"It behooves me to retire to spend some time with Kalidoona," he said.

"Oh?"

"Between you and I, somebody needs to tell that bull-headed fool to shut up and accept *Dalou*'s offer of increased trade," Jaxom said. "Otherwise, he might start a two-front war."

Her smile told him all he needed to know. Jaxom bowed to her now and nodded to his minder.

Kalidoona needed to be brought around. Whatever it took.

THIRTY-SIX

Heather had briefed Phil, Aliza, and Nicu about her conversation with Jaxom the previous night, so they were in better spirits this morning. The shuttle had hauled everyone over to *Storm Petrel*, like yesterday, but folks were more relaxed. Hopefully, that meant that Jaxom had gotten through to the man.

Certainly both Bereoa and Zechiel had smiles for her today that didn't suggest they had mentally stripped her nude when they looked at her. Finally.

As before, Captain Yukimura had escorted everyone. Same decks. Same honor guard. Same conference room.

Same players.

Kalidoona wasn't as uptight as he had been.

"Good morning, Prince Kalidoona," Lady Kugosu said as everyone got seated, aides and guards around the outer wall watching and key operators at the table. "Have you had a chance to review the new treaty proposed?"

Heather was across from him today and one chair closer to the Crown Prince, with Aliza between them.

"I have," the man said in a friendly enough voice. "On the whole, my advisors suggest that it is largely workable in the

221

current form, but that we might need to make a few changes before signing.”

Like the others, Heather nodded at that. Treaties normally took years to negotiate. In the case of *Ewin* and *Dalou*, their last such formal agreement had been more than a decade gestating.

Overnight was too much to hope for.

“Technical details only?” Kugosu asked in voice too mature and well-educated to match such a young face.

Heather wondered if she was dealing with another one that might turn into *Dalou's* first Jessica Keller one of these days. If so, the girl needed to meet Iveta in less-structured circumstances. *Junkyard* had a wealth of things she could teach such a woman. Maybe an invitation to transfer to *Urumchi* for a while?

“Largely so,” Jaxom spoke up now. “Tonnages of ships as classifications for various categories, as the boilerplate language the First Centurion proposed envisions much larger vessels. Additionally, resupply, as *Aquitaine* and *Fribourg* sail much greater distances when making port calls. But those can easily be shifted to an appendix where ongoing teams can nail down the exact details. Taxes on trade might be difficult, but Kosnett has also proposed that both sides charter financial institutions for the sake of maintaining lines of credit and currency arbitrage. This is not something any of us have any expertise at, but Ambassador Torosian has offered to assist all sides as a neutral third-party, at least until such time as the issues that drive us in this current situation are resolved.”

Heather nodded internally, outwardly calm and composed. All going according to script. Now everyone turned to the *Dalou* representatives.

“That pleases me,” Lady Kugosu said with a nod and a smile. “After speaking with my own advisors, perhaps we should simply agree for now on a much broader memorandum of understanding, while our two sides dicker about the finer details that can turn into a superseding treaty later?”

Heather was the only person other than Phil who didn’t

jump a little at her words. Especially coming from someone born and raised in *Dalou*. They didn't do rapid *anything*, let alone politics. And whoever had been whispering in this young woman's ear was at least as sharp as Bereoa, though she couldn't be sure if it was Yukimura, one of his senior officers, or maybe Crown Prince Shingo. For all his youth, the man had struck Heather as being smart. And understanding forms and legalisms better than he generally let on.

It was there in the way some comments didn't confuse him like they did many of his peers.

"Truly?" Kalidoona asked, a bit lost already.

Must have gone off script from what Bereoa had prepared him for again. The man was supposedly a pretty good fleet commander, but Heather hadn't been impressed by his political chops.

"It is my understanding, Duke Kalidoona, that the circumstances which bring us together like this also impose critical timelines on your own operations," she said, impressing Heather up another whole level from before. "This lets you go settle your other affairs without worrying about your rear flanks."

And gives everyone a quick victory that lets *Ewin* settle Russand and maybe Doysan, while extracting a long-term benefit that was still well-balanced.

Kohahu Kugosu was likely to make a dangerous Shogun, one of these days. Maybe Heather needed to lean on Phil to write a letter to Karl VIII? There weren't many women out there that could offer relevant advice to the first-ever female Shogun, after all. And *Fribourg* would be coming here, one of these days, if only to keep tabs on Phil and establish their own trade ports.

Heather caught Phil's eye and nodded to him, like he could read her mind. Maybe he could, considering their adventures on *CS-405* and *Buran*, plus more recent affairs.

"If it might help, perhaps various representatives should all transfer to *Urumchi* for the time being," she offered, nodding to

Aliza. "Prince Kalidoona has asked this full squadron to accompany him to *Ewinhome* as neutral observers. That gives you several days to talk, while still allowing an *Ewin* force to sail to *Ewinhome* while time was of the essence. Would that be acceptable to everyone?"

She watched folks settle into a new frame of mind. Easier to lead that horse to water, according to the old saying, but they wanted to drink, and hadn't figured out how. Now, they could.

"One question," Jaxom spoke up now. "How would Lady Kugosu get a message back to her people? Or did you intend to detach *Forktail*?"

Heather hadn't thought through that one. The Fast Clippers were about, but using one of them to haul messages would throw off her own supply cycle. And while Phil had enlisted *Hollywood* Ward to do things similar, none of her vessels were present.

"Perhaps," Phil leaned in, "if we were to ask Prince Kalidoona to allow us to temporarily borrow one of his frigates? I could put one of my officers aboard, as could Captain Yukimura, and the ship could temporarily fly an *RAN* transponder code as a courier. *Dalou* has some experience with such things, when *Meerut* needed to send me messages suddenly at *Ellariel*-jo."

She watched that reminder ripple around the room. *RAN Varmint* had been hauling the alert that Baron Russand had gotten out of hand, before she and Phil had gone and done something about it.

And it might get *Ewin* strikers used to making non-hostile port calls. Small steps into a new future.

Kalidoona started to say something, then caught her scowl and subsided, turning to Jaxom. Bereoa nodded and Kalidoona settled.

"I think that such a plan of action helps everyone get where they need to be," Jaxom interjected after a moment. "Let us quickly work up a memorandum acceptable to everyone while

Prince Kalidoona talks with his forces. We can reconvene this afternoon sometime and get all the various balls rolling."

Heather nodded. She still wasn't sure why all of these men seemed to defer to her, but perhaps they saw her as some terrible war goddess?

Oh.

Vilahana.

Ground Control.

Yes, she supposed that maybe they did see her as something beyond merely human, after all. Heather kept her grimace to herself.

It was a useful legend, if it kept everyone around here on their toes.

THIRTY-SEVEN

Phil had sent Heather home to prepare Iveta for a new job as a role model, if Heather was right.

And Heather was almost always right when she took the time to express an opinion. That was why he valued her so much.

Plus, he did need to write Casey *zu* Weigand a letter. An invitation to become penpals with a possible future Shogun of *Dalou*, which would eventually necessitate a State visit by *Fribourg* that would further cement better relations across the gulf.

And inside the Cluster.

He wasn't there yet, but Phil could actually see a gap he could thread that would end up reshaping all of the Balhee Cluster into a positive place, rather than breaking them all down into jagged shards, like Jessica and Lady Moirrey had done to *Buran*. Necessary in that latter case.

Balhee wasn't the possession of an angry god.

The players were back in *Storm Petrel's* main conference suite. He got to watch history being made, as two representatives of the *Ewin Principalities* signed the new Memorandum of Understanding with a matched pair from *Dalou*.

He wondered as each took their turn if he was also watching the fall of Doysan IV as king. Duke Godfrey Kalidoona was about to take a warfleet comparable to Phil's to *have a chat* with his nominal superior. If Duke Farouk did the same, there might be a whole second battle for the skies above *Ewinhome*, this one even bloodier because everyone would be prepared.

Kalidoona had gone first, and now stepped off to one side. Phil sidled close and applauded when it was all done. Yukimura's wardroom had even made a sheet cake for the event, weird as that was.

But it made this an Event. Wine and juice came as well.

"I have a question," Phil asked as folks settled and he faced Kalidoona and Bereoa. "When we get there, do you expect trouble?"

"Doysan broke his fleet a week ago," Kalidoona replied. "He is not really in a position to start something now."

Bereoa nodded but was apparently going to let the Prince handle this conversation.

"What about Farouk?" Phil asked. "He'll have had time to do exactly what you intend, possibly with less friendly intentions. Assuming yours are still positive, Prince Kalidoona."

The man might have decided to just sail in and depose Doysan. Farouk might, as well. That hadn't been discussed.

Then what?

"Do I expect you to side with us if someone attacks?" the man asked. "Is that the real question?"

"Your words, but essentially yes," Phil replied. "Am I supposed to take sides in an impending civil war? That could be a public relations disaster, as I have important representatives of *Dalou* flying with me and you've just concluded a treaty with them."

"Speaking in Doysan's name," Bereoa noted sharply as he stepped close, having been listening. "At present, we are transiting to *Ewinhome* so we can deliver the joyous news to our king at *his* profound success."

Phil noted the sarcasm in the man's eyes, but supposed that it was palatable enough as a cover story. Peace, trade, and diplomatic relations were Phil's mission.

"If you are attacked, I expect you to defend yourself," Kalidoona spoke firmly now. "We'll be closer to trouble than you were the first time, or when you emerged here, but I also have heard from my experts that any *Ewin* force attacking your squadron is committing a particularly painful form of suicide, Kosnett. It is my hope that we can buy technology from you at some point so that we are not left entirely behind when *Aditi* and *Dalou* do the same."

"One-sided technological transfers would be even more destabilizing than just blowing up fleets," Phil said carefully. "If you all maintain a certain parity, that reduces the risk of wild card players causing trouble. But trade will do far more because it will change how people think about other nations."

"So the First Minister has reminded me, more than once, First Centurion," Kalidoona replied with a hard smile. "That and Lady Kugosu are what convinced me that I needed to make some drastic changes in how we do things around here. To circle back to your original question, I believe that Doysan IV needs to come to a better understanding of the future that you yourself are already creating, or he must give way to someone else who can. I doubt that Bertrand Farouk is any better than Doysan, but that's not the problem. Right now, they are likely to shatter *Ewin* at the worst possible moment. I won't claim that I have a mandate from Heaven to save the kingdom, but this is also the moment when we have to decide if it is worth saving. Or rather, which parts."

Phil nodded.

"Adequate for my needs, sir," he bowed his head. "I prefer that the *Ewin Principalities* survive as an entity, however messy and chaotic that will be over the short term. I have warned *Aditi* not to meddle in *Dalou*'s affairs. I can extend those warnings to a wider swath of players as well."

"You *warned Aditi?*" Kalidoona asked, somewhat incredulous.

"As you noted, I command a significant military force, Prince of the Eastern Squadron," Phil said in a harder voice. "And I could ask my superiors to send a war fleet sufficiently powerful that perhaps not even *Yaumgan* could resist me, though we have not compared things that closely. *Dalou* has been asked not to violate your borders, and has even signed a new agreement specifically covering that. I will expect *Ewin* to reciprocate. *Aditi* will be reminded. *Yaumgan* does not really bother their neighbors. *Gloran* is too far away to be a problem today, but I expect to sail to *Derragon* at some point as well. There will be peace. Or I will leave you all to implode while we watch from a safe distance and I suggest to my superiors that we not return for a generation before we try again."

Phil fell silent and watched the two men recover. They'd gone a little pale. But then, he'd never spelled out so exactly and so clearly his opinion in such raw terms to anyone local. The Princes of *Ewin* were not threats to him. And if they pissed him off enough, he might decide to sell pulse weapons technology to *Dalou* and *Aditi*, wherein these princes would cease being a threat to anyone.

And he might not warn *Aditi* not to meddle at that point, either.

"I hope that will not be necessary, First Centurion," Bereoa said diplomatically.

"And I as well," Phil nodded. "With that said, let us take this afternoon to celebrate a new beginning. And then tomorrow, we can sail to *Ewinhome* and continue those conversations."

CONFRONTATION

THIRTY-EIGHT

Heather had bent a few rules in order to have Lady Kugosu—Kohahu—seated here on *Urumchi*'s bridge today, in a spot where she could watch everything, including her and Iveta at work. She and Phil had had a couple of pointed discussions with nobody else around, not even Harinder and Aliza, about what she was going to do.

He hadn't forbid her anything except formally enlisting the young woman in the *RAN*. But then, Senior Officer Namrata Nagarkar, technically on loan from the AdCon Cruiser *Aranyani*, had also been qualified to sit bridge shifts, so Heather had them both here today. It helped that Nam was only a decade and some older than Kohahu, while Iveta was old enough to be her mother, and Heather older yet.

But Heather had also gone back and reread everything that had happened with the once and future *Emperor of Fribourg*, when Centurion Kasimira *zu* Weigand had flown aboard Keller's flagship, back in the day.

"Pilot, what's the countdown?" Heather asked across the otherwise silent bridge.

Everyone was in soft suits already, including the two women visitors. Not necessarily an immediate need, but it helped frame people's state of mind, and saved the sixty seconds or longer if combat did break out.

A-team on duty for this. All of her people were better than good, but Leyla, Bozhidar, and Hào were better than that. In any other circumstances, Nam might have sat a watch on the Gunner's station instead of Hào, but not today.

Heather had gotten to pick her Gunner from every man and woman in the fleet who had wanted to apply.

"Three minutes and change, Commander," Bozhidar replied crisply.

Heather found the right switch on her controls and opened the ship-wide comm. Normally Phil's job, but the vast majority of *RAN* ships operated without a Fleet or First Centurion aboard, so better if Nam and Kohahu see how it should be done.

"All hands, this is Command Centurion Lau," she said, listening to her voice echo back from speakers around the bridge. "You have ninety seconds to be at battle stations and prepared for combat actions. We will be coming out hot, so all gun teams go ahead and unlock your systems, but you will not fire without an order, not unless you detect an incoming missile with active targeting lock on *Urumchi*. Let the escorts handle things otherwise. We are witnesses to history today, so I have no intention of starting any fights. I will expect you to finish them. Stand by for Emergence. Tactical Officer, take command."

She cut the line and nodded to Kohahu. Best way to learn this sort of thing was to watch it happen, then do it yourself. Kohahu was too young, but after this, Heather intended to sit her here in the big chair a few times with Iveta on Tactical, and let her work out all the flutters Heather remembered from her first time.

Even with The Professor himself training her, there was always that first.

She looked over at where Nam was watching a gunnery board and caught the woman's firm nod. Senior Officer back home. Equivalent maybe to a Centurion who has just qualified for her second stripe and readied herself to move up into senior management.

And she'd done a good enough job that Heather wouldn't object if the woman requested a permanent transfer to the *RAN*, though Heather rated that unlikely. Much better chance of getting her own *Aditi* boat after a year of serving with the foreigners.

Kohahu was both wide-eyed and shrewd when Heather looked over. Absorbing every detail and fitting things into a matrix that would help a young woman take command of older men that might not be as open-minded to the topic.

"Questions?" Heather asked. She had time.

"Is it always like this?" Kohahu asked. "Ready instantly for combat?"

"No," Heather shook her head. "Rare, as a matter of fact. However, because we are ready to open fire immediately, any surprises tend to be going downrange. Fool who shoots at this double fleet has truly misunderstood the situation. Perhaps terminally."

"Will my presence be a social or political issue later?" Kohahu asked, showing just how mature the youngster really was.

Able to see that having a representative of *Aditi* fleet as well as the daughter of the *Dalou* Shogun on *Urumchi*'s bridge during what might be the start of an *Ewin* civil war could cause problems later.

"They are welcome to send along a female officer trainee as well," Heather said with a smile.

"They do not have such a thing," Kohahu said before pausing and smiling suddenly.

"Whoops," Heather nodded. "Better luck next time."

"Still, you should send notes to *Gloran* and perhaps *Yaumgan*," Kohahu said earnestly. "Invite them to participate in such diplomacy as well. Most will not understand, but some will."

Heather nodded and caught Iveta's nod as well. A most cogent and dangerous suggestion. She needed to reach out to Kaur Singh after this action and thank that woman for sending Nam over in the first place.

It might be another wedge Phil could use to break things open here without destroying everything, because even the *Gloran Empire* allowed some women to be warriors, though it ended up being far less than parity.

Emergence.

"All hands, this is Kosnett aboard *Urumchi*," Phil's voice filled all lines with his smooth tones. "I have the flag. We are on a diplomatic mission to *Ewinhome* at the invitation of the Prince of the Eastern Squadron, here to celebrate the recent treaty agreed to with *Dalou*. All vessels will remain on passive alert unless or until something happens. You will note that we are again high in the orbital sphere of *Ewinhome*. Not as far as before, but also not sailing blithely down to the station, as we might have done elsewhere. Stand by for orders."

He cut the line from his end and Heather nodded. Scanners were already starting to fill in data, with dots and transponders being marked and located on her display.

"Oh, shit," Iveta muttered under her breath.

Heather had to agree, though.

As they watched, more dots appeared. Prince Kalidoona with *Utron Heavy*'s squadron a little ragged as they got organized. Still, one battleship, three cruisers, and nine escorts. Significant force, though not enough to threaten all of the *Aquitaine* team, especially after everyone had trained and fought together.

"Leyla, start flagging folks by your best guess on team colors," Heather said immediately.

"That's *Pride of Kalos*," her Science Officer replied quickly. "Notes from Bereoa mark that as Farouk's flagship. Archer/carrier like *Meynard II*."

"Assume everyone close by is Farouk's as well," Iveta broke

in. "Give me blue on friendly, green on Farouk, red on known Doysan, gold on anyone we can't immediately identify."

"Coming up," Leyla replied.

Heather watched the screen resolve itself almost into pie slices in *Ewinhome*'s orbital space. Farouk had more ships than Kalidoona. Doysan fewer than either, but he'd also just fought a major battle here twelve days ago, so many of them probably still needed time in a repair yard.

They hadn't caught Doysan with his flagship in dry-dock. Man must have learned something from what happened to Russand, though Heather didn't think that *Meynard II* would be all that dangerous. It was merely an Archer-style ship.

Fleet Carrier with added missile racks, going back to when Heather had first been commissioned. Not a lot of titan bolts or Main Guns, because they relied on somewhere around twenty-six fighters and usually a dozen missile launchers, two on each face of the hex, forward and aft.

During the last attack, *Meynard*'s fighters hadn't done much of anything, because it took so long to prepare them for what had been a sudden decision to attack *Gallivant*. *Freewind* had gotten out without much physical damage, but functionally lost their entire flight wing, so Kalidoona had brought the ship along empty.

Like a man returning a lost puppy, rather than a warlord intent on an invasion.

"Lot of gold, boss," Iveta muttered. "Not much red."

"Understood," Heather said. "We're just here to talk for the moment. This is Kalidoona's show. Leyla?"

"Lot of traffic everywhere," the Science Officer replied. "Only about a quarter of it I can't read right now. *Utron Heavy* let everyone know that they signed a new agreement with *Dalou* in the king's name and have come to deliver a copy and brief their monarch."

"Anybody falling for it?" Heather asked.

"Dunno," Leyla said. "No, wait. Oh, wow. Squadron, this is

Ekmekçi, Science Officer aboard *Urumchi*. I have crash launches from most of Farouk's squadron. Those new signals you are picking up are fighter craft being hot-launched from their ready bays. They are not, **REPEAT NOT**, hostile missile launches. Farouk's squadron has an Archer, two Hunters, and three of the Vulture variant of the light bombards as carriers. All three of the destroyers are Escort Carriers, as are four of the frigates. All ships stand by."

She looked this way and Heather just shrugged.

Maybe Doysan and Farouk had been just awaiting their arrival.

THIRTY-NINE

ROYAL COURT, ALLEMAINE STATION, EWINHOME

"God damn it!" Doysan bellowed angrily at the messenger who had just stepped back, cringing. "Has everybody lost their fucking minds? Where's that worthless punk Russand? This is all his fault!"

"He has departed to rally your barons, My King," the man reminded him.

Doysan didn't even remember the man's name. Too many new faces around here lately for him to learn who they were. Instead, he emptied the goblet he had been enjoying with Farouk and held it out for someone to refill. With his other hand, he took the printed message and crushed it.

"What about my First Minister?" he hollered next. "Has that worthless cur come back from wherever he slunk off to last time?"

"I'm afraid not, My Liege," the messenger said. "He departed with the *Aquitaine* squadron previously."

"Your note informs me that they have returned!" Doysan screamed now. "Worse, they went and got themselves a pretender at *Elox*. Probably that scumball duke Kalidoona himself. Come to oust me and take over. I will not have IT!"

He turned his bleary eyes to Farouk. The man had always

reminded Doysan of a son. A better one that any that he'd sired, at that. Maybe a little taller and not as heavy around the middle as some of his kids, but still handsome enough to get all the girls atwitter and throwing themselves at him.

Of course, he'd had to invite the man aboard Allemaine Station. There was precious little Doysan could do these days, with much of his Central Squadron wounded in the aftermath of that stupid ambush Russand had convinced him was necessary.

Or had it been Bereoa who ordered it? The days were blurring together and he had a hard time sorting things out.

"Fill me," Doysan grumbled, putting the messenger out of mind for a moment as he tried to figure out what he could do. As Farouk poured, Doysan pushed the crumpled ball of paper at the man. And hiccupped. "Trouble has come. I'm betrayed on all sides. If you really want the throne, you're going to have to fight Kalidoona for it. Right now."

He took a hefty drink and settled.

"Not much I can offer you," Doysan continued. "Betrayed on all sides. Said that. Squadron's fucked. Russand and Bereoa conniving, I suspect. Should probably put bounties on both their heads and just be done with it."

"You're not still mad at me?" Duke Bertrand Farouk asked now.

His glass hadn't emptied nearly as many times as Doysan's but the man was only a duke. Didn't have the weight of a crown pressing him down night and day.

"Course I'm still pissed at you, Bertrand," Doysan roared. "She ran off with you, didn't she? But those mangy dogs are here to pick my carcass clean. I already apologized. And it wasn't my fault. Bad advisors tricking me into doing stupid things. Should have them killed. Or you should. Fucked this all up. Probably too dumb to be king now. Maybe time to say fuck it and sail off somewhere."

Bertrand smiled. That was good. Doysan's

maudlinnesssseseses…whatever was getting out of hand. Prolly started drinking too early today. Or yesterday, when a big-ass warfleet dropped out of nothing and surrounded him.

Then a second one.

Shit, what was Kalidoona at this point but late to the party? Fucker'd almost missed it entirely, because Farouk was here with ships and Russand and Bereoa had set Kalidoona up to be right proper fucked.

"If I drive them off for you, I'll be back in your good graces?" Bertrand asked cheerfully.

"Nothing I can do at this point but adopt you, m'boy," Doysan smiled grandly back. "You handle Kalidoona and the others and I'll resign this stupid kingship shit and you can have it. Never brought me nothing but grief. Just make sure you destroy Russand and his ilk. And Bereoa. They're here to get even with me for all the shit I've ever even thought of doing to them."

He liked Bertrand's broad smile. Looked like a king. Warm and hearty and bold and strong.

F'rookie had put the bottle down to read the note from… whatsisname, so Doysan grabbed it and went to pour. But shit, the goblets never held enough.

He put it to his lips for a good long draw instead as he heard the man speak.

"Order my squadron to launch everything," Bertrand Farouk said boldly. "And prepare my shuttle to return to my flagship."

Doysan nodded with the rightness of it all. Then he put his head down.

Just a little nap to make it all go away.

FORTY

Iveta had Tactical. Combat command of the single most powerful and dangerous warship in the system today. Possibly the Cluster itself. One that had been designed and built to deal with anything at short or medium range. Twelve Pulse-Two turrets arranged so that usually any nine could hit someone, assuming she didn't roll onto a flank or wing to bring everything to bear. Two of the big Type-4 beams that had originally been solely used on stations, until that silly pirate decided to hunt sharks with them instead.

Around her, four modern corvettes plus *Forktail*, who had been busting his ass to make up for *Morninghawk* not lurking in *Urumchi's* shadow. Big shoes to fill, indeed.

On her flank corners, five mismatched cruisers, one each from the major players, from the light missile bombard in *Shadowbolt* up to the flying man in space *Li Jing*.

Iveta knew exactly what everyone on her flank was capable of, in what was shaping up to be the biggest space battle in living memory for most of these people. Even at *Meerut*, the enemy had been a bunch of small ships, mostly trying to escape from her rather than turning bow on and thinking they were important.

And she was only the flank today. *Utron Heavy* and that battle group were outmatched if everyone over there decided to gang up, but Iveta had her doubts about that sort of thing lasting long. Of course, if that was Duke Farouk, here to claim the throne of *Ewin*, that might be long enough. *Utron* was outmassed a little under two to one.

At least among *Ewin* ships.

Kosnett had opened a team channel that included her, Heather, and the flag bridge set up. Iveta was poised, but didn't have anything to do until somebody got feisty.

Or stupid.

"I have a message from the station, ordering us to withdraw from the system or face the consequences," Phil said. "Signed by Duke Farouk under King Doysan IV's name. At the same time, Prince Kalidoona is transmitting the treaty in the clear to anybody and everybody with a receiver."

"Did we arrive about the time that Doysan was being overthrown?" Harinder asked on the private line.

"I suspect that Farouk has been here long enough to make a case for being reinstated as Heir," Phil offered. "Having arrived with a big enough fleet to make his point. The others might have done the same. Or maybe we have several pretenders. Or folks actually did rally to the throne. Weirder things have happened."

"What about all those fighters?" Heather asked. "Most of Kalidoona's force is designed for close combat with *Dalou*. They simply cannot handle waves of missiles from all sides, like Farouk can do now."

"I'm hoping that things can be contained," Phil said. "That all the various dukes and barons present can sit down at a table like rational adults and talk. I appreciate the smiles all of you are giving me, and that nobody has patted me on the head like a precious toddler, but that might be the best we can get here."

Iveta didn't have much to say, so she was watching her boards rather than Phil's screen. She saw Leyla wave her arms and cut her silence field.

"**Mass launch**," Leyla called simply across the big bridge. "Every fighter has started to blueshift hard. Every one of them has launched at least one missile. Every one of the red or green ships has launched something like a full salvo, along with a chunk of the gold ones I'm tentatively retagging as red for now."

"Can *Utron's* group handle it?" Iveta asked.

"Not on their best day," Leyla replied with a shake of her head.

Iveta nodded to the woman and brought her line live again.

"Phil, we just ran out of time," Iveta said. "Farouk has thrown everything *and* the kitchen sink at Kalidoona. They cannot stand before it, so they must withdraw if they want to survive. That, or I have to get involved."

He paused. Studied her on the screen. Iveta didn't smile, like she might have a year ago. That would have been bravado, like most of these *Ewin* fools tossed around so casually. Nor was it grimness.

There was time for Kalidoona to withdraw. Those missiles would require several minutes to accelerate up the gravity well and swarm *Utron Heavy*. That was probably the exact message Farouk was trying to send.

Back off. This kingdom is mine.

Playground bullies shoving each other.

"Is it worth it?" Iveta asked the First Centurion now as he remained silent. Planning.

It was his call. His name in the history books that would be written about today.

She was just here to make him look good.

"Can you do it, *Junkyard?*" he asked, as if they were the only two people left in the universe.

"Yes, sir," Iveta replied quietly. Firmly.

Professionally.

"Then take the flag," he ordered. "We need to save the *Ewin Principalities*, and I believe that Kalidoona is the best bet on the table."

"Understood," Iveta said.

She cut the field and looked once around the bridge. All her key people that Heather had brought together, plus Nam and Kohahu Kugosu.

Phil Kosnett was known throughout the fleet as *The Professor* for his scholarly and intellectual approach to things, but people often forgot about the combat side of operations behind enemy lines aboard an undergunned scout corvette with a broken JumpSail. Against the entire *Holding of Man*.

And winning.

Iveta keyed the widest channel. The one that would let Kalidoona and his force hear her. Probably most of the enemy fleets as well, but they should know what they had just done by starting the fight.

"All vessels, this is *Junkyard*, aboard *Urumchi*. **I have the flag**," she said, shifting mentally into that other place that Heather talked about. The one where *Ground Control* lived. "*Urumchi*, accelerate on this line. Corvette force, two wings back in an arrowhead formation. *Aquitaine* auxiliaries, follow us in, with *Forktail* in close escort as always. All guns are live. All missiles are to be destroyed. Hold on engaging other warships until they provoke, and then savage them without mercy. Type-4 teams, I have identified the enemy flagships. They will be your primary target if anyone attacks us. Then I will want them broken if it comes to that. All ships, execute."

FORTY-ONE

FLAGSHIP URUMCHI, THE EDGE OF BATTLE

Kohahu blinked as First Officer Beridze spoke. The challenge in that woman's voice. The calm certainty. She had only ever heard something similar a few times in her short life. Each time her father, either on the dojo floor instructing her, or in his council chambers, signaling seriousness that might end in death.

Beridze was about to challenge the combined might of the *Ewin Principalities*, confident that she could not just win, but perhaps annihilate them. Father had warned her that *Ewin* played dangerous games because they didn't always stop and consider what they were about to provoke. They had teased the big dogs, and were about to be savaged.

Today, Kohahu would apparently see it.

Kohahu checked her emergency suit, more out of nervous habit than anything. Helmet attached on a lanyard to her hip. Strapped in.

Around her, she saw the forces of *Aquitaine* ascend to a new place. Kohahu didn't have the vocabulary to describe the thing, but she had watched her father do it on the dojo floor a few times.

And heard stories about the nightmares that Lord Morninghawk had inflicted upon his enemies.

Nobody in the entire Cluster had the kinds of ships that could sail into the storm of missiles approaching. Not even *Yaumgan*, from what she had learned of the humanoid ship flying on the left flank of the formation. *Urumchi* was challenging the very gods themselves today.

Junkyard had become a goddess of destruction.

And Kohahu had a front-row seat. For better or worse.

"Squadron, all gun teams engage at the outermost markers," Beridze ordered. "Wounded might be sufficient for now."

It took Kohahu a moment to understand. The woman was ordering them to ignore any missile that they had hit and move on to the next, rather than pausing. Letting them get through to where the second line of cruisers might engage them. Or perhaps the escorts that had accompanied Prince Kalidoona and his battle group around *Utron Heavy*.

That ship did not impress any of the *Aquitaine* folks, even though it would be a chancy match for anything less than the Behemoth-class super-battleships that anchored entire fleets back home.

Kohahu turned to her station and started adjusting her screens. Nothing at all like what she had learned on as a child, but there were only so many ways to display such information, and she didn't need to push any buttons today.

Merely be a witness to history. And it would be historic.

Kosnett had brought this force to *Ellariel*-jo politely. Had acted with restraint and care for as long as she had known the man. *Ewin* had brought out his temper. Or finally irritated him enough to be made an example of.

"Flag, this is Yukimura aboard *Storm Petrel*," a familiar voice came through the command chatter she had been listening to. "Enemy flagship *Pride of Kalos* is now in the outer engagement range of the condor and closing. Should we fire?"

"Negative, *Storm Petrel*," Beridze replied. "He gets one more chance to behave before I get vengeful."

Kohahu felt a chill descend on her shoulders at the word Beridze used, like a sudden rain squall on a cold day.

A condor at this range would force *Pride of Kalos* to react. To turn away or focus all their attention on the firebird, because cutting off their targeting systems to launch a mimic and hide right now would cause many of those missiles to go astray.

It was a prime *Dalou* tactic when engaging missile cruisers on the *Ewin* frontier. The Princes did the same when facing massed firebirds. Everyone remained at range and dueled.

Except that *Utron Heavy* and escorts were designed to get close and slug it out at much shorter range. Which they could do as *Urumchi's* weapons began lashing out and blowing things up. The escorts engaged as well, using the pulse weapon they called a Type-3, better than Main Guns both for range and damage.

And then massed batteries of Pulse-Two turrets decided that they were close enough to engage.

Kohahu's jaw dropped as the stuttering fire began inflicting massive losses, like a firefighter with a hose knocking down an inferno.

Calm. Focused. Professional.

Deadly.

What had been hundreds of missiles began to thin down even as she watched. The first wave had been launched as a single, massive salvo, with subsequent launches more ragged as various ships had to reload the tubes and enemy captains suddenly had to contend with an angry *Aquitaine* fleet wading into the fray.

"Tactical, we're starting to draw attention," the Science Officer nearby called. "*Pride of Kalos* and others are ignoring *Utron Heavy* and focusing tracking weapons on us."

Kohahu expected the woman to react. To curse, to rail, even to smash her fist angrily on a surface or something. Many of the male captains and councilors Kohahu had known would have done so.

None of them would have smiled. Not like that.

"Everybody?" she asked in a warm, cheerful voice.

"Just about," the Science Officer—Leyla—replied evenly, also not frustrated or fearful.

"Excellent," Beridze announced. "Ghost Mode. Now."

It took Leyla a moment, and then she began to smile equally. Both women almost seemed on the verge of cackling. Kohahu knew a moment of serious fear in the depths of her soul.

"Oh, you're an evil bitch," Leyla replied merrily. "Coming up."

Kohahu's confusion must have been obvious, because Heather Lau turned her way and nodded.

"This is the difference between a century of you folks fighting tiny wars with low stakes and what *Aquitaine* faced, first with *Fribourg* and later with *Buran*, Kohahu," Heather called across the space. "Nobody around here understands scouting like we do, because they don't need to. So they don't build ships like ours."

"What are we about to do?" Kohahu asked. "What is *Ghost Mode?*"

"Jessica Keller invented it, back when she invaded and actually captured a *Fribourg* world," Heather said. "This ship is a survey dreadnought, rather than a line-of-battle ship. We have a tremendous amount of power and range for our sensors and scanner systems, even compared to our ships back home."

"And here?" Kohahu asked with growing dread.

"*Pride of Kalos* and others are about to be blinded by the amount of power Leyla is going to generate and blast in their faces."

"Blinded?" Kohahu asked, confused.

"Imagine trying to shoot, while someone shines a light in your eyes," Heather said. "At the same time that you are walking through a hailstorm. Everyone has locked their targeting systems on us to fire their next sets of salvos, expecting to overwhelm us with target swarms."

"And they cannot see us," Kohahu noted.

"Oh, it's much worse than that, Kohahu," Beridze laughed now. "Many of those ships are wisely flying in overlapped formations defensively, especially the escorts. Missiles launched from second and third lines of the formation might accidentally lock onto their own frigates at point-blank range because they don't know any better and are also blind. *Pride of Kalos* might manage to shoot their own ships in the ass before they stop. That's when the chaos gets ugly."

Kohahu noted that the woman—women—seemed to be planning to pounce, from the feral smiles around her. Kosnett had put First Officer Beridze—Iveta—*Junkyard*—in charge of *everything*, trusting that she could handle it.

Kohahu got the impression that the woman had been planning something like this the first time the squadron sailed into *Ewinhome* orbit, and might have been disappointed that she couldn't spring her trap then.

Duke Bertrand Farouk, speaking for King Doysan IV, was the man who had chosen to stick his foot into Iveta's bear trap.

"Squadron, this is Science Officer Ekmekçi aboard *Urumchi*," Leyla announced. "Stand by for Ghost Mode from the flagship."

On Kohahu's screen, twin yellow beams appeared as animations, broadly pointed at both battleships, *Pride of Kalos* and *Meynard II*, and then locked. Missiles that appeared as solid track vectors aimed at this ship suddenly changed to dotted lines in many cases. Others went black as targeting locks were broken and the missiles weren't smart enough to recover.

Would they just fly off ballistic paths forever, or were they low enough that they might eventually fall back into the atmosphere. Would any become navigational hazards?

Kohahu found that she only cared on an intellectual level. They had come to try to talk sense. To begin a new era in

Ewin/Dalou relations. One that opened the door to trade and cultural exchanges, as Kosnett had intended.

Instead, Farouk had opened fire unprovoked. That suggested to her experience that he was the kind of king intent on ruling *Ewin* with an iron fist later.

Even at her age, Kohahu could see where that would be a long step backwards, at a point in time when the rest of the Cluster was poised to walk into the future.

Some of them, at least.

"And we have the first own-goal, Flag," Leyla called with a terrible laugh. "One of *Kalos*'s Escort Carriers just took a missile in the back. I have secondary and tertiary explosions detected."

Kohahu watched on her screen as closer scans displayed the middle of the three ships suddenly venting plasma and presumably large pieces of hull as earthquakes convulsed the hull.

Tertiary explosions suggested that the flight bay had taken a hit and started to cascade through interior corridors.

"And there goes a frigate," Leyla announced like a sportscaster. "I have complete chaos on Farouk's command channel, because nobody is sure what secret super-weapon we just unleashed on them."

"Let them figure it out in the after-action reports," Iveta snapped. "If they can. *Storm Petrel*, launch your condor at *Pride of Kalos*. Hold everything else ready."

Kohahu noted that the thing called Ghost Mode was still active, even as Farouk's ships and fighters stopped wasting ammunition by trying to attack in a snowstorm. What would it look like when a firebird that size suddenly appeared out of the haze, racing towards you at high speed?

"Update," Leyla called over the noise. "*Kalos*'s formation is turning away. I repeat, redshift detected. Fighters remain in place."

"They can land on the planet if they have to," Iveta said. "Or a handy station. Type-4 Teams, engage *Pride of Kalos* now. Punish him severely."

Kohahu dialed her scanner image around to locate the enemy flagship. Around them, *Urumchi* and all her escorts had kept up a steady woodpecker of destruction at all the missiles in the skies, though few of the fighters had been engaged.

She assumed that was on purpose. Without missiles, they were badly-shielded, undergunned platforms to be destroyed. Yesterday, they had been whole wings of extra missiles that might turn a battle.

Yesterday.

Kohahu was just happy that *Dalou* had never wasted time or money on trying to build similar carrier ships, only to see them rendered so irrelevant today.

Like the rest of *Ewin.*

Pride of Kalos staggered as the first two beams impacted. Heather had pointed out that ships turning to run frequently forgot to spin their Shield Projector around to cover their rear flank, or to reinforce it first, meaning that it was weak.

Farouk had miscalculated.

"Shields down on *Kalos!*" Leyla called.

"*Aquitaine* squadron, fire everything in range at *Pride of Kalos*," Iveta said sharply. "Now, before he can get away."

Kohahu studied the ship and the distance it would take them to climb to any sort of safety. The ship had been deep in the gravity well initially, so they had that much more space to travel to escape, and *Urumchi* was above them looking down, if Iveta wanted to box them in below her.

She might.

Kohahu found that she didn't have sufficient tactical or strategic training or understanding to identify the best solution here.

What she did understand was *killer.*

More explosions on the rear hull and shielding of the enemy

flagship. Titan bolts from a variety of ships. Beams from Pulse-Two through Main Guns and up to the terrible Type-4.

Even a pair of Power Taps, from the *Aditi* ship *Aranyani* as well as *Li Jing*.

The range was extreme for most weapons, but *Aquitaine* was currently sailing in almost a straight line at Farouk, who was trapped in place turning as he tried to run.

Parallax nearly zero, into weakened or destroyed flank shields.

"*Storm Petrel*, give me a spread of your lesser firebirds into the enemy cruisers," Iveta ordered sharply. "*Forktail*, add your falcon but hold the shrikes for now."

Kohahu had watched that one Escort Carrier suffer tertiary explosions, so she understood what it meant when *Pride of Kalos* seemed to lose their gyroscopes and begin to tumble. The rear third of the secondary hull was engulfed in flames like a wall of fire ants climbing forward.

"Boom separation detected on *Pride of Kalos*," Leyla called as the other officers focused on punishing the ship.

"All gun teams with range and arc, ignore the *Energiya* and begin shooting the *buran module* if you can," Iveta ordered. "Otherwise, shift to secondary targets as I have assigned them."

"But he's launched his boom," Kohahu found herself objecting. "He's helpless now."

"And he hasn't surrendered to me," Iveta turned this way with a hard, terrible smile on her face. "Until he does, that is just another enemy warship on the battlefield. One that happens to have an enemy fleet centurion aboard."

Kohahu grimaced. Duke Farouk might not understand that *Aquitaine* didn't recognize boom separation from a doomed secondary hull as a form of surrender. He had to speak the words, or they would kill him. Iveta's face was clear on that topic.

Would he listen to anyone? To her?

"Put me on an open channel to *Pride of Kalos*," Kohahu said.

She tried to make it sound like an order, but she was surrounded by three deadly women in the process of dismantling an enemy fleet like a turkey being served for dinner.

All three of them turned to her with stunned looks on their faces.

"He does not know any better," Kohahu said, trying to sound stern. "He must learn."

"Leyla, go ahead," Iveta ordered.

Heather nodded. Kohahu breathed out carefully as Iveta went back to stage-managing her battle.

"Go ahead," Leyla said in a quieter voice. "Not sure they'll listen, but they acknowledge on this channel."

"*Pride of Kalos*, this is Lady Kohahu Kugosu, aboard the *Aquitaine* flagship *Urumchi*," she said in a calm, deliberate voice, regardless of the sudden pounding of her heart or roaring in her ears. "You will verbally surrender to *Utron Heavy* and Prince Kalidoona of the Eastern Squadron, or *Urumchi* and escorts will destroy you, regardless of your boom separation. You will acknowledge on this line, or you may make peace with God. Those are your current choices. What will it be?"

It helped that one of the Power Taps had locked on the third wave, carving turkey flesh out of Farouk's hull.

It used to be universally understood that forcing a boom separation was the end of action. Most of the important crew had a chance to flee, and the engineers could try to save the aft section before it exploded.

Iveta Beridze was not taking prisoners today. Not like this moron duke might have understood the term. She wanted blood. And he had started it.

Another Power Tap wave impacted. That would be the fourth, but booms were built much less ruggedly than aft sections. More plasma. More hull.

"What are you doing?" a man's terrified voice came over the line now. "Can't you see we're fleeing?"

"*Aquitaine* doesn't care, *Pride of Kalos*," Kohahu said,

drawing implacable strength from the hard women around her. "They are going to destroy you."

"Make it stop!"

"You make it stop, *Pride of Kalos*," Kohahu ordered. "I am just the messenger here. The witness when asked later."

"We surrender, *Urumchi*. Cease fire!"

Kohahu turned to Iveta and Heather now, eyes questioning.

She had no power over these women. Witness to history.

"Nicely spoken, Kohahu," Kosnett suddenly said, nearly making her levitate out of her chair in spite of being buckled in. "Squadron, this is Kosnett, aboard *Urumchi*. *Pride of Kalos* has surrendered. Cease fire on him. Anyone firing anything at us in ten seconds is to be de-orbited in pieces large enough to survive atmospheric reentry. Break. Allemaine Station, this is First Centurion Kosnett. I will deorbit your station next if you don't surrender right now."

Kohahu gulped. Kosnett had called her by her first name, but she had spent several days with the man and understood that to be a form of acceptance. He did the same with Heather, Iveta, and Leyla, as well as Harinder Abbatelli and Ambassador Aliza Babatunde.

He was treating her like one of them.

Was she? Did she even wish to be?

On the one hand, she was the daughter and intended Heir to the Shogunate of *Dalou*. On the other hand, her father was hardly forty, and she only fourteen.

Kohahu could take some time to learn from these people. They would show her a different future, just as they had Lord Morninghawk, not all that long ago.

Then she could be another member of this band of iron-hard women.

Phil wasn't feeling as surly as he might in other circumstances. *Junkyard's* Ghost Mode trick had ended up doing more damage to Farouk's force than Phil's guns had, after mistakes and panic had taken out several of the man's ships. Plus a couple that had fired on him after the order to surrender.

Ewin frigates were eggshells holding a tremendous number of explosive devices in close contact, when somebody kicked you in the face with Type-4 beams at short range. And then fired a fourth set into your cooling corpse after everybody in the squadron had hit you once.

About half Farouk's *surviving* fleet had fled, along with a large chunk of the others of various provenance and loyalty. Normally, Phil would be concerned, but he was beginning to wonder if some of these people could organize an orgy in a whorehouse, to use an old insult his first roommate in school had liked.

Today, orbital space above *Ewinhome* was his.

Well, technically it belonged to Prince Kalidoona, since Phil was here as his guest.

Bodyguard had been a secondary duty, implicit in the fact

that Farouk had shot first and not even bothered to stop and ask questions.

Phil studied the Prince's face in the big projection hovering above his table.

"I still feel that you should accompany me to the station, First Centurion," Kalidoona repeated.

"It would send the wrong signal," Phil replied. "I don't want anyone thinking that I come as a conqueror."

"You come as a diplomat, First Centurion," the man implored instead. "We have a new treaty with *Dalou* to celebrate. Perhaps if I were to make this invitation general, for all the strikers, all the captains of all the nations that have accompanied you, First Centurion?"

Harinder nodded minutely from where she sat across the table. He agreed. That would make it palatable for everyone. This was not *Aquitaine* stomping King Doysan's ally and heir, en route to crowning a replacement.

Phil honestly didn't know at this point what would happen to Doysan. Kalidoona and Bereoa would have to handle that themselves. Preferably after he was gone.

"That would be acceptable, Prince Kalidoona," Phil nodded. "I and Ambassador Babatunde will join you on the station, along with others."

"Command Centurion Lau would also be a welcome addition," Kalidoona said discreetly.

Phil wasn't sure what Heather had done, but Bereoa was right. They treated her like some sort of goddess come to earth when she was around.

"I will ask her," Phil said, signaling that the conversation was done.

Kalidoona nodded and cut the line from his end.

"Phil, I have Kaur Singh for you," Harinder said as he took a deep breath and considered expressing his profanities aloud.

He hadn't had nearly as much time to work with Kaur as before. Partly, that was the trip to *Ishiokoh* and then *Ellariel,* before *Ewinhome*. Still, she was literally his first ally in the Cluster, going back to the day when *Urumchi* had come out of Jump at *Vilahana*.

He took a second breath and smiled as he keyed the line open.

"Hello, Kaur," he said. "With what can I help you today?"

"I have been giving thought to the document that *Dalou* and *Ewin* signed at *Elox*, Phil," she said.

She paused and he nodded. In and of itself, a very general thing. Almost meaningless in that it agreed to nothing new.

"It commits *Dalou* and *Ewin* to getting serious about trade," Kaur continued. "And Morninghawk went to *Urwel* to do the same, drawing *Aditi* in as the third side of that corner, since *Ewin* and *Aditi* worlds are much closer than any *Dalou* colony right now."

"That's right," he said, wondering if she'd figured it out so much faster than almost everyone else. She was a sharp captain.

"As it is a simple Memorandum of Understanding, how would you feel if I proposed to Lady Kugosu and Prince Kalidoona that each execute similar documents with an *Aditi* representative?" Kaur asked finally. "Myself."

"Do you have the authority?" Phil asked, making sure she had an opportunity to back out.

"It is not a treaty, Phil," Kaur smiled at him. "It is a working document that says everyone will get serious about doing a treaty. And in the meantime it sets up rules for how everyone should behave when visiting foreign ports, which we seem to be doing a lot of lately. I've had Arya Chaudhari and my legal department go over it closely. You did a remarkable job of getting people to assume nice things about one another, without any greater penalties for misbehavior than exist now. But it is a framework everyone can work in. I feel like *Aditi* should not let *Dalou* and *Ewin* get a head start in that direction."

Harinder was not visible in the camera pickup. Which was good, because her eyes had gotten huge in the last five seconds.

She nodded fiercely in his direction, which he took as a good sign.

"Well, Kaur, I just got off the line with Kalidoona," Phil replied. "He intends to invite all the commanding officers and myself to a party on the station, after he and First Minister Bereoa sort out a few things. I think it would be an excellent idea if you brought it up with him directly. How's that sound?"

"Wonderful, Phil," she said. "I'm looking forward to it."

He cut the line and leaned back, feeling like Atlas holding the weight of the galaxy on his shoulders after all this.

"You might have pulled it off," Harinder said now that the room was private.

"At what cost?" he fired back. "*Ewin* is poised on the brink of imploding. All we've done is be present when a significant percentage of *Ewin* command hulls got shot up or even destroyed in a few places."

"And you've told me more than once that everyone will need to build new ships, once *Aquitaine* technology becomes available," she replied. "Maybe *Ewin* surrenders their cultural addiction to missile carriers and becomes less of a threat to the others?"

"That's too much to wish for," Phil said. "Unless we start those transfers right now."

"So why don't we?" she asked.

Phil started to say something tart. Something possibly even rude, which he could do because at the end of the day she knew him almost as well as Xue Yi did. Maybe better, because Harinder saw him day in and day out while Xue Yi got him when he was home trying to be a civilian.

But he reconsidered. Harinder never spoke out of turn. Never got as radical as some of his other senior advisors. Always had a plan.

Always had a plan?

"Talk to me," Phil retorted, focusing on the woman. "What have you gamed out?"

Her smile did little to comfort him. Felt like he'd walked into some ambush she'd set up. At least it was Harinder.

"*Dalou* already discovered that firebirds are not particularly effective when facing our Type-3-Pulse, Pulse-Two, and Type-4 batteries," she nodded. "*Ewin* has had it painfully rammed home that Pulse-Twos will utterly annihilate their dreaded missile swarms, though they surrendered before we needed to sweep the skies clear of all those snubfighters they carried. Probably just as well, because they might develop an inferiority complex if we had. Luckily they think and fight those little hornets defensively."

"Bedrov originally designed beam-only strike fighters," Phil pointed out. "Didn't work against *Buran* for reasons that were obvious in retrospect."

"True," Harinder agreed. "But again, the Pulse-Two on a warship renders them much less effective. *Aditi* and *Gloran* carry some missiles, but tend to use titan bolts and Power Taps as primary weapons. Even there, though, they are better off pulsing things, but none of their ships are currently built to take advantage of such things, unless you remove your heavy weapon mounts on the bow and trade rapid fire beams for slower, harder hitting."

"Okay," Phil nodded. "With you so far."

What had she seen that had eluded everyone? Because she had. It was there in her eyes.

"So what happens if we make Type-1-Pulse available?" she asked. "Better, what if we made all three technologies available to anyone who wanted them?"

"*Ewin* would have to rebuild their fleet completely," Phil said automatically. Then it hit him like a pallet of bricks. "So would everyone else. You realize that it might become something of an arms race at that point?"

"Perhaps, but at the same time, everyone takes five to ten years to gut and replace their fleet," Harinder said. "That's an expensive proposition. Meanwhile, *Dalou* and *Ewin* have a trade treaty. *Aditi* already wants in. Morninghawk is building up *Urwel*. I expect Cruiser-Captain Khan to suddenly wake up in the next seventy-two hours and demand a piece of the action for the Empire. *Yaumgan* doesn't trade now, but would they then?"

"Shit, that's a truly mercenary solution to preventing war," Phil smiled at her. "I knew there was a reason I hired you."

Harinder smiled and leaned back. She had gone bigger than even him on this one. Dangle the apple out there, without people realizing until too late that it was slightly poisoned. Only slightly.

At the same time, it would fulfill First Lord's secret orders that he not bring the entire Cluster down in fire and devastation. She didn't necessarily hold with the school of thought that predicted Imperial *Aquitaine*, but if Denis Jež was right, it also wasn't likely to happen in her lifetime, let alone her time as First Lord of the Fleet.

Tomorrow's problems, in more ways than one.

But a stable, *secure* Balhee Cluster that was modernized was not at risk of being invaded by such an imperial policy. Too far away for serious logistics trains, for one thing. Those were easy to break at that kind of distance, unless *Aquitaine* built up a tremendous highway of advance bases to protect transports running so far into the darkness.

Phil considered her idea from a variety of angles, but none of them looked bad in this light. And doing so would provide significant credit from all the big players, cash that he could use to found a couple of banks for commerce around here. That would just draw even more flies in with honey.

"What if they have their own Yan Bedrov?" Phil asked. "Or Lady Moirrey?"

"Then we better be on good terms with everyone, shouldn't we?" Harinder replied tartly. "Everyone was already looking anyway. If they find such random creatures, our remaining friendly means that we have the chance to take advantage of developments and carry them back to *Ladaux*. We have a strong edge now, but we're about to let everyone catch up some. Better if we keep at least a little edge, correct?"

"Correct," he nodded. "Everything works better if everyone can get rich, rather than a special few decided by contacts or blood relations. That was what let the Republic keep the *Fribourg Empire* at bay for so long. Jessica Keller was a lower-middle-class kid who came out of the scholarship program, along with a great many of her famous subordinates. They didn't have to be scions of noble houses to be put in command. *Aditi* has something similar here, which is why they have developed ahead of the *Dalou Hegemony*, the *Ewin Principalities*, or the *Gloran Empire*. *Yaumgan* is more like us, the more I learn about them. But their culture is too isolationist. At least for now."

"Will they change?" Harinder asked.

"I need to have a conversation with Captain Xue," Phil decided aloud. "That has suddenly become a critical question."

FORTY-THREE

Heather groused, but only inwardly. She was getting tired of being a show pony, but understood that the backward-ass hicks of the Balhee Cluster didn't quite understand that any woman could be the equal of any man, regardless of birth.

As with all hostile situations, Phil had crossed to the station aboard one of his GunShips, with all the rest of the GunShip force and the whole squadron ready to shoot first, shoot survivors, and melt wreckage if anybody so much as sneezed in Phil's direction.

The locals had already lost two major battles in the last month, so Heather could count on them being a little gun-shy for a bit. Helped that Iveta had *Urumchi* bow-on at optimum range to sign her name on the station hull with the Twos, to say nothing of punching daylight through with the Fours.

Nobody would misbehave.

Inside, they were met by two Honor Guards. The folks who had traveled with Prince Kalidoona were the only ones armed with more than belt knives right now, but station authorities weren't really in a position to complain.

Food was all being provided by Chief of the Wardroom Rei

Bottenberg and their crew, having come over several hours ago and taken over one of the big kitchens.

Even the Chief wasn't going to take any shit today.

You would be loved, and like it.

Because that was how they cooked.

Heather listened to Kalidoona and Bereoa make quick speeches thanking everyone for being here. She half-bowed when they introduced her, ignoring the usual gasps that the flagship commander had breasts.

The horrors, right?

The local welcoming party was missing the king, but Phil had informed everyone that they were calling on the man to inform him of the success of his mission sending the First Minister to *Elox* to negotiate a new trade and welcome treaty with *Dalou*.

A good enough fig leaf for now. Wasn't like Doysan IV was in a position to complain or abrogate it. Not when Kalidoona had the biggest squadron remaining around here and *Urumchi* was guarding the hen house against any foxes dumb enough to try their luck with Phil.

Heather followed the mob through hallways that struck her as a little dreary. Been too long since they'd been painted, to the point that grime and atmosphere had faded everything, like a layer of yuck brushed on to make it look poor.

Was that it? Doysan just didn't care anymore, so had let things go a little to seed? She'd heard rumors and suggestions, plus measured Kalidoona and his captains against the locals.

She'd heard more than one person on her own staff talk about bullies in sandboxes to describe what was happening in *Ewin*. Punks, the lot of them.

Inside the reception hall, the Chief and their marines were guarding the food and assuring that it was safe to eat. Even Phil would have a few things, because he'd brought Sam and *Stunt Dude* over, and she had a full medkit discreetly on her hip.

Heather went through the reception line, nodding and

smiling at locals suddenly discovering the real meaning of *force majeure*. Small sandbox. Small people. Big fucking hammer in her hand.

The king would be along later, one presumed. In the meantime, Kalidoona and Bereoa had gone ahead to a private meeting where all sorts of things would be hashed out for later public consumption.

She and Phil were here to be seen by the locals, and very obviously not involved in twisting any arms. Just celebrating a new treaty.

Heather got a little finger food and a sealed can of sweetened tea from *Urumchi's* stores then made her way to a tall table in a corner where she could be away from people and scowl at anyone wanting to get too close.

For the most part, these men sized her up as a sex object, saw her scowl, and thought better of introducing themselves. Heather was okay with that.

She wasn't surprised that Captain Xue had ended up at the same mental spot and joined her after a short time. Their combined scowls kept the rest of the event at a polite distance.

Farther away than Heather wanted to chase anyone propositioning her to…*whatever*.

They munched in companionable silence. Dao Zhiou Xue wasn't as much an introvert as Heather, but she was also *Yaumgan*, and the locals had their own superstitions to keep them at bay.

"I have a question," Dao Zhiou said after a time. "Assuming that *Ewin* is settled for now, what's next?"

"Ready to be home?" Heather asked.

"On the contrary, Heather," Dao Zhiou smiled. "I've been more places and seen more things than just about any other officer in the forces. More than most diplomats. At this point, *Derragon* is the only capital left we haven't seen, unless I can talk Phil into finally traveling to *Kyulle*."

"You might, actually," Heather nodded. "I have the distinct

impression that we're as done here at *Ewinhome* as we can get without a long-term mission. And Phil's mostly been making this up as he goes since the day we came out of Jump at *Vilahana*."

"Anything at all like you expected?" Dao Zhiou asked.

"*Ewinhome* this time around was much closer," Heather admitted. "Lots of folks see a fleet like ours and assume we're here to cause trouble, when it's never us shooting first. Or even second in a few cases."

More conversation was precluded by the First Centurion himself emerging from the mob of folks circling that Heather had largely blocked out of her perception.

She was here because Kalidoona and Bereoa wanted her seen. Fine.

At the same time, Kohahu and her bodyguards were causing more consternation, but over in another corner, because she represented *Dalou*, the known enemy. And she had samurai with swords with her.

"Good, I actually wanted to chat with both of you," Phil said as he stepped close and put a small plate and can on the standing table.

Markus and Xochitl Dar took up positions nearby facing out, causing the currents to shift farther away like a tide receding.

Heather took a drink of tea and waited. Phil could have asked her on the ship at any point, so she presumed he'd been looking for something like neutral ground to have a chat with Dao Zhiou.

"I had a meeting with Kaur Singh, off *Aranyani*," he began, talking mostly to Dao Zhiou, as Heather expected. "She has expressed an interest in signing a similar Memorandum of Understanding with both *Ewin* and *Dalou* as they previously executed. One binding *Aditi*, for now, into something of a triumvir of trade, presumably largely centered on *Urwel*, *Toulouse*, and *Belamel*."

Heather nodded and inwardly shrugged. Not her business. She handled Phil's flagship. And occasionally moved worlds when he needed it.

Dao Zhiou had grown attentive, but didn't speak when Phil paused.

"I have a bet going with Harinder as to how long it is before Cruiser-Captain Adham Khan demands the same for the *Gloran Empire*," he continued. "What nobody can answer for me is what the *Yaumgan Domain* will want, if the other four suddenly discover that trade can be useful and start building such networks."

Heather watched the woman think, but Dao Zhiou gave nothing away. That was to be expected, as the Philosopher/Kings had specifically chosen her to accompany Phil's original mission against the pirates, before it had morphed into…whatever it was now.

Showing the flag at every capital? Only *Derragon* and *Kyulle* remained at this point.

"I am only a captain, First Centurion," Dao Zhiou replied carefully.

"Acknowledged," Phil said. "However, you are my primary contact to *Yaumgan*, at least until such time as *Hollywood* Ward gets her messenger network set up and running. Until then, I can send notes to your ambassadorial staff at *Aditi* and have them answer, but more likely they will also have to contact their superiors, as where I'm at right now has gone far beyond the original specifications that saw your ship attached to my force."

"Yes, and no, First Centurion," Dao Zhiou replied.

"Call me Phil when it's just us," he countered. "Heather and the others do when things aren't official."

"Phil," she nodded. "And I am Dao Zhiou. It is my great pleasure to meet you, Phil. But I would argue that your original mission against the pirates was always intended to forge greater ties with the locals of the Cluster. In doing so, it was implicit that each of them would in turn forge greater connections. What you have done at *Elox* was simply another seed that any who had been paying attention might have expected. Certainly I was not surprised. Nor would I expect my superiors at *Kyulle* to be."

Heather watched him chew on that for a moment. He had an unfair advantage on most of the Cluster, since he was used to smart women speaking their minds around him.

"And if the seed sprouts and begins to send runners?" Phil asked.

"Then the garden becomes a better place," Dao Zhiou smiled. "*Yaumgan* has little trade, mostly conducted with neutral merchants flagged and operating out of *Aditi* ports. That is not the same as none. *Gloran* and *Ewin* on our flanks are too warlike, much of the time, so we have had to maintain stricter relations there. At the same time, I am not empowered or even emboldened to sign a similar treaty on behalf of the elders, but I would reject the notion that more trade would be unwelcome."

Heather smiled as she parsed that. Dao Zhiou Xue had obviously been selected for her ability to talk circles around anybody but a lawyer. It took Phil a moment as well.

"Understood," he finally said. "However—and I would ask that you not share this widely beyond your own superiors—one of the topics that has come up now is the possibility of licensing pulse technology to any government in the Cluster that wishes to acquire it. We will restrict such things to governments, but you and I are aware how easily it might slip through whatever controls are established. With the *Zen-Mekyo Syndicates* largely broken, piracy will hopefully decline as a problem."

"I do not see where *Yaumgan* needs such a technology," Dao Zhiou said.

"Oh, I would expect that your scientists will want access to it, if nothing else," Phil countered quickly. "Whether you use it or not is up to you. I expect everyone else to want it."

"And what do you think they will do with it, Phil?" she asked pointedly.

Heather was looking over his shoulder for listeners, so she was surprised when he did the same before he continued.

"Harinder, my Flag Command Centurion, believes that it will cause *Ewin* to rebuild their entire fleet from scratch, adapting to new forms and tactics," Phil leaned in and said in a quieter voice. "And that *Dalou* likely does the same. At that point, *Aditi* and *Gloran* will join in. In a decade or two, pulse weapons become the standard for all warships in the cluster. Possibly excepting *Yaumgan*, because you might have something even better that you have never mounted on a ship seen by outsiders."

"Better?" Dao Zhiou asked, a little taken aback by the way her voice got louder and higher.

"When we killed the god *Buran*, Lady Moirrey used a weapon she referred to as a Type-6 beam, Dao Zhiou," he said quietly. "Given how range and power scale with numbers, and you've seen me use the Type-4, you can imagine what she invented. I am just glad that she destroyed all her working notes afterwards and will not explain to anyone how to rebuild the device."

"Type-6?" Dao Zhiou gasped. "But that could…"

"It was used to slice apart a battle station even larger and more sturdily built than this one," he cut her off. "It is too terrible to be used in any lesser role than *deicide*."

They all fell silent at that. He'd hit that nail square.

Too terrible to use. Yaumgan might have notes about how to build such a thing, but hopefully had never actually gone so far as a demonstration model. The next generation of dreadnoughts that the *RAN* had started designing incorporated a whole series of breakthroughs that Bedrov and others had dreamed up, out at distant *Petron*. Keller's honeymoon flagship supposedly put *Urumchi* to shame, and it was a civilian yacht.

That was an arms race the galaxy didn't need to pursue.

"I will convey your thoughts to my superiors," Dao Zhiou said soberly now. "However, I think it would be best if you communicated them directly yourself. And not just letters, Phil. At some point, you need to talk to the elders at *Kyulle*."

"Understood," he nodded. "Up until now, I have been reacting to circumstances thrust upon me. It is my hope that from here I will have liberty to return to my original plan of visiting many worlds and working on opening up trade."

"We still haven't dealt with Giscard Russand," Heather reminded him. "He got away."

"No, Heather," Phil turned to her with a hard scowl. "He only got a head start."

FORTY-FOUR

ROYAL COURT, ALLEMAINE STATION, EWINHOME

Jaxom hadn't dreamed big enough, when considering what had happened to Doysan IV since he'd last seen the man.

Less than three weeks ago?

How much had changed.

Jaxom Bereoa had been compelled by this stupid drunkard to go out and demand to know what the outlanders wanted, because nobody else at Doysan's Court had the balls.

In the last few hours, Jaxom had reached out to a few friends and allies who had survived the purges. Right now, he was almost angry enough to strangle the drunk fucker himself.

They were in Doysan's private quarters. Jaxom, Doysan, Kalidoona, and Kalidoona's bodyguards. Nobody else's were allowed. A persnickety few had nearly gotten themselves shot objecting, but the room was clear.

Jaxom could count four empty bottles in plain sight, plus a mostly-empty rack on the wall behind the man that had been full a month ago.

A month?

Jaxom wondered how close the man's liver was to exploding from alcohol poisoning.

Kalidoona had frozen just inside the door. Probably never

been in a situation like this. Or if he had, he'd been the one passed out drunk, face down on the table.

Jaxom turned to one of Kalidoona's goons.

"Get me a pitcher of cold water," he ordered. "NOW!"

Apparently, his rage was sufficient, as the man jumped and fled.

"What are you going to do?" Prince Kalidoona asked carefully.

They knew it had gotten bad. But Kalidoona didn't know anybody on the station who had been thrown in prison. Or fired. Or possibly killed for loyalty to a First Minister making the best of an impossibly-bad situation.

"Waking this doddering, drunk fool up!" Jaxom growled.

At this point, he was almost past caring that Kalidoona was a Prince of *Ewin*. One had only to look at men like Farouk or Doysan IV to determine that inherited aristocracy wasn't the most optimal solution to humanity's needs.

The guard returned. Jaxom tested the water with a finger, found it just barely above freezing.

Adequate.

He poured the entire thing on his nominal king in one go, watching the man emerge sputtering and coughing.

"What the hell do you think you are doing?" Doysan screamed as his eyes finally focused.

"Getting some sobriety into you," Jaxom snapped at the man. "You knew we were coming, and when, so you have no excuse not to be prepared for the ceremony."

Doysan's bloodshot eyes narrowed.

"Just kill me," he growled in a voice that might have been heavy and dreadful a decade ago, but now was just tired and weak.

"Not a chance," Jaxom snarled at the man. "You get to remain king. At least for a time. We didn't come here to overthrow you. That won't fix anything. Hell, it might make fools like Farouk more ambitious, because they will learn the wrong lesson from all this."

"What lesson?" Doysan asked, starting to process that all the men around him wore Kalidoona's uniforms. Not Doysan's.

"Kosnett came here to apologize for destroying that jackass Russand, you fool," Jaxom grated. "He came here to open up trade relations with *Ewin*. And warn people not to bother *Meerut*, or he would do to them what he did to Russand. And now has done to you and Farouk."

"He came to overthrow me!" Doysan started to rise, but seemed to realize how drunk and weak he was, because he almost collapsed back onto his stool.

"Nobody gets to overthrow you!" Jaxom raged back. "Even if you do deserve it, you worthless grump!"

"What?"

"We're here to guarantee the crown, Doysan IV," Jaxom snarled. He gestured Kalidoona closer now. "This man negotiated a trade and friendship treaty with the daughter of the *Dalou* Shogun. We came to *Ewinhome* to deliver the joyous news that you have peace on your Eastern Frontier and can start sending merchant ships to *Dalou* worlds. Farouk opened fire without even pausing to ask why Kalidoona was here. At that point Kosnett had to get involved. You're just lucky that he chose not to destroy you. Even Farouk survived, though his boom suffered so much damage that they nearly didn't land on the planet below in one piece."

"So what do you want with me?" Doysan asked, his voice modulating down now as the cold water and adrenaline worked to burn out at least the brandy the fool had apparently drunk today.

"You will remain on the throne, in spite of everyone baying for your head," Jaxom said. "That's the deal I worked out with Kalidoona and Kosnett. However, at some point, maybe a year from now, you will announce your retirement and abdicate. Until then, you will be nothing but a figurehead. All decisions you desire to make will be approved by myself and Prince Kalidoona. Farouk can keep his head if he agrees to retire to his estates and passes the duchy powers on to someone else. Otherwise Kosnett's folks want him to answer for attacking them without provocation."

"Coming here was provocation enough!" Doysan snapped.

"Not if you'd bothered talking to the man!" Kalidoona snapped angrily, stepping close and using his enormous size offensively. "I've spent a lot of time talking to him and his people. They are all killers in ways that I don't think anybody in *Ewin* understands. But they came to trade. The daughter of the *Dalou* Shogun travels with him and signed the treaty, as did the Crown Prince."

"Daughter," Doysan said dismissively. "What good is a daughter?"

"She aims to be the next Shogun, King of *Ewin*," Kalidoona spoke in a cruel voice. "And seems to have an alliance with the Imperial House such that they will help her achieve it."

"So what?"

"So we can make friends with them now," Kalidoona said. "Or I suppose you can abrogate everything I've done in your name to try to bring peace to our realms. Farouk can try his luck again. Or Agrimond. Or Russand. Maybe you insult her sufficiently that she asks Kosnett's help in simply **ending** *Ewin*. He's made no bones about the fact that he could do it, if anyone pissed him off enough. However, if you make that choice, I will not support you. Nor will the Eastern Squadron. You can have peace, right now, or you can try your luck with a civil war, where outlanders like *Dalou* or *Aquitaine* will likely side with me. What will you have?"

Jaxom watched the blood flow out of Doysan's face as Kalidoona spoke. The realization that the old ways had failed. And failed so badly that traditional *Ewin* braggadocio wouldn't impact on people like Kosnett or Kugosu one whit.

"Will you set yourself up as the next king?" he asked in a

peevish voice.

"I doubt it," Kalidoona surprised Jaxom now. "I'm as old and set in my ways as you are, Doysan. Just not as big a drunkard and fuckup at the end of the day. We will need new blood, to be certain, but it might be better if we had someone like Gotzon Solo in your place. He's worked with Kosnett and the others and proved himself to *their* standards. Maybe he is the one to guide us to wherever *Ewin* needs to go if *Dalou* and *Aditi* are already making plans."

Kalidoona turned his way now.

"Do not tell Solo I said that," he ordered. "The man must yet prove himself worthy."

A Prince of *Ewin* could technically give that order. A Duke and Prince of the Eastern Squadron doubly do. Jaxom had spent some time around Solo, early in this mission. And had recommended the man when Doysan had been looking for a sacrificial lamb to send to *Aditi*.

Solo was the quiet, methodical one among loudmouthed *Ewin* captains, for all that people like Heather Lau considered him to be an irritable blowhard.

But there was a whole spectrum of such things, and *Ewin* rated Solo somewhat introverted, compared to men like Kalidoona or Farouk, weird as that might seem to an outsider.

Even Jaxom wouldn't have put it that way a month ago.

Only a month ago?

How much could change in so little time.

Still, he nodded to Kalidoona. They would keep this little conspiracy quietly. One that might see Gotzon Solo the Quiet made King of *Ewin*. Jaxom had his doubts, but Ministers only advised, even today. Even as angry as he was at what Doysan had done.

Princes of *Ewin* made that decision when gathered in conclave to name a successor to a departed king, whether dead or retired.

He had a year to set the groundwork.

FORTY-FIVE

Phil had convened a meeting in the conference room closest to his flag bridge. He could have done it on Allemaine Station. Doysan IV had certainly been much more polite that Phil had expected, when he finally emerged from his hibernation to greet all of his probably-unwelcome guests.

However brittle the man had been at the time, with an angry, avenging angel named Jaxom Bereoa never more than arm's length away.

Phil didn't figure he'd ever get that story. Nor did he care. The Princes at *Ewin* would solve themselves. Or not.

If they decided to be a problem, he might go ahead and embargo pulse technology to them, while making the others a deal. Type-3-Pulse turrets would mount well in the space freed up by ripping out a falcon firebird. Maybe put a Type-1-Pulse where the shrikes were. Or shift a few things around and put in Pulse-Twos.

Little Escorts like *Forktail* merrily annihilating *Ewin* missile swarms at range.

Kohahu Kugosu, for instance, would have useful things to say about the relevance of the *Ewin Principalities* at that point.

He smiled at the thought. Captain Tahn Sugawara had worked hard to live up to the legend of *Morninghawk*, and hadn't done that bad of a job.

Still, he was unfortunately being compared to a living legend.

Phil had all his command centurions present physically. Captains, Cruiser-Captains, and Strikers included. He rapped his knuckles to end the little side conversations folks had been having.

"We are, again, about to significantly disrupt the Balhee Cluster," Phil announced to his assembled team, old timers and locals alike. "Or up the voltage. *Dalou* and *Ewin* have a new treaty. *Aditi* will shortly sign something similar with both. *Gloran* has asked to participate. *Yaumgan* is in consultation with their superiors back home before proceeding, but we will assume the friendship part of things, even as trade is worked out with the Domain."

Good, he had their attention. Heather and Harinder both knew what was coming as did Captain Xue, Dao Zhiou. Time to drop the other shoe.

"With the settlement of the new treaty binding *Ewin* and *Dalou* into closer alliance for the time being, *Aquitaine* will begin licensing pulse technology," Phil continued, watching the other faces light up or panic as was their normal constitution. "Those factories will take some time being built and tuned, so nothing much will be expected for the next year or three, depending. However, that future is coming, and I want you to communicate that to your various fleet headquarters and political bosses with your next message home."

"Doesn't that jeopardize a wider war, First Centurion?" Adham Khan asked carefully.

Gloran saw themselves as warriors first, unlike *Ewin*, for example, who announced that they were aristocrats of the blood foremost. True *Gloran* pirates had been rare in the time before, simply because they considered preying on the weak to be dishonorable, much of the time. Raiders and youngsters out to make names for themselves was something else.

"It may," Phil nodded to the man.

Man. *Gloran* wasn't as urbane and sophisticated as the *Aditi Consensus* or the *Yaumgan Domain*, but at the same time they weren't nearly as sexist as *Ewin* or *Dalou* had been. Female captains were perhaps ten percent of their fleet on a good day, but he'd drawn a fierce male when he asked for a battlecruiser to hunt pirates.

"At the same time, I expect that the new technology will cause all players to step back for a time, while they work out new tactics, strategies, and logistics," Phil continued. "While that is happening, I want trade to bloom."

Nods from folks. They had all heard the speech a fair number of times.

However, this time it meant something more.

"Does this mean you are breaking up this squadron, First Centurion?" Khan asked, strong emotions present, but Phil wasn't sure which ones.

Phil considered it.

"We assembled this team for the purpose of hunting the pirates of the various Syndicates, I will remind you," he responded, more musing aloud than anything. "That led us to *Meerut* eventually. From there, *Ellariel* to honor Morninghawk. Russand attacked us and provoked my wrath, so he had to be dealt with. That brought us to *Ewinhome*, *Elox*, and back to *Ewinhome* finally."

He paused to look around the room and study the faces. It was so much nicer to have them all physically present, minus the four that were currently off having their own adventures in various places.

He landed back on Khan and studied that man's eyes. Hard-ass warrior who always carried something longer than a steak knife and shorter than a sword on his belt. Probably slept with it. Might have showered with it.

The *Gloran* were a warrior culture that occasionally put him in mind of the ancient Spartans, or the Imperial Americans who conquered so much of the homeworld in their time.

At the same time, Khan embodied a hard code of honor that Phil could respect.

Then he saw the man's fear. Except that fear was the wrong term. He didn't fear for himself. He feared for his Emperor, as weird as that was.

Yaumgan wouldn't care if Phil dismissed everyone before finally making his way to *Kyulle*, but it might be considered an insult to *Gloran* if this squadron didn't make the long trek across to *Derragon*. This fleet of ships had, after all, called on each of the other capitals, something nobody alive had done as far as Phil knew.

"Actually," Phil smiled at Khan now. "My hope is that you will remain with me for a time yet. I'd like to take the *Gloran* Emperor up on his invitation to visit, and bring this entire force with me so that each of you get to meet the *Gloran* people on even footing."

Khan deflated a little, but you'd never know unless you happened to be staring at him. Phil wondered if Khan would be dishonored otherwise. He knew that the rank of Cruiser-Captain could be revoked just as quickly as it was awarded. Frigate-Captain could be what he was reduced to. Or even just Frigate-Commander.

Interestingly, he could also be promoted right back up again, depending on how well he did at some lesser command.

Phil was given to understand that they had an entire fleet's worth of so-called Penal Ships where you served a sentence for dishonor, before being transferred back to the main fleet after a time.

Completely insane, but that wasn't Phil's call to make. If it worked for them, bully. He actually found himself looking forward to seeing it in action, just to learn how they managed it.

"However," he continued. "We are not done here."

He paused as everybody perked up again, having relaxed some.

"Yes, Duke Bertrand Farouk has been captured and generally disarmed," Phil noted. "Godfrey Kalidoona is likely the heir-designate, though that has yet to be worked out and I don't care what they do. That's an internal matter for *Ewin*. Doysan has competent advisors again and everything is about to become even more jumbled as the fleets of the Cluster start thinking about the future I have promised them. There is one issue left to resolve."

"Russand," Heather called from her spot, next to Harinder.

"Correct," Phil said. "He eluded us here, wisely understanding that I'd come back when I was good and ready. At times, I wonder if he set Farouk up, knowing that someone was coming along to crack skulls together. But he's still out there. Still scheming. According to First Minister Bereoa, the rivalry between Russand and Doysan goes back decades, so I don't expect our little termite to change his behavior anytime soon."

"Is there a bounty on the man?" Gotzon Solo asked now, a little nervous.

"No," Phil replied. "This is personal. And he is, as far as I'm concerned, perhaps the last of the pirates who need to be dealt with, if the Balhee Cluster is to truly know peace in this generation. As that was your original mission, helping me with the piracy problem, I ask your assistance now to see if we can break them once and for all."

That got smiles and a few cheers. Fists thumped on tables. They'd been with him at *Meerut*, both at the lagoon and the moorage. And helped him pull off the rudest practical joke Phil could ever remember at *Jacoby*.

"The *Ewin Principalities* are not safe as long as men like Baron Giscard Russand are running around causing trouble,"

Phil pronounced. "I can't stop all of them, but if enough of such men spend more time looking over their shoulders, perhaps they won't misbehave as badly as they have. It is probably too much to ask that they grow up, but if they fear my wrath, then perhaps the rest of you can work on building a better Cluster than you inherited. That, ladies and gentlemen, is all any of us can ask."

FORTY-SIX

BARONIAL RETREAT, UPPER MALSH FOOTHILLS, WEST PYKONG

Giscard was enjoying himself on the veranda that wrapped around Baron Valéry Garnier's weekend estate, up in the mountains where the rest of the world was kept at bay. It was an ancient place, hardly updated in more than a century. Not isolated, but remote enough that Giscard had been able to keep Garnier's attention focused on important things, like the garden that spread out in front of them as they watched the sun approach zenith.

The Baron's garden was a thing of beauty, with plants from a variety of worlds that his sire and grandsires *ad nauseum* had brought here and installed. The late morning sun was shaded by just the perfect amount of marine layer clouds on the verge of burning off.

Hot tea would give way in perhaps an hour to fresh lemonade.

Giscard studied the man seated across from him. Servants and guards kept a discreet distance. Observant, but silent.

"And that, Garnier, is why I think we should rethink this whole kingship thing," Giscard concluded, taking another sip of the tea, as he'd spoken at great length this morning and was a touch dry. "Too often the Dukes seem to just share it amongst themselves and ignore the fact that every world has a Baron who is just as perfectly qualified to sit on the throne at *Ewinhome*."

"What of Doysan's heir?" Garnier asked.

He was a short man. Almost rotund. Bald on top with a tremendous amount of beard that might have never been trimmed. Black for now, but gray and white was starting to thread it slowly. If Giscard remembered correctly, Valéry should be about forty now.

Right at that age where he had outgrown most of his youthful exuberance and was looking forward now with greater sobriety. The kind of men Giscard would need, in order to pull down that fool Farouk when he convinced Doysan to adopt him again.

"Doysan is old, tired, and drinks far too much," Giscard derided that pompous fool. "He was mad at Farouk because a woman had the audacity to want to bed someone with more enthusiasm and less of a pot belly. I'm sure that by now that they've reconciled and Farouk is back in the man's good graces. Fine. Wonderful. Another Sector Duke will become king, just like the last three. We need new blood, Garnier. Someone who isn't a duke to take the throne and shake things up around here."

"You?" the man asked pointedly.

"Hardly," Giscard scoffed. "I'm almost as old as Doysan, and loathe to give up my delights at *Jacoby*. No, what we need is someone younger. More virile, because all of our neighbors will be feeling frisky after this. Meddling in our affairs when we should be the ones meddling in theirs. The Barons need to stand up and speak with a unified voice when it comes time to replace that old fart."

"Younger?" Garnier asked with a helpful tone in his voice.

Giscard smiled at the man.

"It will be a challenging task, Garnier," he said. "And something that will take a generation to complete. No, this should be handled by a young man at the peak of his game. I envision myself merely offering sage advice from the role of an elder statesman who brings experience and competence to the room."

"The Dukes won't like it," Garnier rumbled now. "Too much of a threat to their traditional hold on things."

"Exactly my point, my good man," Giscard nodded. "They get everyone wound up in the regionalism of supporting their own sector duke against some other duchy's candidate. What we should be doing is speaking as Barons. There are far more of us than there are of them. Even more so if we recruit all the Princes who have nothing but blood."

"What would you offer them, Russand?" the man asked.

"If we revitalize *Ewin*, and acquire all this new technology that the outlanders threaten us with, I see no reason we couldn't go carve off a large chunk of *Dalou* for ourselves. It's not like they have any use for those worlds, having left them fallow for so long. Plus, those rapid-fire beams are murder on firebirds. My own spies have reported that from *Vilahana* and other places."

"Won't they do the same against *Ewin* missiles swarms, Russand?"

"No," Giscard stated flatly. "Any competent commander can overwhelm such defenses, just by layering launch windows and timing variable-speed strikes. Nothing can stand before the *Ewin* fleet. And once we can brush *Dalou* aside, then all those full-blooded princes who don't have their own baronies to look forward to might be able to claim conquered worlds."

"We haven't conquered them yet," Garnier reminded him.

"Because Doysan is old, stupid, and drunk much of the time," Giscard retorted. "This is exactly what is wrong with *Ewin*. Why we need new blood in charge, and not just another old, worthless duke whose turn is next when it comes time to elect a king. Men like you, Garnier."

He sat back now and watched the play of emotions across Valéry Garnier's face. The man was popular among the Barons, but not all that smart. Not that sneaky.

He would make a useful foil. A figurehead who could

challenge men like Farouk and tear the Principalities apart, pitting region against region and dukes, barons, and unlanded blood princes against one another.

The result should be half a decade of complete and utter chaos, at which point the Princes would be baying for a new leader to depose either Farouk or Garnier and save the kingdom from anarchy.

Giscard would be sixty-one at that point. A true elder statesman. Just what *Ewinhome* would need to lead them back from civil war and get everyone focused on expanding at the cost of *Dalou*'s flank. And *Meerut* would be taken, with everyone there executed for embarrassing him as they had.

Giscard just needed someone else to propose all those taxes that would build a new fleet. Someone else to start wars between all three levels of the Princes.

Someone else to take the blame.

Then he could waltz right in and save the day.

Giscard happened to be facing the northern sun, just up the valley from Garnier's reclusive estate, so he saw a dark spot appear silently.

At first, he thought it was a bird, but it was too far away, and flying wrong. It moved more like a shuttle dropping out of orbit, but Garnier forbade any craft from flying anywhere near this estate, let alone landing.

He himself had been forced to take a railroad, of all things, though it was certainly luxurious as befit his station, and ride south from the nearest port, eventually being deposited like a common laborer on a long, wooden wharf called a train station, where a ground vehicle rolling on actual wheels carried him in state up into the mountains.

Valéry Garnier liked his seclusion. Whoever was flying this way was likely to be arrested and imprisoned.

As it should be. A baron's word was law on his world. That was the explicit promise of the *Ewin Principalities*.

The thing got larger, but still flew silently. It took Giscard a moment to appreciate that it must be traveling faster than sound, the image arriving before the noise of it.

And it was still plummeting hard.

"What in the blazes?" Garnier snapped, putting down his own tea to stand, facing the approaching craft.

Giscard rose as well, towering a bit over the man but keeping enough of a distance not to be noticeable.

Baron Valéry Garnier turned to a servant who looked older. Perhaps a senior aide of some sort, but Giscard hadn't been paying attention. Bollvize had slept in, then spent the morning under orders, working on turning double agents by recruiting Garnier's staff with the promise of financial rewards.

The usual activities when two Barons got together.

"What the devil does that fellow think he is doing?" Garnier roared now, one pudgy arm pointed at the approaching shuttle.

Because it was a shuttle. And approaching at potentially-insane speeds. Larger than a missile, which had been one of Giscard's fears. Assassination by remote control, as it were.

Clean hands later, and all that.

The servant turned and had the audacity to shrug.

"I do not know, Baron," he replied quietly.

"Then FIND OUT!"

Garnier was angry now. As he should be. Giscard would have the fool flying arrested. And possibly *disappeared*, along with his entire family, just to make a statement about bothering your betters.

The shuttle wobbled at this point. Air brake wings deployed and it seemed to suddenly hover.

A few moments later a tremendous explosion of sound like thunder rolled over the estate, an earthquake that caused a breeze to stir where there had been little before.

The scale of the shuttle became obvious as it swooped in to land, looking like it would settle right in the middle of the garden for a moment before the pilot somehow found a clearing wide enough to allow it to only crush ground.

Skybeast. A gray dragon of a style Giscard had never seen before, with six landing feet deployed from the belly of the long, angular form.

At the very last, it spun in place, presenting the blunt tail, which turned out to be a landing bay as ramps dropped with crashes of sound audible even one hundred and fifty meters away.

Everyone was paralyzed. The audacity was a monumental insult to Baron Garnier.

Heads would roll.

The bodyguards had sprung into action, forming a line across the bottom of the steps to the grass. The house itself, while vast, was a manor, not a fortress, so Giscard didn't suggest retreating inside. It would do no good.

Plus, they were Princes of *Ewin*, he and Garnier. Men of the blood. To retreat now would be to face accusations of cowardice from their fellows. Just exactly what Giscard didn't need, if he was going to throw Garnier as a sacrificial lamb to the Conclave, when Farouk thought he had the election wrapped up.

Nor later, when Giscard rode in to save *Ewin* from defeat at the hands of whatever stupidities he had been secretly whipping up.

No, he would face this like a Prince.

Figures were exiting the shuttle. Many of them. Dressed in gray and possibly green, though it was hard to tell at this distance.

They came at a hard jog, covering the distance quickly, but moved in four columns, feet striking the ground in a unison that sounded like a drumbeat.

Garnier was beside himself with fury, practically frothing at the mouth as two hundred pairs of armored boots ruined his yard and garden. Giscard moved off to one side, where he wouldn't be struck in the face if the man began gesturing as madly as the curses under his breath suggested.

The invaders came to a halt about twenty meters short of the line of bodyguards. Eight bodyguards. Two hundred heavily-armed strangers.

The four lines split sideways suddenly on some unspoken command, flowing outward before forming two lines across, one kneeling and one standing. All were armed with rifles of a sort Giscard didn't know, though none were pointed this direction.

Yet.

Two hundred of them might destroy the house itself if they opened fire at this range.

A figure separated from the lines and began to walk forward. It appeared to be tiny, compared to the others. Curves suggested it was a woman in some sort of armor.

Garnier stomped loudly down the stairs and shoved one of his bodyguards out of the way to meet the figure midway. Giscard followed, but paused, then moved just outside the line of protection.

Never let it be said that he held back when Garnier charged the enemy. That would never do.

"What the hell do you think you are doing?" Garnier roared.

Even as short as he was, he towered over the stranger by half a head.

The woman flipped open a mirrored faceshield now and studied the baron. She had a rifle slung across her back, and a pistol on her hip, but drew neither. Instead, she looked around, seemingly marking the baron, the servants, and the bodyguards. Then her eyes alighted on him.

Giscard saw the smile take root. It did not bode well.

"Are you Baron Valéry Garnier?" she asked in a hard voice, turning back to the man.

"I am," he snapped. "I will have you executed for this insult to my honor!"

"Hardly," she replied. "You are under arrest by order of King Doysan IV of *Ewin* and First Centurion Philip S. Kosnett of the *Republic of Aquitaine*. You can do this the easy way or the hard way."

Giscard wasn't sure what she meant, except that Garnier stepped forward as if to grab the woman by a shoulder and shake her.

Then he was laying on his back, having performed a perfect somersault in the air so quickly that nobody could react.

The bodyguards started to stir and the two hundred invading troops—*Aquitaine* combat forces—suddenly let out a bark of savagery to intense that Giscard found himself holding his ears.

Eight against two hundred as rifles came down.

The tiny woman stepped past Garnier and walked right up to Giscard. He towered over her like a building, but she didn't seem to notice.

Giscard started to say something, but she suddenly grabbed him and he was tumbling through the air. Then all the air rushed out of his lungs as he slammed into the ground.

"Been looking everywhere for you, you son of a bitch," she said pleasantly.

EPILOGUE: KOSNETT

DATE OF THE REPUBLIC JANUARY 12, 412 RAN
URUMCHI, PYKONG ORBIT

Phil wanted to be cross with Xochitl Dar, but the Centurion was so proud of herself that he couldn't bring himself to it.

"Was that really necessary?" Phil asked as her video of the arrest concluded and he put the tablet down on the conference table. He ignored Heather and Harinder around him and concentrated on Xochitl.

Hell of an operation. Both Barons flat on the ground. The estate surrounded and taken without any other casualties besides those men.

"He was resisting arrest, First Centurion," Xochitl grinned at him. "I found it necessary to bring both threats down quickly, employing minimal force, in order to control the situation before anybody decided to open fire."

"Uh huh," Phil grunted, rather skeptical.

Her smile broadened.

"Dismissed," he ordered.

Dar bounced merrily out of the conference room, leaving him, Heather, and Harinder seated at the table.

"Markus, I could use some fresh coffee," he said pointedly to the man.

Markus was smart enough to follow Xochitl out, closing the hatch behind him.

"Now what, Phil?" Harinder asked.

"I think we might be done here," he said, pausing to rub his eyes. "We'll let *Freewind* transport the man back to *Ewinhome* in chains for now. It was only fair that I let them come with us, since they were the only ones who tried to do the right thing in the first place."

"And Markus not being here?" Heather leaned forward, pointedly nodding to the door.

"Looking at the future, Heather," he replied. "I might have to promote the boy to Centurion over his complaints, just so I can assign him to some of those tasks he was working on when he had to come to *Ellariel*."

"He still has all ten fingers," Heather reminded him. "That might be seen as a punishment detail."

"Then I need a better suggestion," Phil said. "Someone who understands our sensors well enough to guide those teams rebuilding *Viking*'s array. Someone who can take Iveta's idea of a modified Shield Projector that might be an extra nasty variant of Ghost Mode we can use to distract enemy missiles and firebirds. I have a number of other projects that require a redneck engineer."

"What about Nam?" Harinder asked.

Phil wondered if the gravplates in here had just blipped. He turned to her and blinked a few times.

"What?"

"*Aditi Consensus* Senior Officer Namrata Nagarkar," Harinder grinned at him impishly. "She's almost one of us anyway these days. And has a clearer understanding of the Shield Projector technology than anyone on this ship. Plus she understands the walls of the Balhee Cluster better than any of us born elsewhere. Why not see if she's interested in fully stepping over to run a project for you when we get back to *Meerut*?"

"Shit," Phil muttered. "Think she would?"

"She's been serving with us almost from the beginning," Heather spoke up. "Qualified on the Pulse-Twos and sat bridge watches. Plus, new weapons we invent are going to make the locals even more twitchy, so it might calm them down if we had a local involved. I have lots of engineers I could send. As does Barnaby, if you ask him. Technical redneckery was something we selected for in building out our crews, Phil. You know, out beyond the edges of the map, where we have to buy, steal, or repurpose something because we can't just stop at a friendly base and they'll have it in stores?"

He shared her smile. Sounded like something they'd both done, once upon a time. Plus Markus.

And he would have been pissed to have to go act like a grownup. Especially since he still had all ten fingers.

Markus appeared now, opening the outer hatch and just sticking his head in rather than entering. Phil nodded to the man and Markus stepped fully in.

"You have a guest, First Centurion," he said, coming to rest to one side with a fresh vacuum flask in one hand. Phil waved at him to continue. And whoever. "Lady Kugosu?"

Kohahu paused at the threshold when she appeared, as if uncertain of herself. He doubted that. She was generally calm certainty, even when she wasn't.

But she was an outsider on this ship. Not one of them. Not like Nam had turned into.

Phil waved her close and pointed at a chair next to Heather. She walked in and carefully sat. Markus set the flask on the table and retreated silently to his normal chair by the door.

"What can I do for you, Lady Kugosu?" he asked formally, unsure who she was representing at present.

He watched the young woman study Harinder and Heather before turning to look at him. He started to comment, but she already knew that those two women were his closest advisors. Even Aliza was a distant third, as she generally focused on the ambassadorial corps he had brought along.

"After *Ewinhome*, it is my understanding that you intend to visit *Derragon?*" Lady Kugosu spoke carefully

"That is correct," Phil replied. "However, I need to first spend a month or two in port at *Meerut*. My ship and my squadron have been operating at a high level of alert for some time, and need a rest. Plus, the ships themselves need to be inspected and probably repaired. As we are keeping Russand's dry-dock, that can best be handled there. But you are correct. I do intend to send messengers to the *Gloran* Emperor ahead of time, so that he doesn't panic when we arrive suddenly. What are your plans?"

She was attached to the squadron because she had attached herself. Phil understood that she was measuring the Crown Prince for a place in her intended future, but she had transferred to *Urumchi* more recently, and begun to learn how the *RAN* worked.

"I was present to represent the *Dalou Hegemony* while you continued to operate with one or more of our vessels," she said delicately. "If that is to continue, then I expect to travel with you, messages from my Shogun notwithstanding."

Phil nodded at that. His four Fast Clippers kept up a regular series of runs, with two newly-assigned vessels just running directly from *Aquitaine* Fleet Bases to his station outside the Cluster. Phil hadn't even had time to circle back to *Vilahana* to negotiate an operating base agreement with them, though that was slowly coming together according to reports.

From there, *Mexicali*, *Ensenada*, *Tecate*, and *San Quintin* made regular runs in to *Meerut*, staging more materials there before chasing him down to resupply in motion. Complicated, and nothing the locals had ever needed to create, because they were rarely more than a few days from home port.

Getting messages to Phil Kosnett in motion required a little luck and a lot of planning, unless you were First Lord of the Fleet. All the more reason he hoped that *Hollywood* was having luck setting up her own pony express to haul messages back and forth.

"I will presume that you will be able to communicate with the Shogun while we rest at *Meerut*," Phil nodded.

"What happens after *Derragon*, First Centurion?" she asked next.

Phil leaned back and considered. She hadn't been present when he'd spoken to the command centurions, but no doubt Yukimura had passed things along.

"After that point, the only capital left to visit is *Kyulle*, Lady Kugosu," he replied. "I will presume that the various ships attached to my force will wish to join me, assuming that *Yaumgan* doesn't object. As you might still be with us after *Gloran*, I would expect that you also traveled to *Kyulle* with this force. After that, I truly expect that my expedition will be ready to wind down, having visited every capital, deposited ambassadors, negotiated or assisted in various treaties, and helped advance the peoples of the Balhee Cluster."

He paused there and watched the play of emotions in her eyes. They were muted, but present. A young woman who hadn't fully mastered the art of lying with her eyes.

"What future does Kohahu Kugosu foresee?" he asked.

She gasped a little, but he'd addressed her as a person, rather than a title, a rank, or an alliance.

Lady Kugosu was still only fourteen. He remembered what his kids had been like at that age, especially his own daughter, Yi Wen, now studying at the Academy to follow in his footsteps.

"*Aquitaine* brings revolution," she said in a voice much older than her fourteen years. "Lord Morninghawk understood that and risked everything in order to prepare the rest of the Hegemony for that, lest we fall so far behind the *Aditi Consensus* and *Yaumgan Domain* as to become a second-rate power. Or third-rate in this case."

Phil nodded. An accurate description, when you boiled away all the dross.

"I believe that it would greatly assist the *Dalou Hegemony* to better understand how the *Republic of Aquitaine* and its Navy operates, so that we can face that future with greater confidence," she continued. "I have watched Heather and Iveta in battle. Spoken with Harinder and Nam Nagarkar and others. Plus, I have read about the woman who is *Emperor of Fribourg*, and who once served with many of you in *RAN* uniform."

Phil couldn't help but smile. His orders had been to turn Nam into one of them like Casey Weigand had once done. *Dalou* and *Fribourg* were much closer to one another culturally, in that neither had envisioned a galaxy where a woman might rise to power.

Kohahu had fallen silent now, watching him primarily for signs. It was his mission. His fleet. His word, at the end of the day, because the *Aquitaine* Senate had granted him Plenipotentiary powers to act as a governor of and ambassador to a region not under *Aquitaine* control. They had understood that the lag between communications would make any orders they gave almost irrelevant as situations changed.

At the same time, First Lord Naoumov had spent years letting him prepare for this grand adventure.

"You have not asked a question, Lady Kugosu," Phil pointed out distinctly.

Let her speak the words. They might bind her fate even harsher than her possible alliance with the Imperial House that could yet spawn a revolution in *Dalou.*

Another one.

For good or evil.

"If I chose, would I be allowed to temporarily enlist in the *Republic of Aquitaine* Navy, First Centurion?" she spoke clearly. "In a manner such as Nam has done. Or Kasimira *zu* Weigand of *St. Legier?*"

Phil didn't let his surprise show, but he felt it. The *Aditi Consensus,* for all their republican values and openness, still struck him for the corruption that he had felt, just below the surface. Nam wouldn't be able to change that.

Kohahu Kugosu, however, might turn into the Shogun of *Dalou*. The *Hegemon* herself, one of these days.

What she learned from him right now would flavor that forever.

Phil turned to Heather for an opinion. Kohahu would serve on her ship. He was just the First Centurion around here.

Heather nodded quickly, so it must have been a topic of conversation with her and Iveta at some point. Or several points. And several other officers. And Heather would remember Casey, though neither he nor she had ever been close to the woman before she pinned medals unto both their chests personally.

Phil fixed his intent on Kohahu finally.

"Under two conditions," he pronounced.

"They are?" Kohahu asked, her head coming up some as her chin went out.

She looked remarkably like Heather when she did that.

"First, you will get the formal permission of the Shogun," Phil said.

"And second?"

"It will be something you want for yourself, Kohahu."

She blinked at that. Probably driven her entire life by duty as she interpreted it at each stage. But if she was going to become one of them, she needed to be doing it for herself.

"It is, First Centurion," she said. "I have much to learn."

He nodded at Heather.

"And I have the right person to teach you," he said.

READ MORE

Be sure to read the next books in the First Centurion Phil Kosnett series!

Encounter at Vilahana
Consensus at Aditi
Hegemony at Dalou
Princes at Ewin
Empire at Gloran
Domain at Yaumgan

Available at your favorite retailers!

ABOUT THE AUTHOR

Blaze Ward writes science fiction in the Alexandria Station universe (Jessica Keller, The Science Officer, The Story Road, etc.) as well as several other science fiction universes, such as Star Dragon, the Dominion, and more. He also writes odd bits of high fantasy with swords and orcs. In addition, he is the Editor and Publisher of *Boundary Shock Quarterly Magazine*. You can find out more at his website www.blazeward.com, as well as Facebook, Goodreads, and other places.

Blaze's works are available as ebooks, paper, and audio, and can be found at a variety of online vendors. His newsletter comes out regularly, and you can also follow his blog on his website. He really enjoys interacting with fans, and looks forward to any and all questions—even ones about his books!

Never miss a release!
If you'd like to be notified of new releases, sign up for my newsletter.

http://www.blazeward.com/newsletter/

Buy More!
Did you know that you can buy directly from my website?

https://www.blazeward.com/shop/

Connect with Blaze!

Web: www.blazeward.com
Boundary Shock Quarterly (BSQ):
https://www.boundaryshockquarterly.com/

ABOUT KNOTTED ROAD PRESS

Knotted Road Press fiction specializes in dynamic writing set in mysterious, exotic locations.

Knotted Road Press non–fiction publishes autobiographies, business books, cookbooks, and how–to books with unique voices.

Knotted Road Press creates DRM–free ebooks as well as high–quality print books for readers around the world.

With authors in a variety of genres including literary, poetry, mystery, fantasy, and science fiction, Knotted Road Press has something for everyone.

Knotted Road Press
www.KnottedRoadPress.com

www.ingramcontent.com/pod-product-compliance
Lightning Source LLC
Chambersburg PA
CBHW060239100726
47907CB00003B/700